THE AFTERLIFE OF WALTER AUGUSTUS

HANNAH LYNN

Don't miss out on your FREE full-length novel.
Details of how to claim it are at the end of the book.

Text copyright © 2018 Hannah Lynn

First published 2018

ISBN: 9781980909682

Imprint: Independently published

Cover design by Cherie Chapman
Cover photograph by Cherie Chapman
Edited by Emma Mitchell @ Creating Perfection

For Jake and Elsie

CHAPTER 1

*T*HE AFTERLIFE smelt of cut grass and fresh laundry.

This was not an aroma that had been landed upon lightly. Countless alternatives had been suggested over the millennia, such as ground coffee, frankincense with a hint of lemon, freshly baked bread, sea air with a whiff of slightly soured buffalo milk, spiced cinnamon and ginger, morning frost, rhubarb and spearmint and, obviously, chocolate. However, when all had been decided, newly cut grass and freshly laundered linen were deemed the most appealing scent for the wide range of clientele that passed through this interim aspect of existence. After all, it didn't matter if you lived your previous life in the meadows of fourteenth century Eastern Scandinavia or grew up in a tower block in 1984 listening to Michael Jackson on your Walkman. Cut grass and fresh laundry smelled good wherever and whenever you came from. Unless you were Walter.

In Walter's defence, he'd spent the first century of his afterlife revelling in the starkly clean comfort of the scent. Even now, the occasional whiff could tickle his senses and unexpectedly transport him back to a more pleasurable time. However, lately those moments had become few and far between. In truth, it was not the dewing aroma that Walter Augustus had grown sick of in the last few decades, more the interim in its entirety.

While alive, Walter had been considered an attractive man. His hair was sun-bleached to the colour of straw and his skin was tanned and weather-beaten in the way that skin that dealt with the elements often was. His slight shyness – and acute awareness of his position in society – meant he often avoided eye contact, but in a manner that came across as endearing, rather than rude. He had been a reserved, hard-working and appreciative man in life, and for the longest while these characteristics had travelled with him into the interim. Unfortunately, like the love of his post-existence aroma, he could sense that within himself these characteristics were also starting to fade.

Walter's current abode was an exact internal replica of the house in which he'd lived during his adult physical years; one up, one down, with bare stone walls and a hearth that occupied the majority of the downstairs. He had opted out of its original view – a large and unfeasibly pungent manure pile – and instead selected a cliff top position, complete with winding pebble path and distant, cawing seagulls. The garden outside was home to a selection of vegetable patches and fruit bushes, while his trusted wicker rocking chair was, if possible, even more comfortable than it had been during his corporeal years. These decisions had not been a conscious selection, of course. The interim would have never worked in such a prosaic manner.

Walter pulled a cast-iron poker out of the fire. He plucked the toasted bread from the end, took a bite then coughed as the bitter tasting charcoal covered his tongue. Spluttering, he swallowed and took another bite. Not until he was halfway through the slice did he remember that whether he ate or not, it would have no bearing on his day. He sighed, opened the window and threw the remaining toast outside.

Since his great-granddaughter had passed on, Walter had stayed almost entirely in his little corner of the interim. He kept no company and his existence had become a day-to-day monotony of habit and routine. That said, he had ways to keep himself occupied and tried to mix things up now and again. Along with strolls down to the beach, sometimes he chose to rest in the long grass of the cliff tops and scribble odd verses into his little blue notebook. Occasionally, he would saunter over to the workshop and hammer out an odd piece of ironwork should it so take his fancy. He had no desire to see how humanity had changed since his passing or to see how his afterlife existence could be in any way expanded or updated. Walter had resigned himself to live out the rest of his existential existence on his own, in his own way. Particularly now.

For the first time in half a century, Walter was genuinely excited. This was not the sort of excitement felt for everyday events – like the thought of a good meal after a strenuous day's work or discovering long-forgotten money in the lining of a seldom worn summer jacket. This was the type of excitement that only resulted from years, if not decades, of anticipation. It occupied every waking thought and continued to bubble through his intestines at night. Bigger even than the birth of his children or Edi's arrival in the interim. Walter's excitement was almost beyond containment.

A day, a week, one month at absolute most, and he would be moving on, leaving the interim for whatever awaited him in the next stage of the afterlife. It was just a matter of time.

$\mathcal{L}$etty rubbed her eyes and groaned. Every muscle from her ankles to her wrists throbbed, but it was her knees and back that were the worst. They had been on dodgy ground for a while now, with too many clicks and aches to mention, but today, they were burning. Simply bending down to pick up one of the many discarded welly boots was enough to cause a shooting pain to sear right through her thigh, all the way up to her spine. No doubt the extra weight she'd piled on in the last few years hadn't helped, but she was fairly sure that age – not Mars bars and millionaires' shortbread – was the overwhelming culprit. She groaned again, hoisted herself up using one of the low square seats designed for fittings, and placed the boot back on the shelf.

'Why don't you do the till?' Joyce said as she straightened up the sales rack. Joyce was a slightly vacant but sweet eighteen-year-old that had started as a Saturday girl and had a penchant for revealing more information about her relationships than Letty deemed necessary. 'I can finish tidying up. Might as well get the vacuum out too. I don't think we're going to get anyone else in now.'

'You're probably right,' Letty said and glanced through the open doorway. The afternoon sun had started to dip and the sky had taken on an orange hue. After a moment's consideration, she nodded her agreement and started towards the till. En route, she paused to straighten up a size four patent girls' school shoe and two rows of men's loafers before continuing over to the counter. 'Let's see how we've done today,' she said.

Shoes 4 Yous was a small chain of shoe shops that provided mediocre quality merchandise at a slightly less

4

extortionate rate than its nearby competitors. Set midtown –
equidistant from the swanky bistros with their oversized
wine glasses and the kebab shop where meat was of an
unspecified origin – it attracted a range of clientele, particularly at this time of the year. With the start of the school year
only days away, the shelves were packed with sensible
looking black footwear, from slip-ons, to triple Velcro and –
for those parents who still had the patience to teach bunny
ears or the like – old fashioned lace ups. The aroma in the
shop was one of faux leather and carpet cleaner, and while
the soft lighting had been intended to create a homely
inviting atmosphere, Letty was fairly certain that it had also
resulted in her need for reading glasses since the age of
thirty-five.

Still, there were worse places to work, she reasoned.

Now fifty-four, Letty had worked as the Senior Manager
at Shoes 4 Yous for the best part of three decades. Prior to
that, she had worked in a Woolworth's store, which had been
converted into a discount furniture shop selling cut-price
sofas. There was nothing about insoles, insteps, and upper
leathers that Letty didn't know. She could tell a child's foot
width from a cursory glance, the condition of a woman's
arches by the state of her heel, or whether a man wore a size
nine or ten, regardless of which he asked for.

'Letty,' Joyce said, cutting the vacuum only minutes after
starting it. 'You wouldn't mind if I skip out a bit early, would
you? Kevin's taking me out tonight and I wanted to go see if I
could get my bits waxed first.'

'Oh. 'Course. You get off.'

'He doesn't like it if I don't, see. He says it's like kissing a
hamster down there.'

'It's fine. Please just go.'

'I'll finish the 'oovering first.'

'Don't worry about it. Just go. Honestly, I'll see you Monday.'

'Cheers, Letty,' Joyce said, dropping the vacuum where it was and blowing Letty a kiss. 'You're a right star, you are.'

As Joyce disappeared down the high street, Letty turned the sign to closed, locked the front door, then got about balancing the till.

The day's takings were good. Other shops were finding it hard now, with online shopping and supermarkets managing to undercut them at every corner, but shoes were different. People liked to try shoes on before they bought them. And rightly so to her mind. In Letty's opinion, one could never underestimate the power of good or bad fitting footwear. So, while other clothes and retail shops were closing up all over the place, Shoes 4 Yous was about to open its fifth branch. Not that it affected Letty at all, just a few more trainees to get up to speed here and there.

After balancing the till, Letty went about the rest of the jobs. That night, it included restocking the shelves, pulling used tissues out from inside a pair of high-heels, and wiping off a dubious green substance from the underside of the mirror. Once that was finished, she picked up the vacuum to finish where Joyce had left off. The old red Henry growled as the nozzle pushed against the faded blue carpet, it's heavy thrum drowning out the sounds of the radio and the high street beyond.

Due to the noise and Letty's concentration on the job in hand, it was a solid minute before she finally registered a heavy knocking sound coming from the front of the shop. Glancing over her shoulder, Letty started at the sight of a face pressed up against the glass.

A second later, she offered a short wave of recognition. 'One sec,' she called, before craning over and switching

6

Henry off at the plug. She scuttled over to the door, unlocked it, and opened it with a jingle.

A woman with frizzy brown hair stood in the doorway, rocking a stroller back and forth. 'I'm so sorry I'm late. He wouldn't settle.' She gestured the pushchair in her hand. 'It's like he knows I've got things to do.'

'No, not at all. Perfect timing. I was just off in my own little world, that's all. You hang on a sec. I'll go and fetch it from out back.'

Letty ambled across to the back of the store and through the heavy white door marked Staff Only. A minute later, she reappeared, a large white box in her arms.

'Do you want to have a look first?' she said. 'Check it's all okay?'

'Thank you,' said the woman, who then took to jostling the stroller with her foot.

Letty prised away a small piece of tape and lifted the lid. The woman gasped.

'Oh, it's perfect. Thank you so much. You are so clever.'

'Oh, it's my pleasure,' Letty said. 'How is he, by the way? Over that tummy bug?'

The mother rolled her eyes. 'Finally. Honestly, I thought it was never going to pass. Craig's come down with it now.'

'Oh, I am sorry. Will he be alright for tomorrow?'

'He doesn't have much choice.'

Letty offered a polite little chuckle then took one final peek inside the box. She was proud of this one, even if it was simple. The coloured triangles of the bunting were the neatest she'd managed, and the little blue bear and toy box were easily as good as some she'd seen in magazines. Two tiers. Hand cut letters too.

'It's forty pounds, right?' The woman took the box and carefully squeezed it into the base of the stroller, before slipping her handbag off her shoulder. After a moment of rummaging, she pulled out her purse and extracted two twenty-pound notes.

'That's great. Thank you,' Letty said.

'No, thank you. Honestly, you should open a bakery. You're brilliant.'

'Maybe one day.' Letty felt a flush of colour rise to her cheeks. Fortunately, any possible embarrassment was averted by a sudden interlude of bawling that erupted from the stroller.

'Not again. I swear he never sleeps.'

'It's no problem. You get off. And have a lovely day tomorrow.'

'I'm sure we will. Thanks again.' Making a variety of shushing noises, the woman headed back down the high street. After a moment more watching her, Letty shut the door with another jingle and went back to the vacuuming.

CHAPTER 2

*T*HE CORRIDOR IN the interim was by no means your standard corridor. In fact, it would not, by the average lay-person's standard, qualify as a corridor at all. A sea of free-standing doors stretched out endlessly into an infinite landscape which – like the doors themselves – would change and transform almost daily. It was easy to see how people found pleasure in the unexpectedness and beauty that rose from this magnificent panoramic backdrop which was so central to the interim afterlife. Although Walter was not one of those people.

Today, the doors were a heavily stained cedar, from which rose an earthy and damp perfume that blended perfectly with the cut grass and linen aroma. The floor, by contrast, was an infinite expanse of powdery sand that shimmered and glinted in the soft light and from somewhere far off came a light-fingered mastery of the mandolin. The destination of these doors was, to Walter, as elusive as the manner in which they were constructed.

Perhaps it was his age, or the cynicism that had grown from being alone for so long, but to Walter, the interim no longer possessed the irrefutable prestige it once had. There had always been the odd rancid egg – those that had difficulty letting go or found pleasure in the obscure and, of course, those whose memory lived on for the most abhorrent reasons – but it was the vast quantity of them still hanging around that was worrying. Men calling themselves actors, gathered in droves, discussing the time they had a walk-on part as a half-eaten zombie or laughed about their pet cat on ice going viral, whatever that meant. Wives of ex-cons gossiped and whinged about the good old days over frozen margaritas and manicures, not in some secluded doorway, but out in the open, for everyone to see. Gamblers, addicts, and musicians: once their time here had been brief, but now, they never seemed to leave. Yes, in Walter's opinion, the prestige of the interim had most definitely deteriorated.

Walter kept his head down as he hurried through the corridor. He had visited Betty often since she'd moved into the home and barely needed to lift his eyes to find the way. After a few minutes and having successfully avoided the gaze of every person on his route, Walter found the door he was looking for. He twisted the handle and stepped through.

Elizabeth Mabel Green was the last person on Earth who knew who Walter Augustus was. She'd read *Seas, Swallows and all but Sorrows* – the only remaining copy – in the early sixties, and while some parts of her memory had given way to time, she'd remembered his name as clearly as she remembered her own. She remembered how she chewed on a crumpet while her father read the poems over breakfast and how the melted butter dripped down her chin as she listened. She remembered the coarse woollen blanket that covered her knees while she fought off the cold and re-read her favourites in the first home she'd ever owned. She did not remember every word of every poem, but she remembered the way they made her feel.

Once Pemberton had departed the interim, Walter assumed he would not be far behind. But Betty continued to cling to his name and his poems. Even now, in her last days, Walter could feel the tugs as he flitted through his memory. After all, Walter was family.

Betty Green's hospital room was adorned with several bunches of flowers. It sported a small white cabinet and plug-in air fresheners at every available socket, although they did little to camouflage the scent of Dettol and urine that rose from the carpets and bed sheets. Betty lay beneath a powder blue blanket that, at a casual glance, appeared motionless, although Walter – and any person who cared to sit and study it long enough – could see there was still life in the old girl yet. Walter watched the faint rise and fall. He could hear a gentle hiss as the air was drawn in and then expelled from his great-great-great-great-granddaughter's lungs and the weak double thud of her fading heartbeat.

'Are your kitchen tiles a nightmare to clean?'

Walter jumped back from the bed.

Behind him a small black box was affixed to the wall, inside a tiny woman was on her hands and knees scrubbing the floor. She looked out at Walter, opened her mouth and spoke. Beads of sweat began to bubble on his forehead.

'You need to try Fleazy Klean.'

The woman's voice, rather than coming from her mouth, came from another little black box, two feet to the right. Walter shuddered. A television. Even avoiding the present day as he did, Walter had not managed to evade this unnatural source of wizardry. One glimpse of the shiny black glass was enough to send his post-organic frame rigid with tension and his surplus-to-requirement pulse into overdrive. He sidestepped away – keeping half an eye on the mini-man who was now on screen, apparently trying to sell him some kind of dental apothecary – and focused his attention on Betty.

Walter knew there must be pain; there always was at that stage, but for now, she seemed at peace.

'Don't worry,' he said, leaning over and whispering. 'It's not the end. Everyone's waiting for you.' Betty mumbled softly. Walter reached down and stroked her forehead. 'Take all the time you need,' he said. He waited another minute, offered a final uneasy glower to the man with too many teeth on the television, then opened the door and stepped back into the corridor, a spritely spring in his step as he walked.

~

*L*ow slung clouds shrouded the sky as Letty strolled up the high street. The evening was cool, and a light breeze carried an aroma of oak trees, honeysuckle and the slight hint of motorbike fuel. Donald would be glad of rain, Letty thought. The humidity of the last month had played havoc with his joints too. A little way up the high street, she stopped. Resting her arm against the yellowish Bradstone wall, she kneaded the base of her spine with her knuckles. In one of the stores across the road, the back-to-school sales signs were already being pulled down and replaced with pumpkin banners ready for Halloween. Letty's stomach churned. If the thirty-first of October marked everyone else's Halloween, Letty's personal day of nightmares came a few weeks earlier each year.

Despite living less than twenty miles apart, Letty and her sister Victoria saw each other an average of three times a year; Christmas, the twins' birthday, and once in July to remember their mother's birthday. Occasionally, they would place a meeting somewhere between January and July to bridge the sixth month gap, but that was not always the case. As it was, Victoria had cancelled the July meetup this year, as the twins had a last-minute gymkhana competition they simply couldn't afford to miss.

There were various reasons that meetings with Victoria tended to be tense, one of the overwhelming factors being money. While Letty suffered from an affliction of saving money, the same could not be said for her sister.

'It will just be a short-term loan,' Victoria said the last time. 'And the interest we'll give you will be far better than any you'd get at the bank.'

'But what about Mum's inheritance?' Letty said. 'That was over twenty thousand pounds.'

'My thoughts exactly. And I'm guessing it's just sitting in your account earning you nothing. If you look at it that way, we're actually doing you a favour. Think of it as an investment opportunity.'

Letty had mumbled something unintelligible as she shifted uncomfortably.

'Great,' Victoria said. 'Do you want me to set up a bank transfer before I go?'

'What's she doing with all their money?' Donald said when Letty told him of the conversation a couple of days later. 'And what happened to her share?'

'I didn't want to ask.'

Donald huffed. 'Well, you know how much you've got left of that money. If you think we can lend her a couple of grand, then it's up to you. But don't go leaving yourself short.'

That had been over a year ago, and Letty had neither seen nor heard anything of her investment opportunity since.

The other point of tension came from the children. As anyone who had witnessed Letty at work could testify, she had an uncanny affinity for small children. Be it screaming toddlers or sulky teenagers, somehow Letty could bring the best out of them all. All children, it seemed, apart from her nephew and niece.

While some may have seen fit to liken the pair to characters from a Stephen King novel, Letty would have considered this unfair, given the possible moral redeemability of the bloodsucking clowns and killers Mr King portrayed. Likewise, adjectives such as spirited and boisterous seemed far more suited to rescue puppies than to the double delinquents with whom she somehow shared DNA. Born after years and years of trying, Victoria viewed her children as nothing short of miracles. Throw in the added guilt she felt at being an older parent and a father who was barely home, and it was clear how Victoria and Felix had raised nothing short of monsters.

Every visit included a fight. Sometimes, these involved weapons, such as a plastic Buzz Lightyear or a conveniently placed lamp. Other times, it was simply teeth and nails.

'They're energetic,' Victoria said. 'Lots of intelligent children are like this.'

Letty wasn't so sure. The twins' birthday was the singular time of year when Letty truly considered giving up baking for good.

The cake thing had become somewhat of a venture lately. Twelve months ago, she'd been doing one order, maybe two, a month. Now it was more like that a week. And gone were the days of simple round cakes with a little bit of pipe work. In the last month alone, she'd created one Peppa Pig cake, two M&M piñata cakes, a Louis Vuitton handbag, three cupcake wedding towers, and a hen-do cake that even now turned her cheeks scarlet at the memory. Of course, the area manager had dropped by for a chat on the morning she'd taken that one into work. The meeting had been tortuous. Letty sat nodding, her mouth bone dry, beads of sweat trickling down her forehead as the box sat perched above his head resting on top of the size twelve men's brogues.

'There's really no need to look so worried,' the manager had said. 'Everyone's numbers are down on this time last year. You should see Stroud's numbers.'

Letty nodded mutely.

When he finally left, Letty had told Joyce she was taking an early break, at which point she collapsed onto a box of lime green flip-flops, red-faced and trembling. No more hen party cakes, she decided after that one. Not unless they were picked up from home.

'You should be charging proper money for these,' Donald said, almost every night as she stood in the kitchen rolling out fondant and mixing up buttercream.

'I'm not doing it for the money.'

'Well, maybe you should be. You're wasted at that shop. And we can't rely on my wage forever. I'm getting old.'

Despite Donald's concerns, Letty was savvy enough not to be out of pocket. She charged enough to cover the ingredients and a little bit more so that people felt they were getting quality. In her opinion, people always became suspicious if they thought things were too cheap.

The sky twisted with soft greys and lilacs as Letty ambled towards the crossroads. Somewhere, a bonfire was burning, and the tang of pine drifted through the air. She glanced down at her watch. Five thirty-two. Friday night meant Donald would be out for drinks with the other men from the water board. A homemade pie was defrosting in the larder, and a large apple crumble awaited them for dessert. She had a little time to spare. With one last glance at her watch, Letty changed course and crossed the road. Thirty seconds later, she was standing inside the bank.

Letty preferred these bank machines, as unlike the others on the high street, they were tucked away inside a building. Whenever she used the outside ones, it felt as though someone was there, peering over her shoulder, trying to steal her PIN code or tutting if she took too long. That afternoon, only one of the machines was in working order, and when a young man with a toddler in tow stepped through the automatic door only a moment after she did, Letty waved him in front.

'Honestly, you go,' she said.

'Are you sure?'

'Of course, of course. It's no problem.'

Letty stood what she considered a suitable distance behind, while the man did his business. After he finished, she offered him a polite smile and watched as he exited the room. Only after the automatic doors had closed and she felt certain that no one else would be entering for at least a minute, Letty moved to the cash machine, inserted her card and tapped the screen.

Entering her PIN was a reflex response. After all, she'd used the same four numbers for every card that she'd ever owned and had no intention of changing it anytime soon. A series of options, including Cash or On-Screen Balance, appeared in front of her. She selected balance.

As she waited for the figure to appear, she withdrew a small notebook and pen from her handbag pocket and wrote the date at the top. A moment later, a number appeared. Sixty-seven thousand, six hundred and sixty-eight pounds and twenty-four pence. Letty wrote it down in her notebook. After confirming with the machine that she did not require any more services, she withdrew her card, placed it back in her tattered old wallet, and selected another.

This second account gave a similar reading to the first, as did the third and fourth she checked. The fifth came in slightly lower, at only twelve thousand, two hundred and nine pounds and thirty-three pence. She was about to check her sixth when a cough behind her caused her to jump.

'Sorry,' Letty gasped. She pulled out her card and hurriedly backed away from the machine. 'I'm all done now.'

Two minutes later, when she was back on the street, Letty's pulse pounded. Her money situation was out of control, and she was going to have to tell Donald sooner or later. She just had to find the right way to word it.

CHAPTER 3

*I*N THE MID 1800s – when Walter James Augustus had been at the pinnacle of his living existence – he, like those around him, held to the concept of a finite life and an infinite afterlife, be it eternal bliss or equally, if not more so, eternal damnation. His belief was perhaps slightly weaker than those around him; he would not feel the need to chastise himself too greatly should he forget an evening's prayer for instance, yet he never considered allowing his children to forgo their prayers, just in case. Like his fellow men, he'd believed – somewhat naively, he now realised – that his passing would take him to his final resting place, where he would spend all eternity surrounded by those he loved. If only it were that straightforward.

Back in the cottage, Walter took a sip of tea. A melancholy groan escaped his lips. Overly-sweet tea, exactly the way Edith would have made it.

It had been one hundred and twenty-four long, long years since Edith had been with him in the interim, yet he could still see the shy, embarrassed flush that coloured her cheeks whenever she caught him watching her. He could still feel the way her hands would work out a knot at the base of his neck after a hard day at work and how she, exhausted from running around after the children, would drift to sleep beside the fireside, her crochet hooks still delicately held between her fingers, the balls of yarn unravelling at her feet. He could remember it all, and soon, he would be able to live it all again.

For three years, when he'd first passed, Walter watched over Edi as she carried on her life without him. Unbeknownst to her, he was there by her side when she woke each morning and stayed tucked up next to her at night as she slept. He read poems to her of an evening as she sat crocheting small bonnets for the grandchildren and would take walks with her around the village and down to the bay and even to place flowers by his headstone.

When Edith's time came to join him, they took up the mantle together, keeping a watchful eye on their ever-expanding brood. Similarly, Walter and Edi were never far from their children's thoughts.

Generally, tugs for Walter occurred somewhere between his sternum and his belly button. During those first few decades, he'd been acutely aware of them all. On a few occasions – like Edith's passing or the arrival of a new grandchild – the sensation had been more like a knife through the gut. Most of the time, it was more of a gentle twist around the appendix. Still, each time Walter felt that belly-binding sensation, he, like all other inhabitants of the interim, knew he was being remembered down on Earth, and as long as the bond between him and the Earth remained, Walter, like all other remembered spirits, was bound to the interim.

While alive, Walter J Augustus had been many things, including, a churchgoer, a husband, and a father with a tendency for over-indulging his three daughters. He had grown up during the tail end of the eighteenth century in the small town of Eastleigh Leach, on the North Somerset coast – a pretty village with a shingle beach, a quaint church, and excellent bakers. It was there that he'd met and married Edi, raised his girls, and even written a short poetry anthology. This anthology, as it happened, was the cause of his post-mortality quandary.

During his pre-eternal existence, Walter had been a farrier. While others of his intellect may have dwelled on the limitations of his modest beginnings, Walter, in this temporary existential state, had never been one to brood. He had taught himself to read and write for betterment of himself and his family yet had had no desire to progress above his current situation in life. He did not wish to travel up to Birmingham to work with the ironmongers, nor did he wish to study veterinary arts with the scholars in Camden town. The idea of spending his days gorging on such rich and fatty obscenities as to cause his legs to swell with gout – as it did with so many of the people whose horses he shod – was to Walter a source of constant bewilderment. Walter Augustus had a good life and one he treasured.

Despite that, work was not easy. Walter spent his days by a skin-singeing furnace, with smoke that choked his lungs and caused his eyes to stream. By the time he'd finished his apprenticeship, his arms were puckered and pink with scars, and he'd developed a cough that would put a chimney boy to shame. But of an evening, when the sun had sunk so low that even Pemberton deemed it time to shut up shop, Walter would head home to his family, where he would be surrounded by laughter and warmth. Sundays, after church, they would head to the beach to fly kites or sail model ships and eat blackberries that they'd foraged en route. And if time permitted, as occasionally it would, Walter would write.

Storytelling was an art Walter had honed as a child. As the eldest of six, he was often required to entertain his siblings for extended periods of time and quickly discovered that a well-spun tale of a heroic family adventure – with several misdemeanours, blood thirsty battles, and the occasional dragon – could keep them occupied for far longer than, say, a game of marbles. As an adult and with the sudden rise in popularity of rural poetry, Walter saw a new avenue for his creative streak. Initially, his poems were little snippets or phrases scribbled in the margins of Pemberton's day-old papers, but then Edi saved up money from the house-keeping and bought him his own little notebook. He had promised to think of her with every word he wrote in it, and that he did.

Walter had trained under Edward M Pemberton, a man whose face was so long and pinched it appeared to be made almost entirely of nose. He was the type of person who spoke twice as slowly as he needed, thus sounding like he viewed everyone he spoke to as an idiot. With Walter, he spoke three times as slowly. Pemberton – who almost always had a boiled sweet in his mouth, thus extending his pinched look even further – had apparently inherited the Eastleigh Leach Farriers from an uncle, although he had no children or family to speak of.

He would bark orders at men he deemed below his station, treating them with as much civility as he did the horse manure that amassed outside his workshop. To men above his standing, he was polite, but often curt in a way that would make Walter flinch. As for women, from what Walter saw, he refused even to acknowledge them. If Pemberton ever saw the glowers he received, he paid them no mind, for it was of no consequence to his business. Despite all his flaws, Edward Pemberton shod horses with the best shoes between Bristol and Barnstable, and he knew it.

The frost had been thick on the ground for nearly a month and the air outside tasted of ice and fog. Pemberton was unusually absent, attending to business in Bristol, and Walter felt no guilt as he blew the bellows at the forge and made the coals glow a little redder. Winter was the time of year that Walter was grateful to be in the shop amid the warmth of the forge. Trips outside resulted in chilblains and numb feet, rigid joints and arthritically slow fingers. Everyone was more irritable in the snow, the horses included.

The doors to the shop were pushed open, and a strong draught blew the snow in from outside. During the previous few weeks, business had been so slow that a lesser man than Walter may have taken advantage of their master being away for the day and closed the doors, but Walter had not. He had, however, positioned himself close to the flames, tucked away from the entrance and out of the biting wind. Making the most of the quiet, he took out his notepad and began to write.

Walter's pen sped across his notepad. His teeth bit down on his bottom lip as he tried to keep pace with the flurry of words in his head. He was thinking of Edi, as he'd promised, gleaning inspiration from the way she curled a strand of hair around her finger when she was nervous.

'What is that you're writing?'

Walter shot up from his seat and banged his elbow on an anvil.

'Sorry, I ... I ... Sorry, sir, I didn't see you there.'

The young man was similar to Walter in age and build. He was dressed in jodhpurs and a fitted jacket that, no doubt, cost more than Walter would earn in a decade.

As the son of one of the wealthy estate owners, the man was a familiar face in the village. He was far more affable than those in his position tended to be and always offered a wave or a smile if Walter happened to see him out and about. Walter had even seen him racing around, giving piggyback rides to the local children.

The man waved Walter's apologies away, stepped into the shop, and shook off some of the cold.

'Please don't apologise. I shouldn't have startled you.'

Walter blushed and slipped the open notebook onto the workbench behind his back.

'You shouldn't have come out in this weather, sir,' he said. 'I'd have come to the house.' Walter crossed the workshop and peered out the doors to see a bay horse racked up against the fence post. Its cinnamon coat was dappled with snow. 'Mabel again? She thrown another shoe?'

'Yet another,' the man cast a glance outside. 'I have to admit the weather didn't look nearly so ghastly when I left.'

'Why don't you head back up to the house?' Walter said. 'I can come up in the morning. Or tonight if it's desperate.'

'No, no, it's not desperate.' The man threw another glance towards the swirling sky and shivering mare. 'Perhaps you're right. Maybe I'll hold on a minute, though. See if it's going to pass.'

'As you wish, sir.'

The gentlemen took another step into the workshop.

'Please. Come in by the forge,' Walter said.

'Thank you, I will.'

Letting the man pass, Walter pulled the door to, then took a moment to flatten down his apron and wipe a little of the ash from his hands.

'Is there anything else I can get you?' Walter said, stepping back inside to where the man stood facing of the forge.

'Actually,' said the man, turning to face him. 'I would very much like to have a read of these.'

CHAPTER 4

*L*ESS THAN A minute after the key clicked in the lock, the heavens opened. Letty cursed herself for dawdling. Even with her knees playing up, she could have gotten home in half the time, but her mind was elsewhere, back in the bank and the mystical numbers that had risen beyond all realms of possibility. She took off her shoes and placed them on the shoe rack, straightening Donald's beside them.

The house was the same one Letty and Donald had moved into when they married, and her weekly salary at Woolworths had been a paltry one hundred and fifty-two pounds. Paltry, at least compared to the three hundred and eighty pounds that Donald had earned at the water board. Back then, the house smelled of newness – the latest kitchen appliances and wood chipped walls. Now, it smelt of dated decor, hidden cobwebs, and icing sugar.

Donald had insisted he pay for everything when they married. The mortgage – though in both their names – came out of his account, as did the gas bill, the electricity, and the television license. Despite earning her own salary, he'd insisted on giving Letty house money for groceries and any incidentals and maintained that Letty keep her own money for when she wanted to, 'Buy herself something nice.'

Donald's funding of their life was something Letty kept to herself. She could have found it demeaning, but Donald had never meant it like that. He had wanted to look after her, give her everything she needed. Paying for things was his way of doing that. He couldn't give her what they'd really wanted, of course, but neither of them had known that at the start.

That was where the saving had begun. Each week, Letty had put aside the lion's share of her earnings in an account, ready for when the pitter-patter of tiny footsteps finally arrived. She was in no rush when they were first married, and there was an exciting buzz about the moment she'd be able to reveal to her husband that, not only was he about to become a father, but that she'd already saved enough money to kit their little one out with everything he or she would ever need, including the best Silver Cross pram that money could buy. As the years progressed, the money increased, although the pitter-patter never arrived.

It was her bank who advised her to open a second, then third, fourth, fifth, and sixth account as her savings expanded. Most banks, she'd learnt, now had a protection limit of eighty-five thousand pounds. However, Letty never really felt comfortable having that much money in one place, so separate accounts seemed like the best idea.

At their suggestion, she also set up a couple of low-risk savings ventures and, after a conversation with Felix over a decade ago, she'd bought herself some premium bonds – once again, all with the initial intention of surprising Donald.

But the bond winnings only made her secret-squirrelling

even more disconcerting and any time she tried to broach the subject she felt her palms turn slick with sweat and her chest begin to palpitate. Letty Ferguson had single-handedly amassed herself a small fortune of over half a million pounds. The thought made her nauseated.

Letty switched the kettle on at the plug then went back out to the hallway to hang up her coat. She was back in the kitchen and halfway through pouring when the phone rang.

'The Ferguson residence,' she said.

'Oh, Letty love. I'm glad I caught you. I was worried you might be out for the night.' The voice came through with an unusual breathlessness.

'Jean? Everything alright?'

'Yes, yes. Well, no, not really.'

'Oh.'

'You see, it's the party at the shop tomorrow. For the staff. Two years already, can you believe that?'

'That has gone fast.'

'Well, I've just realised I'm the one who said I'd bring the cake. Of course, I'd bring the cake. I'm the bloody owner. I meant to ask you weeks ago.'

'It's fine—'

'I'd get one from the shop. I mean, I can if you'd rather. Only I know that Angela's bringing one of her homemade quiches, and Phil says he's to bring a fish pie—'

'It's fine I can do it—'

'It doesn't have to be anything fancy, you know. Just a sponge or something. We're only shutting up the shop for a couple of hours. Maybe a bit of icing—'

'Honestly Jean. I'm having a baking night already; one more won't be a problem.'

'You're a lifesaver, really you are.'

'It's no trouble at all.'

There was a slight pause down the line. Letty waited for the final request.

'And I don't suppose you could pop it down to the shop, could you? Only I've got to shuffle things around over there. Make a bit of room.'

Letty was almost positive that at no point in their thirty-year friendship had she ever said no to any of Jean's requests, yet still she let the silence hang for a teasingly long fifteen seconds.

'Of course,' she said. 'What time do you want it? Ten? Nine-thirty?'

'Ten would be a dream.'

'No problem then. How many people is it for?'

'Oh, not too many. Ten. Twenty, perhaps, if they bring partners, I suppose. Perhaps a couple more.'

'Well, I better get baking then. And I'll see you tomorrow.'

'Thank you my lovely. I owe you one.'

'Don't mention it,' Letty said, then she hung up the phone and went upstairs to fetch a clean apron.

The addition of Jean's cake meant Letty was a little later than planned in getting the pie into the oven. Fortunately, Donald was home from the pub a little later than planned.

'Good day, dear?' she said.

Donald grunted, kicking his shoes off into the middle of the hallway.

'Well you're home now, you can put your feet up.'

He gruffed as he wiped himself clean. Like Letty, Donald had aged substantially since their early days. His once slender frame had extended around the middle, and his previously dark hair was now much more salt than pepper. Letty leant forwards for her back-from-work kiss. Donald, seemingly oblivious, twisted his shoulders and began up the stairs.

'I'm going to have a bath. I take it you'll be cooking all night?'

'Oh, okay then. I've got a few jobs to do,' Letty said, suddenly feeling guilty about agreeing to Jean's last-minute request. 'Are you alright, dear? Is something wrong?'

Donald paused, turned back and removed his glasses.

'Just tired, that's all,' he said. Letty studied his face. The wrinkles around his eyes had deepened lately, as had the frown line between his eyebrows. It was age, she told herself. It happened to the best of them. A good meal and he would be looking right as rain again.

'Well, dinner can keep in the oven for as long as you need. Why don't you go upstairs and have a good soak? Take as long as you need.'

Donald grunted and began back up the stairs. Letty watched on, feeling peculiarly helpless.

Conversation over dinner was stagnant. Letty's mind was elsewhere – mainly on how she could tell her husband about the secretly amassed small fortune – while Donald spent the majority of the time gazing at the wallpaper and pushing peas around his plate. It was the type of response that would normally have left Letty wondering if she'd forgotten to season the meat, although it tasted spot on to her.

'Are you sure you're alright, dear?' Letty said as the gravy began to show signs of coagulation.

'What?' Donald's head sprung up from the plate. 'Oh, yes, yes. Do stop fussing. Do stop fussing.' He closed his eyes. 'Sorry, love. It's not you. It's me.'

'Are you sure you don't want to talk about it?'

'I'm tired; that's all. There's really nothing to talk about.'

Letty paused.

'Well, make sure you tell me if there's anything I can do,' she said.

'You know I will.' His hand reached across the table for hers. 'I've always told you everything.'

A dull throb twisted in Letty's gut.

Letty had spent a good part of her married life trying to figure out how she could tell Donald about the money. She'd debated surprising him with a round-the-world cruise or a month long Safari to see the gorillas in Africa. But Donald wasn't one for foreign food, and truth be told, the flight over to Guernsey for their honeymoon all those years ago had been enough to put her off flying ever again.

She considered the possibility of early retirement, but what would they be retiring for? With no grandchildren and the rest of his family up north, there was only so much time Donald could spend at the bowls clubs. Besides, he liked his job, and so did she, most of the time. Soon, she thought, as she picked his shoes up off the floor where he'd dropped them. She would definitely tell him soon.

It was after she'd loaded up the dishwasher, while checking the current situation of cake orders, that Letty flipped over the calendar from August to September.

'Donald?' She called through to the living room. 'Donald dear?' Donald appeared in the doorway.

'You know it's the retreat next week, don't you?'

'What was that?' A confused expression graced his eyebrows.

'Your retreat. The water company one. It's next week. Or at least that's what the calendar says.' She pointed at the faded pencil marks scratched into the paper.

'I, Well ... Well ...'

'You hadn't forgotten, had you? That's not like you.'

Donald's cheeks flushed pink.

'Of course, I'd not forgotten. I'd ... I'd just decided not to go.'

'Not to go? I thought it was the highlight of your year? All those homebrews and card games.'

Donald mumbled something.

'Love, are you sure you're alright? You don't seem yourself tonight.'

'Honestly.' Donald's hands flew into the air. 'What have I done to deserve all this nagging? I said I don't want to go. Is that such a big issue?'

Letty's jaw dropped, and an unfamiliar heat bloomed behind her eyes. 'Donald?'

Donald's face was set in stone. A moment later he shook the expression away with a sigh.

'I'm sorry, love. Really, I am.' He kneaded his temples with his knuckles. 'I need a little time out. Is that okay? Just a couple of drinks. There's no need to fuss.'

Letty nodded with the minutest of movements. 'Of course. I've got all my baking to do anyway.'

Donald leant forward and planted a kiss on her forehead. His lips lingered there. Letty raised her arms to embrace him.

'I won't be late home,' Donald said, stepping away from Letty and her hug. 'But don't stay up if you don't want to. I love you, Mrs Ferguson.'

'I love you too, Mr Ferguson.'

With Donald at the pub, Letty got on with the cakes. She fussed. She knew she did. Perhaps it would have been different if they had had children. It was no wonder he got a little annoyed now and again with all her pestering and bothering. This week, Letty decided, as she dug out a bottle of toxic green food colouring, she would make sure Donald had all the space he needed and absolutely no nagging. Satisfied that this was the solution to her husband's problems, Letty took out her weighing scales and got started in earnest.

Of all the cakes she did now, the stress linked with these

two birthday cakes was by far the worst. In fact, Letty considered, as she set her oven temperature and tied her apron, she would rather have done another two-hundred-person wedding cake, completely with five different sponges and gluten free flour, for the stress they caused her. But she'd agreed to it, as she always did.

Victoria had called the house phone weeks before to ensure all preparations were in place.

'I want to make sure you haven't forgotten that it's the twins' birthday next month,' she said, her tone overly jovial, in a manner that always meant she was after something.

'Of course not,' Letty said.

'Because they'll be ever so disappointed if you're not there.'

'We wouldn't miss it.'

'Well, they'll be so pleased to hear that.'

A slight pause punctuated the conversation. Letty held her breath as she waited for the next bit. It didn't take long.

'And you're still happy to make the cakes, aren't you?' Victoria said. 'Only I know we didn't manage to meet up for Mum's ... you know, but if you aren't, then we could have done with a bit of extra warning you see.'

'Yes, I'm still happy to make the cakes.'

An audible sigh of relief rattled down the phone.

'Well, that's good.' There was another pause. This time, Letty was unsure who was supposed to fill it. She opened her mouth ready to say something about the weather, but Victoria cut her off before she could start.

'Of course, you know the children have a series of designs. I've sent them through to your email. I'm sure you must have seen them already.'

'My email?'

Letty's stomach dropped.

There was no way she was going to get through this one unscathed. 'The thing is ...' she started.

'You don't have to follow the pictures exactly. They're just a guide.'

'No, it's not that, I don't mind pictures—'

'If it's size, we've invited forty, but there's bound to be more. You know what these things can—'

'No, it's not that.'

'Then what is it? What's the problem?'

Letty swallowed. Admitting to the problem was going to cause another problem she really did not want to face. Not admitting it would probably end in disaster. Letty mumbled something into the phone.

'What was that?' Victoria said. 'You're mumbling. Speak properly.'

'I'm not ... that's not to say I can't, it's only ...'

'For God's sake, spit it out, Leticia.'

Letty coughed, cleared her throat, and gripped the phone receiver as tight as she could.

'I don't know how to use the emails yet,' she whispered.

A prolonged silence hung down the end of the line.

'What do you mean you can't use email?'

'It's just ... you see—'

'What about the iPad we got you for Christmas?'

'I know. That was very kind of you—'

'Do you know how much they cost?'

'I'm sure it—'

'Have you even used it?'

'Of course,' Letty insisted with a heavy dose of indignation in her voice. 'Only, well ... when Felix showed me, it was a little while ago.'

'A little while ago? That was Boxing Day, Leticia.'

32

Letty hung her head. 'I'm sorry,' she whispered down the phone, sounding decidedly younger than her fifty-four years.

As she waited for a response, her stomach squirmed and tightened. Finally, Victoria spoke.

'I'll put the pictures through your letterbox,' she said. The line went dead. Letty sighed. It could have gone worse.

CHAPTER 5

ALTER WATCHED the horse and rider disappear in the swirls of snow and mist, wondering whether he should laugh or cry. He had objected to a point – after all, what would a man of his position want with a simple farrier's notebook – but in the end, Walter had had to concede. Even with the strongest will, he had no standing in a situation like that, and they both knew it.

'I'm sorry,' Edi said when he told her of the turn of events. 'We'll save. I'll get you another note book.' Her words did little to console him.

The girls were asleep in front of the fire, their arms snuggled around one another for warmth, a soft amber light from the hearth casting shadows on their skin. Condensation slid down the window and walls causing puddles to gather on the ground. Walter bent down and kissed his daughters then plucked another log from the pile.

'They're probably sat around in their slippers, drinking mead, laughing at the stupid blacksmith who writes.'

'I suspect that's the last thing they're doing,' Edi said. 'You said he read them all. He must have liked them?'

Walter dropped the log on the flames, where it sizzled and spat.

'Perhaps,' he said.

*W*inter finally gave way to spring and a new bloom of bluebells blanketed the grass outside the workshop. While the air inside the shop retained its typical stench of soot and sweat, outside was clean and crisp, and choruses of bird song drifted in through the open doors. There was newness to the land, a feeling that anything could happen. Those were the types of days Walter enjoyed the most. Particularly, given the current absence of his employer.

Pemberton was apparently attending to urgent family business in town, although given that he had not once mentioned a single member of his family to Walter, Walter couldn't help but wonder exactly how urgent the situation could be. These absences had become atypically frequent of late, and although he would have previously deemed it impossible, his employer's mood had also deteriorated. Nowadays, Pemberton barely spoke to Walter unless in a coded manner of grunts and tuts. It was of no loss to Walter. If anything, he preferred this more muted Pemberton as opposed to the one who fired insults every thirty seconds.

Walter stood elbow deep in leathers, hammering out a strip of red-hot iron over the anvil. Every strike sent a thousand glowing embers into the air. When he'd first started his training, each one felt like a needle as it singed his skin. Now, his nerves were dead to them. His mind wandered as he worked, words drifting in and around his thoughts, but he'd not written since the pilferage of his notebook. He wasn't sure he would ever write again. The idea of men mocking his innermost contemplations was more than he could bear.

A little after midday, a carriage drew up outside the gates. Hearing the horses coming down the drive, Walter placed the metal down on the bench and ambled outside.

'Augustus. Fantastic. You are just the man I was looking for.' The gentleman grinned as he disembarked his transit. He was dressed in a buttoned coat with velvet facing that cinched in at his waist and a pair of gas pipes so white that Walter's immediate concerns – besides the gentlemen's unscheduled appearance – fell on whoever had to try to bleach them at the end of the day. In his arms, the gentleman carried a small box.

Having not seen hide nor hair of him since the winter, Walter assumed the gentleman to be wintering in London. Now, with his unscheduled and unexpected return, Walter found his fists tightening in his pockets and a definite corkscrewing somewhere in the region of his gallbladder.

'Do the horses need to be shod again, sir?' Walter said, making a beeline for the animals.

'No, no. Nothing like that. Nothing like that at all. This is purely a social visit.' The man strode towards him.

'Social visit, sir?'

'Yes, I have a gift for you.'

Walter stopped. 'A gift, sir?'

The man arched his eyebrow. 'Are you deliberately repeating everything I'm saying?'

'Repeating sir?' Walter blushed. 'No, sir. Sorry. I mean, I was repeating, but not—'

The gentleman waved him silent.

'It's fine, Augustus. I have come to deliver these. I wanted to see your face personally when they arrived.'

Walter eyed the box in the man's arms. Sized a little

bigger than a shoebox and wrapped in brown paper, the string around it was slack indicating that whatever was inside had already been inspected. A nervous prickling spread up through Walter's belly.

'Please, it's nothing bad. Take a look and see.' The man motioned to the workshop with a flick of his chin. 'Shall we?'

With his nerves on edge, Walter headed back into the shop and cleared a space on the workbench between the horseshoes and hammers. The gentleman placed the package down.

'After you,' he said.

The tingling spread to Walter's hands. His fingers quivered as he tugged on the string and loosened the knot. With one sharp pull, the string fell limp and the paper collapsed down the sides.

His breath caught in his lungs. He was either going to pass out or vomit, he thought. Or perhaps both, simultaneously.

'I don't understand,' he said.

The gentleman coughed and cleared his throat.

'Well,' he said. 'I took it upon myself. It's nothing spectacular, mind you. Only twenty copies. And I have already taken one for myself. But that leaves nineteen for you.'

'Sir, I don't know what to say.'

'There is nothing to say. In my opinion, your poems are easily as good as Duck and Thompson and deserve to be read. And if not by many, then by a few who have the integrity and intelligence to know a good thing when they see it.'

Walter picked up one of the small blue books. *Seas, Swallows and all but Sorrows*, it said. Beneath that was his name "Walter J. Augustus".

'I hope you don't mind. I had to take some liberties. The poem of that name was a particular favourite of mine.'

Walter's eyes filled. In a quick sweep, he brushed the tears aside, drew his eyes away from the book and lifted his head.

'Sir, I ... I ...' A lump had formed in his throat and was prohibiting him from making any further comment. He looked upwards and hurriedly wiped his eyes for a second time.

'Ahh, and before I forget ... Your original, for I would hate to be branded a thief.'

The man delved inside his coat and pulled out the pale blue notebook. The pages appeared a little more thumbed than Walter remembered, but it was definitely his. He took it, conveying his gratitude the best he could through a single nod.

Silence followed as both men were unsure where to look or what to do next. Regaining his professionalism, Walter cleared his throat and held out his hand.

'I am indebted to you, sir,' he said. 'You have my most heartfelt thanks.'

'And that's all a gentleman ever needs.' The gentleman smiled and turned to leave. 'Please excuse my hurried departure,' he said. 'There is a meet over in Aldsworth and if I'm quick, I may make second horse.'

'Of course.'

Walter followed the man to his carriage. He gripped the copy of the book, holding it firmly at his side. When they were a stride away from the horses, the gentleman stopped.

'Oh.' He pivoted back around to face Walter. 'And about those liberties. You'll find another one inside.'

'Sir?'

'Dedications are all the rage, you see. And I thought it would be rather forthright to place myself there. But I am sure you will be pleased with my selection. Anyway, I had best be off. I'll be sending a boy down in the next couple of days with some fillies we've just bought. I've let your employer know.'

'Thank you, thank you, and thank you again, sir.'

'My pleasure, Augustus. My absolute pleasure.' With one final half-wave, he leapt aboard the carriage.

Walter stood and watched them until the horse had reached the end of the road and then continued to stand rooted to the spot until the clop of hooves became too faint to hear. He glanced down at the book in his hand and ran his fingertips over the cover. It was beautiful, pristine. The most pristine thing he'd ever known, and it was all his. Every word. The lump reformed in the back of his throat as his thoughts moved to Edith and her reaction. Pemberton hadn't said if he was coming back that afternoon, but for the last few weeks, his absences had been days rather than hours. Today would likely be no different. Walter dashed across to the workshop, checked the forge and, still clutching the single new book, ran back outside and bolted the door. He would be fifteen minutes. Twenty at most. Halfway out the gate Walter remembered the gentleman's final words. He turned to the first page of his book. It read;

'To E.M. Pemberton. For his guidance.'

CHAPTER 6

$\mathcal{T}$HE PREVIOUS evening's rain had brought with it an aroma of damp earth and dandelions, although as was the custom on Saturday mornings at Letty's, these aromatic nuances were met with a heavy injection of bacon fat. She'd been up since seven putting the finishing touches to Jean's cakes. While her initial idea had been a simple congratulations cake with a bit of coloured bunting and some piped wording, she'd let her imagination run away with her. In addition to her original plans, the final masterpiece was crowned with a small square shop front, complete with yellow front door, red brickwork, fondant icing Jean, and an array of bric-a-brac. The door even had a white fondant note, with *back in 5 mins* scribbled on it.

'What's your plan for today, dear?' Letty asked as she dropped three crispy bacon rashers into the centre of Donald's plate, beside four buttered triangles of brown toast and half a grilled tomato. 'Are you planning on coming home for lunch? Only the kitchen's going to be out of bounds 'til I get the cakes done.' Letty went back to the frying pan for the sausages, which she placed directly onto the toast. 'But I can make you some sandwiches if you want.' She made the final trip to the countertop for the fried mushrooms.

'Well?' she said. 'Do you want me to?'

'What's that, dear?' Donald blinked.

'Lunch? I said do you want me to make you lunch?' Donald continued to stare blankly. 'To take to the club? So, I can get on here and work.'

'What?' Donald said, shaking his head. 'Sandwiches?'

'For your lunch. Did you hear a word I said?'

'No, sorry. I mean yes. It's fine. It's fine.'

'So, you'll get lunch out?'

'What? When?'

'This morning!'

Donald scrunched up his eyes and shook his head.

'I don't know. Does it really matter at this precise minute?' He pushed his fingers against his head and inhaled loudly.

Letty stepped forward and placed her hand on his shoulder.

'Are you alright, love?' she said.

Donald let out a groan. 'I'm fine. Just tired, love; that's all. Stop fussing, really.'

Remembering her vow to herself, Letty bit down on her lip and did what she was told. This no fussing was going to be harder than she'd first thought.

The kitchen was kitsch, seventies style with minimal updates other than white goods. The tiles and counters were fawn coloured, the cabinets a deep beige, and although the flooring had been replaced three times since their arrival in the seventies, it had puckered and split in various places.

Letty tottered about, tidying away while Donald finished his food.

'That was delicious as always,' he said, using his last bit of toast to mop up the juices on the plate. When he was finished, he stood up and moved to place his plate in the sink.

'Sorry I've been a grump, love,' he said. 'You never know, this week might be just the thing I need to get me back on track.'

'So, you are going?'

'Why not, eh?'

'Hopefully, you'll come back a bit happier.'

He reached out one arm for an embrace. Letty hesitated, then stepped towards him.

'Ow!' Letty stopped in her tracks. 'Donald Ferguson. Why is this in here?' Her back clicked as she reached down to pick up a steel-toe boot. 'Honestly, if I'd have known I'd be picking up shoes from here, there, and everywhere for thirty years, I might have made you put that in the wedding vows too.'

'Too late for that now,' Donald said. He grabbed her waist and pulled her in, nuzzling his chin into his neck. Letty blushed. At this rate, she'd never get the other cakes done.

*O*utside, a misty drizzle was hazing up the sky. While the shop was well within walking distance, it took only a brief moment's deliberation for Letty to opt for the car. The last thing she wanted was to ruin the cake on route. Donald had already headed to the bowls club, his mood a marked improvement since breakfast.

Jean's shop was what she deemed *nostalgic bric-a-brac*, selling a range of collectables and vintage paraphernalia from books and clothes to furniture and toys. Positioned between a recently vacated kebab shop and a Chinese take-away, it sat beneath a neon sign that flashed, Mystic Moiras. (Letty wasn't entirely sure whether Mystic Moiras was some form of clairvoyance service, or a perversely specialised brothel, although the lack of apostrophe in the signage had her leaning towards the latter).

Letty parked and gathered the cake from the passenger seat. Carrying was normally Donald's job. They often joked that if she did ever set up a cake shop he would definitely be in the running for a position as a delivery driver. With Letty's concentration fully focused on the cake, it was not until she was standing directly in front of the vivid yellow door that she noticed the scrap paper stuck to it. Letty groaned. She knew she should have rung beforehand.

'I'm here! Sorry, I'm here!'

Halfway up the street, a woman with silver hair was waving her arms, her bright orange jacket flapping as she ran towards Letty and the shop.

'Sorry,' she said as she whipped the *back in five minutes* note off the door and stuffed it into her pocket.

'I had to dash out for a second. Margo at the cafe managed to get herself locked in the toilets. All sorted now, though. Honestly, that woman.' Jean unlocked the door and held it open for Letty to step through. 'You weren't waiting long, were you?'

'No, I just got here.'

'Oh, thank goodness. I was worried you'd been stuck outside for ages.'

The inside of the shop had been prepared for the upcoming party. A Happy Birthday banner was strung above the cash register and various clothes rails and display cases had been pushed to the sides to make a little more. Letty viewed the scene sceptically. In her opinion, they would have been better off waiting until the evening and having the function in someone's house, but Jean had never been one to stick to the obvious. Her shop was a testament to that.

An old gramophone with a dented horn overwhelmed

the far corner, while multi-coloured scarves and retro sunglasses hung around the frame of a spray-painted mirror which marked the dressing room. There were faux-fur coats, flared jeans, and books by the hundred. Stacks of retro board-game boxes – containing everything from Guess Who to a battered old Ouija board – filled the shelves along the back of the store and on the floor sat various vintage sideboards and mismatched chairs.

Letty found herself in the shop almost every week chatting to Jean but save for a few pretty scarves she'd found as presents for Victoria, it wasn't a place she shopped. For one, the trousers and skirts lacked the elasticated waists that she'd become accustomed to over the last few years.

'Letty, you're a saviour,' Jean, said, dropping the keys on the counter. 'Here, let me take that from you.' She pushed her finger into the box to take a peek. 'May I?' she asked.

'Be my guest,' Letty said and then, because people's reaction to her cakes – and friend's reactions in particular – always caused her to blush, she busied herself with a box of antique looking books beside the till.

'These look lovely,' Letty said, picking one at random off the top. The powder blue cover was faded and tattered but held a patina reminiscent of a much more regal age. A smell of aged motes and damp cardboard wafted towards her. She flicked open to the first page, her eyes half-heartedly scanning across the dedication.

'Oh I know, they're beautiful, aren't they?' Jean was struggling with the tape on the cake box. 'I picked them up at an old lady's house clearance. Probably all tat, but you never know. Perhaps there's a first edition in there somewhere.' Then, changing her point of focus, exclaimed, 'Oh Letty, this is beautiful. Absolutely lovely.' She threw her hands up to her mouth. 'You didn't have to go to this much trouble.'

Letty's cheeks coloured.

'It's nothing.'

'It's amazing. A whole miniature shop. And is that me? Oh, I hope my skin looks as good in real life.'

Letty fondled the book in her hand. 'I'm glad you like it.'

'It's perfect. How much do I owe you?'

Letty put the book back on the top of the box. 'Don't be silly; it's a present.'

'What? No, I asked you to do this. You have to let me pay you.'

'I do not. It's my birthday present to the shop.'

'You can't do that.'

'Yes, I can.'

Letty planted her hands firmly on her hips, the way she did when she was dealing with snotty four-year-olds in the shop. Jean mirrored the action, adding a pout to her response.

'Well, you have to let me give you something,' she said.

'Honestly—'

'Here, take this then.' She reached across Letty, plucked the pale blue book back off the box and pushed it firmly into Letty's hand.

'Take it.'

'I can't.'

'Go on.'

'It might be valuable.'

'Then sell it, and you and Donald can take early retirement.'

Letty squinted at the book. The cover was so faded she could barely make out the title, let alone the author, and it certainly didn't look like the normal type of book she would have picked out to read. But Jean's face was resolute.

'If you're sure?'

'Positive.'

'Well, thank you. Thank you very much then.'

Letty helped Jean get the cake safely out of the box before making her excuses to leave.

'Are you sure you don't want to stay? People are going to start coming in a minute and I know they'd love to meet you after seeing this.'

'Thank you, but I really need to get off,' Letty said. 'It's the twin's birthday party tomorrow and I need to make sure I get their cakes done.'

Jean's eyes bulged. 'Good luck with that.'

Letty laughed. 'Have fun.'

CHAPTER 7

'WE'LL KEEP ONE copy for us,' Walter said. His chest still wheezing from the run. He had sprinted down the road, keeping the book clutched close to his chest, worried that it may slip out of his hand or be blown away by some heavy gust of wind. 'And keep one for each of the girls. The rest we can give to family.'

'I'm not sure how many of my family can read,' Edi said.

'Then we can teach them.'

Edi moved her fingers from the book to Walter's cheek.

'I'm very proud of you,' she said. 'It's an heirloom. For our children and our children's children. All of them will know what a clever man their grandfather was.' She took the book from his hand and placed it above the hearth. 'I want it where I can see it always,' she said.

Walter nuzzled her neck and a warm bubble of fluffiness rose up from his toes. Generation after generation reading his book, knowing his name; surely that was all any man could ever hope for.

Walter skipped his way back to the workshop, whistling a

tune the entire time. A book. He had his own book. No longer was he some silly farrier who scribbled and daydreamed and spent his free time in a fantasy world of prose and poetry. He was an author. A published – be it limited – author. Now that he'd told Edi, he wanted to tell the world. He would start handing them out that evening, he thought, but he needed to make a list first. With only fifteen copies to spare, it was important he made his decisions wisely.

He turned off down the little lane that led to the workshop, his thoughts still adrift with possibilities of his newfound fame. It was only when he reached the bank of bluebells that the tickling excitement in his stomach twisted slightly. His pace slowed as he studied the view. Walter squinted. Something was different; he just wasn't sure what.

Ten feet from the workshop, Walter realised what had him on edge. He took a tentative step forward, trying to convince himself it was merely a trick of the light. The blue wooden door, with its heavy metal padlock was now ajar, a russet chunk of fire-light gleaming through the gap. Walter swallowed. He distinctly remembered closing the door, for he'd secured the book in the crook of his arm and had been terrified of dropping it into the dirt. Perhaps he'd been too focused on the book, he thought, for it seemed unlikely that the wind could have caused it to blow so far open.

He placed his hand against the wooden frame and pushed the door inwards. Half a step in he froze.

'Augustus. How nice of you to join me.'

Pemberton stood in front of the newly stoked forge. The light fell in such a way that it caused long flame-speckled shadows to rise up from above his temples, giving an appearance that was dramatically infernal.

'I assume you have an excuse?' he said.

Walter swallowed. Sweat beaded down his neck. His throat grew tighter and tighter by the second.

'Please, humour me,' Pemberton said. 'A death perhaps? Although, disappointingly, I see not your own.'

'I ... I ...' Walter stuttered as he tried to find a reason for his absence. His eyes were still fixed on the devil horns that protruded from Pemberton's head, while the sweat from his neck had now soaked through his collar and ran down his back.

'I will not deny I am disappointed,' Pemberton said, moving for the first time since Walter's arrival. 'Of course, I was under no illusion of your stolidness. Your lethargy and day-dreaminess have been a burden since your arrival. But this ... this negligence. This outright impertinence ...' Pemberton let his voice fade into the fire.

Walter gulped.

'Tell me, Augustus, what would you do in my situation?'

'Do?' Walter's insides flipped.

Racking his brain for a suitable response, Walter remembered the paper package with the remaining books that he'd placed on the workbench. His pulse knocked harder. Pemberton pulled a crisp brown packet of pear drops from his pocket and Walter's adrenaline spiked. If Pemberton had not seen the package, then any slight movement by Walter could draw attention to it. However, had he not, then this could be Walter's only chance to save them. His job was as good as gone now – of that Walter was certain – but he still had a chance to save his work. With a sharp intake of breath, Walter's eyes darted to the side of the room. He frowned, and then scoured from one side of the room to the other. Forgetting the imminent threat of dismissal, he lifted his feet to continue his search.

'Are you looking for this?'

Pemberton's lips curled at the corners as he bent down beside the forge.

Walter's stomach plummeted.

'Please, they are—'

'Stolen I assume. You know, Augustus, I thought you were a lot of things. Lazy, slow, stupid beyond belief. But a thief? No, I'm afraid that one skipped me by.'

'Please...' Walter inched forward, his hands outstretched and quivering. 'They're—'

'And books. Why on Earth would a man steal books?'

'They're not stolen; they're—'

'I'm sorry,' Pemberton silenced him with a look. He lifted the books from the ground, hovering them in front of the flames. 'I can't have it. I can't have a thief in my workshop no more than I can have stolen property. I'm afraid this is the end. For you and your contraband.' He twisted his arms towards the fire.

'No!' Walter shouted and made his one and only lunge for his employer.

Walter J. Augustus was unequivocally not to blame for the death of Edward John Pemberton. The event – which happened in Walter's presence and with him as the sole witness – was caused by a massive heart attack, which, in turn, was brought on by a hereditary defect. Pemberton was well-aware of this defect and had been seeking medical treatment for over a year. His local surgeon and apothecary and even a specialist in London were all informed on the matter. Walter was not. Edward John Pemberton was laid to rest three days later in the cemetery of St Lawrence's parish church.

Pemberton was an only child, who had no traceable kin and had left no will. He had no friends to speak of, and even the pastor could not recall the last time they'd spoken. The police and courts – and those landed gentry whose main concern was having adequately shod horses for the remaining few months of the hunting season – deemed the most sensible thing to do was leave the shop in Walter's capable hands, on the stipulation that should an heir become apparent he must immediately vacate the premises and hand over any profits that he'd procured. The physician, with which Pemberton had been in regular consultation, testified to Walter's amiable disposition and the esteem in which he was held by the late Pemberton, who according to the doctor, viewed Walter more as a son than an employee. After the event, Walter wept to his wife, while his sole remaining copy of *Seas, Swallows and all but Sorrows* sat upon the hearth beside them.

~

*I*t was simply a matter of deciding which cake to finish first. Dakota's cake (the first D in the double-degenerates) was a fairly standard princess dress, variations of which she'd requested for the last three years. This year, the princess of choice was Belle from *Beauty and the Beast*. It was a slight deviation from the stereotypical Disney Belle, given that this princess was to have a short, blond bob, along with a Gucci watch, flower print boots and a piebald pony beside her. Even with those additions, it was fairly straight-forward, and in a little under two hours, it was done and dusted. The second cake was less clear-cut.

The print outs Victoria had stuffed through the letterbox had over a hundred samples of dinosaur cakes, ranging from two-foot T-Rexs to three tier fondant covered volcanoes with handcrafted pterodactyls and buttercream waterfalls. Unlike the princess cake, where exacting instructions had been scribbled down on the paper, Letty had been left to her own devices. It was nerve-wracking to the point of heartburn. On a piece of paper, she sketched out possible designs and colour combinations, and after half an hour or so of going back and forth, she settled on a reclining T-Rex hybrid, made from purple fondant with red spots and stripes down its back.

Letty hummed along to the radio as she cut and moulded the different colours. This was her favourite part of the work – the creative part. There was so much freedom. She spread her tools out on the tawny worktop, selecting each one as and when she needed it.

Halfway through the spots, she glanced up at the clock and was amazed to see that two hours had passed. Her stomach growled as if confirming this fact. Putting down the cutters, she covered the icing then headed to the fridge to fix herself a quick meal. That would be another advantage to owning her own bakery, she thought, unlimited snack breaks.

Letty took her lunch into the living room to eat and while chewing on the bread remembered the gift that Jean had given her as payment. She retrieved her bag from the hall, pulled out the book and flicked it open to a random page. Her stomach sank. Poetry. She'd never been a fan of poetry, not since being made to cover it in excruciating detail at secondary school. She tossed it onto the coffee table in front of her and returned to her sandwich, opting instead to read the weekend newspaper Donald had picked up. Ten minutes later, she was back in the kitchen, putting the finishing brush of glitter on the scales and talons, the book all but forgotten under the Saturday paper and its copious number of supple-mentary magazines.

*D*eciding to make the most of what was possibly his last day in the interim, Walter gathered a loaf of bread and a small bottle of ale from his miraculously stocked larder and placed them into his satchel. He was dressed in his usual attire of a twill woven shirt and breeches but had abandoned his apron for the day. Maybe people didn't even wear clothes in the next stage, who knew? With a light-hearted jaunt, he stepped out through his back door and strolled to the end of the garden.

A narrow path lined with daisies and buttercups materialised and meandered down to the bottom of the cliff. His feet crunched on the aromatic grass. He couldn't have asked for a better day.

A little way away from the shingled coast, Walter stopped. He stared and blinked and felt his pulse hasten in his veins. Dampness built on the palms of his hand, and a noose-like sensation tightened around his throat. Standing on the shore was a figure. This was his beach. Why would anyone come here? Who even knew about it? Walter's pulse cranked up another notch. He scanned the area. It was definitely his beach, his place alone, his private corner of the interim. Perhaps it was a mistake, he thought. With silent steps he trod forward. The grass gave way to sand dunes and then to shingle, all the while his eyes locked on the shadowy figure. He was less than six feet away before the air was knocked from his lungs.

'No,' Walter gasped.

The face turned around to look at him. It was a long face, so long it was difficult to see where his nose ended, and chin began. His cheeks were hollowed, as if sucking on a sweet, and the smell of pear drops that emanated from his breath appeared to confirm this. In one fluid movement, the body went from sitting to standing and then peering straight down his nose to Walter.

'Well, Augustus,' he said his voice patronisingly slow. 'What have you done this time?'

CHAPTER 8

*P*EARLESCENT CRABS skittered across the pebbles, while pale blue waves lapped quietly on the shingle beach. Pemberton stood over Walter. His face harboured a look that could have rendered the most tumultuous of harpies mute, while his lips squeezed and pulsed around a hard-boiled confectionery. Walter could not say precisely how long he'd stood there, gawping like a washed-up sardine, not only because time was an abstract matter in the interim, but because the whole of existence appeared to be completely out of whack.

'Well?' Pemberton said again. 'I assume you're to blame for this.'

'This ... this?'

'This? My relocation.' Pemberton swept his arm in acknowledgement of his whereabouts.

Walter was dumbfounded. When at last he managed to find his voice, his words came sporadically in fits and starts.

'You were? You're here? But you, you ...' The stutter continued. 'You moved on. You were ... you were ... how? Why? You were there?'

Momentarily forgetting the disastrousness of the situation, his heart performed a syncopated skip beneath his rib cage.

'What's it like?' Walter said. 'Is it what we imagine? Is it perfect? Do you get to—'

'Really?' Pemberton dismissed him with a sniff. 'What may or may not be is not the matter for discussion. What I need to know is what you're going to do about it.'

'Me?'

Walter continued to stare. Pemberton, his employer, the man he'd avoided like the plague in both life and afterlife, was somehow back and standing in Walter's personal domain. It made no sense. Pemberton had moved on from the interim. People didn't come back. Not unless they'd somehow been re-remembered down on Earth. Not unless ...

The realisation hit like a rogue gelding. His knees wobbled like semi-set jam. Simultaneously, he was sweating and freezing, gasping for air, yet unable even to draw a breath. Pemberton, on the other hand, was as rigid as a rasp.

'And at last, you realise. Of course, I was there. I was in it all. I was—' Pemberton stopped. He pressed his lips together in a line and refocused his glare. 'And now, I find myself here. And I suspect we both know the reason why.' There was an accented pause between each of his words.

'I ... I ...' Walter tried.

'What I want to know,' Pemberton said, 'is how, exactly, I ended up back in the thoughts of someone down there, and precisely what you are going to do to remedy it?'

*O*utside was dusk and the sea breeze carried the scent of evening jasmine in through an open window. Although purple clouds gathered in prominent soufflés and the sun sat low across the horizon, the sky showed no more signs of completing its darkening than it had when Pemberton had arrived several hours ago.

Walter sat on the window ledge, his head bowed. He had offered various alternatives in food and beverage, but his former employer had declined them all, with a curt, yet highly efficient, 'No.'

Currently, Pemberton was standing by the stove. His cheeks were pinched to vertical as he sucked on yet another pear drop from his unending supply and his eyes had spent the entire duration narrowed in a scowl. Walter shuffled uncomfortably.

It felt like he'd shot back nearly two centuries, his belly rife with knots and whirls.

'What do you mean you don't know where it is?' Pemberton said for the umpteenth time. 'Do you not think it might have been wise to keep an eye on the thing? God damn it boy, what have you been doing all these years?'

Walter mumbled something about waiting and spending time on his own and missing Edith. Pemberton snorted his rebuff.

'We need to find it. Immediately. Do you know how long people live nowadays? We could be here another sixty years. Together. And that's a good scenario.' Pemberton crushed the pear drop between his molars with a splintering force. Walter flinched.

'Let's start where we can. Where was the book when you last saw it? You can remember that, surely?'

Walter's cheeks took on an even deeper shade of scarlet.

The problem with being in the interim so long was that it was particularly easy to lose track of time. Walter could remember asking Edith's father for her hand in marriage like it happened only that morning. As it was with the birth of his children and grandchildren and the day his eldest, Vera, first sang in the parish choir. But those more recent events – and particularly those he'd witnessed since his passing – span swirling around his memory, like a drunken deluge of déjà vu. The death of his youngest granddaughter, for instance; he couldn't tell you where that happened, or her age at her time of passing, yet he could remember the surge of emotion at her arrival in the interim and the blissful burning in his daughter's soul at the reunion.

The tugs he felt from Betty were echoes now. It wasn't like she was still reading the book, or had it tucked away under her hospital pillow; although, thought Walter, he might do a quick check there, just in case. Maybe if she'd had some direct thoughts about the book, he could have helped, but as far as he could tell, there was nothing he could do.

Walter was still busy dwelling in his abyss of self-deprecation when a thought struck. He sprung up from the window ledge.

'What about you?' he said. 'It was you that was brought back. You were thought about, not me. I didn't feel a thing. No one new is thinking about me at all. It's you. It's all you!'

Walter pointed his finger in glee before dropping it in an instant. He stepped back hastily.

'I'm, I ... I didn't mean ... I'm, uhm ...' He shut his mouth. The warranted spike in his adrenaline was undoubtedly on account of Pemberton's previous death under such similar circumstances. Their current metaphysical states did little to relieve his anxiety.

Pemberton pouted. His lips squeezed so tightly around the sweet it made his eyes bulge outwards and nostrils flare. Walter continued to wait. His metaphysical heart drummed in his metaphysical chest as the silence prolonged, and after almost a minute, Walter couldn't wait any longer. He opened his mouth to speak, but Pemberton beat him to it.

'For once,' Pemberton said, 'I think you might be right.' Then he swivelled on his heel and marched towards the door and out. Walter stood in stunned silence. Two minutes later, Pemberton's elongated head appeared back in the doorway.

'Well,' he said. 'Are you coming?'

Walter grabbed his coat and hurried after him.

~

*L*etty wished she could hold Donald's hands, but, like hers, his were weighed down with an oversized, precariously balanced cake box. 'We could just drop the cakes off and leave,' Donald suggested. 'Ring the doorbell first, then leg it. You'll have to do the sprint part while I get the engine running.' Letty ignored him.

The hedge around the house had been pruned to precisely three feet, excluding the corners where a specialist topiary expert from London had been hired to create four five-foot monoliths with cascading rhododendron. A smell of wax and leather polish rose from the BMW, which sat taking up far more room than needed on the driveway. Victoria's runaround Fiat appeared to have been tucked out of sight in the garage, Letty noticed.

Letty was met by her second Happy Birthday banner of the weekend, although this one was double the size, made entirely out of metallic helium balloons, and fully covered the doorway. She used her elbow to push them to the side, took a deep breath, and pressed the doorbell. A series of screams and yells drifted out through the letterbox.

'I was expecting you twenty minutes ago,' Victoria said, swinging the door open. Without so much as a second glance, she spun back into the house, leaving the door to close back on them. Donald jumped forward and caught it with his foot.

'Oh, it's been such a stress. I rang the caterers to check the order yesterday and they'd completely forgotten about Dakota's gluten intolerance. It was an absolute disgrace. Well, Felix got on the phone to them then, and you can imagine how that went. So anyway, they redid it all – and obviously, we're not paying – but honestly. What a palaver.'

'I didn't know Dakota had a gluten intolerance,' Letty said, her biceps suddenly trembling with the weight of the fully wheat-filled cake in her arms.

'Well, I don't know if she does. But that's not the point, is it?'

After struggling to remove their shoes without the use of their hands, Letty and Donald followed Victoria into the kitchen, where she was adding a healthy glug of wine to an already half-filled glass. Finally, she turned to face her sister. Her eyes widened.

'Oh, the cakes, of course. Right, they need to go in there.' She pointed out into the conservatory, where a large table was covered in numerous varieties of neon confectionery. 'And they have to stay in the boxes until we light them. The last thing we need is a vindictive nine-year-old with a Nerf gun to find these. That's the problem when you're as bright as my two. They make friends so easily, but how can they ever really trust anyone when everyone is secretly jealous of them?'

A loud thud reverberated across the ceiling and was followed by several profanities that, even when said by eight-year-olds, caused Letty to blush.

'I told you about the incident with the underpants, didn't I?' Victoria continued.

'I think—'

'All jealousy. Complete jealousy.'

With the cakes safely relocated, Victoria led them back into the kitchen, where she finally attempted to commence her role as host.

'Donald,' Victoria pecked her brother-in-law on both cheeks. 'Felix is in the games room if you want to join him. He's got a few bets on this afternoon, so I said he could sit in there until the guests start to arrive. Not that you count as a guest, of course.'

'Actually, I'm fine—'

'And you can take him a drink too,' she said, pushing a tumbler into Donald's hand. 'You know where it is, don't you? Down the hallway, past the drawing room, and next to the study. Just yell if you get lost.'

Donald looked to Letty, who shrugged apologetically.

Now that Donald had gone, Letty felt even more conspicuous. She'd spent a substantial amount of time that morning deciding what to wear, and though she'd been happy with her final decision – cream linen trousers with a blue paisley shirt and navy sandals – when leaving the house, she was now feeling rather hot around the collar.

'Drink?' Victoria asked, shaking a bottle of wine bottle in Letty's direction.

'Maybe later,' Letty said.

Victoria had gone for the layered look, wearing a draped scarf over a pair of nude trousers and a white top. Her nails were painted a vivid red and a sizeable collection of glittering stones finished the look. The scarf, Letty noted, was not one of the ones that she'd bought her over the years.

'You look nice,' Victoria said.

'I ... I ... Thank you,' Letty said, the surprise causing her to emit the words as a high-pitched squeak.

'Honestly, I really do admire how well you hold your weight. Whenever I put on a few pounds, I get all these horrible lumps and bumps and I look terrible. But you always carry it so well.'

The corners of Letty's mouth stretched tight.

'So,' Victoria said, disappearing out of the kitchen then reappearing with an oversized handbag. 'I bought this perfume the other day. Tell me what you think.'

Letty watched as Victoria emptied the contents of her handbag onto the draining board. First came the makeup, then the children's toys and then a ghastly looking wallet that appeared to be fabricated from a collection of dead crocodiles.

'Ahh, here it is.' With a pinch of her fingers, she plucked the lid off a yellow coloured bottle and sprayed the contents on her wrist. 'Have a sniff,' she said, thrusting her wrist under Letty's nose. 'What does it remind you of?'

The smell hit Letty right at the back of the throat. First, was merely an unkind assault on the olfactory system, but after a few seconds, the tones began to sink and mellow. Letty frowned and bit her lip. Peonies and plumeria drifted into her memory and stirred up long-forgotten images of family trips to the coast. She could see her mother so clearly spritzing herself from a small turquoise bottle and Letty watching on as the same delicate hands then proceeded to apply soft strokes of mascara around her bright green eyes.

'It ... it ...' Letty fought to find words.

'It smells like Mum, don't you think? I couldn't believe it when I first smelt it. Some woman was wearing it at Felix's work, and of course, I had to ask her where she got it. Anyway, it turns out it was this private little perfumery, and they only make twelve bottles a year or something, but I said to Felix, I said Felix ...'

Victoria's voice faded into the background. In Letty's mind, she was seven again, sitting on her mother's knee while she brushed her hair.

'You have beautiful hair,' her mother was saying. 'Girls would pay to have hair like this, so don't you go cutting it all off on some silly whim.'

'I won't,' Letty promised.

'Good. Silly whims won't help you in the long run. Believe me.'

'I do.'

'Letty. Letty? Are you even listening to me? Did you hear a word I said?'

Letty's eyes fluttered as she brought herself back to the room.

'Well?'

She shook her head, trying to shake the ache from her chest, yet desperate to cling to the memory that was already slipping out of reach. A heartbeat later, the moment had gone. Across the room, her sister glared.

'Yes, sorry,' Letty said. She cleared her throat and wiped her eyes with the back of her hand. 'Tiny perfumery, twelve bottles a year ...'

'Well obviously, I'd never wear it out of the house. It's vile. I'll probably end up binning it. Unless of course you want it.'

'I ... I'd ... yes. Yes, please,' Letty said, her voice once again starting to wobble. She could see the cafe now, the place they used to go to feed the seagulls. And the fair that would visit and procure all their coins in the promise of winning a goldfish. The heat was rebuilding behind her eyes, and a large swell was obstructing her airway. She needed to think of something else. Victoria was not one for tears at the best times and the last thing Letty wanted was a lecture on oversensitivity.

'That's a lovely wallet,' Letty said, turning her attention to the first thing that caught her eye. 'Is it snakeskin?'

Victoria's smile crept upwards. 'Crocodile actually. It's designer, just shipped over from Northern Laos. The man in the shop said that actually ...'

Letty let Victoria's voice drift once more into the background, the smell of peonies still rising from her wrists.

~

'*Y*ou can help, you know,' Pemberton said as he gripped another metal doorknob only to let it go again without so much as half a twist. 'We're close. Can you honestly not sense it?'

'Perhaps a little,' Walter lied.

In truth, he couldn't sense a thing other than the nervous moiling in the pit of his stomach and the feeling that an attack of some sort or another was imminent. Being out in the corridor was never a relaxing affair, but at least he usually knew where he was heading; Betty's or home. For the last half-century, they were the only routes he took. Today, that was changing.

That afternoon, the doors were made of twisted, fiery-red, wrought copper, which shimmered in the blue-green light as people weaved in and out of them. All sorts of people, including some exceptionally unsavoury looking folk. One gentleman, who had all but a central spike of his hair shaved clean off and holes as big as sixpences in his earlobes, caught Walter's eye and offered a wave. Walter hurried up to Pemberton, only to smack square into his back.

'This is it.' Pemberton had stopped outside a door.

'Are you certain?'

'Of course, I am.'

'How do you know?'

Pemberton did not warrant him a response.

The door in question was identical to all the other doors, and Walter could not identify a single feature that would have drawn Pemberton to this particular one, rather than the other thousand they'd passed, but Pemberton was firm with self-assurance. He turned the handle and stepped inside. Walter hesitated. Even when Edi was here, he wouldn't have stepped through an unknown door. He glanced over his shoulder and saw the man with oversized earlobes petting a dog with a studded metal collar.

'Here goes nothing,' he said.

CHAPTER 9

WHEN HE FINALLY found the courage to open his eyes, Walter discovered they'd stepped from one corridor into another, albeit a substantially diminished and lacklustre alternative. Cream fabric sank beneath his feet, while aromas of sweet bread wafted from the room beyond. Something flickered beneath his chest. Spices meant exotic lands. Carpets, like those of Persia, perhaps? Had his book made it all the way over the ocean? India? China?

'Eastleigh Leach,' Pemberton sniffed.

'What? Eastleigh? Are you sure? How do you know?'

'How do you not?' Pemberton replied.

Walter stuck to his former employer's heels as they crept forward through the house. The hallway opened into a living area, filled with two well-padded navy sofas and an equally comfy looking armchair. There was a coffee table, a glass light fitting and set above a wooden cabinet sat a thin black box. A little red eye blinked on and off at the bottom. Walter winced.

'You start on the bookshelf,' Pemberton said. 'Even you

shouldn't have difficulty with that one. I'm going to search the rest of the house.'

Walter studied the room around him. He had seen modern rooms before – Betty had lived in a two-bed bungalow before she'd moved into the home – but Walter had never visited, much preferring the comforting solitude of the interim to the unknown coldness of modern life. This room, however, exuded comfort. Perhaps it was the wedding photo above the fireplace or the empty cat basket placed beside the armchair. He would like the people who lived in a house like this, Walter decided.

'Any luck?' Pemberton said, reappearing far quicker than Walter had anticipated.

'Um ... ah ...' Walter's eyes darted across the lacquered wooden shelves of the bookcase.

'It's not here,' he said, fairly certain his post-existence eyesight was good enough not to let him down.

'It's not in the kitchen either,' Pemberton said. 'Nor the master bedroom, spare room, study, bathroom or downstairs closet.'

'You've checked them all?' Walter asked.

Pemberton rolled his eyes.

'I was sure this is where it was. It doesn't make sense.'

He was halfway through retrieving a pear drop when his expression tightened. He pursed his lips.

'Augustus, did you look anywhere other than the book-shelf?' he said.

'Not exactly. Why?'

Walter followed Pemberton's line of sight until his eyes fell on a small tattered blue book. In fairness, it was fairly well hidden beneath a pile of newspapers, but nonetheless central to the room and the coffee table.

'How on Earth did you make it to adulthood?' Pemberton said.

The book was in a far worse state than the last time Walter had seen it; the cover sagged away from the pages, the vibrant blue had faded and the paper inside had turned to the colour of hay. An ache akin to mourning rolled through his chest. It had survived. After all they'd been through, his book had survived. And at the same time as rejoicing in that fact, it was the one thing that wounded Walter most deeply.

'I guess we'd better work out how to burn the damn thing,' Pemberton said.

Walter turned rigid.

'Burn it?'

'Unless you have a better idea.'

'You, you—'

'What were you thinking?'

'I don't know. But not that. You can't burn it. You can't.'

It was Pemberton's turn to stiffen.

'What do you mean, I *can't*? It's what I should have done all along. If that bloody thing had gone in the fire with the rest of them, we wouldn't be in this predicament now.'

Walter shook his head repeatedly.

'No. We can't. Surely there's something else we can do? Bury it? Hide it?'

'What, so it can reappear to ruin my afterlife for a second time?'

'Well, we're not burning it; that's final.' An extended pause lengthened into a tense silence.

'No,' Walter said with a certainty that almost matched the conviction he felt. 'We can't burn it. Not in someone's house anyways. For now, we should just move it somewhere out of sight. Under the cupboard maybe.'

'What good will that do, exactly?'

'It might buy us a little time.'

Pemberton huffed and crunched the sweet between his teeth.

The longer the silence extended, the more certain Walter grew. You couldn't go burning down people's houses willy-nilly. It would cause absolute havoc. One way or another, Walter would have to convince Pemberton that he was right.

'Alright,' Pemberton said splintering the silence and terminating Walter's internal monologue.

'Pardon?'

'I said alright. Yes. If you think the book needs to be moved, then I think you should move it.'

'Excuse me?'

'You heard me. I agree, it's a good idea.'

'I'm sorry, I—'

'It is your book. You are the proprietor of its contents, the master of its creation. If you think the book should be moved, move it.'

Pemberton stepped back away from the table to reinforce his point. A small smile formed on his lips.

Walter had almost no experience with these situations. The only time he'd successfully managed to move something as a spirit was an extremely unfortunate affair involving his great-granddaughter's pet hamster. The incident was entirely accidental, but a century later and the story still floated around the interim as advice to the newly deceased on how not to be a poltergeist.

This situation, however, was entirely different. Walter's entire afterlife was riding on his ability to slide a slim, hard-bound, non-living book off the table where it lay and to a more discrete destination. He had to do it. He simply had to.

With his pulse pounding, Walter studied the view. The shortest route would be under the sofa, but the stumpy chair legs could prove a difficult obstacle to manoeuvre. The television cabinet was flush to the floor, and the space beneath the armchair appeared to be already taken with a mixture of cat toys and forgotten sweet wrappers. Under the bookcase was definitely his best option. He crouched on the floor and weighed up the maths. A couple of short sharp pushes was all it would take, provided he got the aim right. Having decided on a distinct goal, he steadied himself for the task at hand.

'Concentrate,' he told himself. 'You can do this.'

*A*n hour later and nothing had happened. Pemberton – who had headed back up to the interim several times to replenish his supply of sweets and reading material – was currently on the armchair, stroking a grey and white cat, who purred contentedly at the attention. Outside, the sky was darkening with inky rainclouds, while the scent of hawthorn drifted in from nearby hedgerows. Walter had removed his shoes and socks and was currently on all fours chanting at the withered pages of his life's work.

'Please,' Pemberton groaned. 'For all our sakes, give up. This is embarrassing.'

'I think I just saw a page flicker,' Walter said. 'I'm sure it did. Yes, yes! Watch, it's doing it again. I'm doing it again.'

Pemberton sighed. 'And I suppose you're also responsible for moving those?' His eyes drifted across the room to where the curtains were swaying ever so slightly. Behind them, a half open window. Walter groaned.

'Fine,' he said. 'You have it your way.' He lifted himself to standing and brushed himself clean. 'I can't do it. Is that what you want to hear? You win. I failed.' A dull ache circulated around his sinuses. Pain, in a physical sense, wasn't something experienced in the interim; nonetheless, this was hardly a pleasant experience. He rubbed his cheeks in an attempt to rectify the sensation.

'Well, back to my plan I suppose.' Pemberton heaved out the words with a dramatic sigh. 'Not that you didn't give it your best shot. Of that I am certain.'

In the two decades he'd worked for Pemberton, Walter had learnt to dismiss almost everything his employer said as unnecessary insults, and on any normal day, he would have let the comment slide. But today was not a normal day. Today, he'd discovered that his proudest work had become little more than would-be kindling. Today, Walter had learnt that a reunion with his family was only hours away from total devastation; and, at the heart of it all, the only man Walter had ever truly despised was back, delivering this news with no more compassion than if he were delivering a cup of milk. Walter flipped.

'Why?' Heat inflamed him. 'Why do you always have to have the last word?'

'Pardon?'

'What is it exactly that makes you think you are so above other people? Over me?'

'I would never—'

'Does belittling people give you pleasure?'

'I can—'

'And why do you even want to get back to the other side? It's not like you've got anyone waiting for you. You don't have a family. You don't have children. You have no one.'

It was Pemberton's turn to turn red. He opened his mouth to speak, but Walter was on a roll.

'And I'll tell another thing,' Walter said. 'You think because of what happened in life that you can say what you want to me over on this side too? Well, you can't. Not anymore. Enough is enough. This is my book. My afterlife. And you're not ruining it.' Then, to reinforce his point, he lifted his foot and kicked the leg of the chair where Pemberton sat. Hard.

The wood and the cushions and all other matters pertaining to the chair stayed entirely stationary on the impact; however, the grey and white cat did not. Arching its back and hissing, it sprung from Pemberton's lap and jumped squarely on the coffee table, landing with enough force to send a single book – a small tattered and blue specimen – flying into the air from under a pile of newspaper. Said book landed with a thump. It hit the ground and bounced back upwards. On its second bounce, it twisted around on its spine, before falling back down and finally coming to a rest, right side up, smack in the middle of the carpet. Both men stared dumbfounded.

'I think we're going to need a little help,' said Pemberton.

CHAPTER 10

*V*ARIOUS BANGS and thuds shook the ceiling above them. While Letty jumped at every one, Victoria continued to sip her drink, without so much as a raised eyebrow. Meanwhile, Donald had disappeared into the ether.

Only after Victoria had poured her second glass of red wine did she inform Letty that the actual party was not due to start for another hour and a half.

'Well, I wanted to make sure there wasn't a problem with the cake,' Victoria said, meticulously folding a napkin. 'Not that there ever is, mind. It's such a gift you've got. The children love them so much. They're the highlight of the parties; they really are.' A well-timed thud, shriek, and stream of expletives thundered down from upstairs. Victoria's smile tightened, as did Letty's throat.

'I'm glad,' Letty said.

'Of course, of course.' Victoria took another gulp of her drink. 'Besides, I rarely get to see you. I thought it might be nice if you came a little early, so we could catch up.'

Letty baulked. The offer of the perfume had started her

nerves tingling, as had the compliment of the cake, but the last time Victoria had said it was nice to see Letty, she'd just had the twins and fifteen milligrams of morphine still pumped through her bloodstream. There was only one reason Victoria ever said something nice to Letty. Spying a pile of carrots on the draining board, Letty sprung forward.

'Do you want me to chop those?' she said, marching over to the sink and picking up a chopping board on route. 'Are they for dips? Shall I do them into sticks?'

'Sorry? Oh, oh yes, I suppose,' Victoria said, clearly disorientated by the sudden change in conversation. 'That would be helpful. You'd think Felix would know to buy ready chopped. One job I gave him to do. One job.' She slid open one of the long white kitchen drawers and pulled out a large and completely impractical knife.

'Do you have a peeler somewhere?' Letty suggested.

Victoria frowned and pulled at a drawer. 'I'm sure we have one somewhere.'

After two minutes of clattering, Victoria had opened and closed every door and drawer at least twice and was starting to empty the contents onto the counter.

'Don't worry. I'll use this,' Letty said, indicating the ludicrously long knife.

Victoria stopped looking and got back to her drink.

Peeling carrots with a nine-inch knife was not a task Letty would have found easy at the best of times, but having her sister perched by her shoulder was making the job close to impossible. While her hand quivered slightly, the blade – at almost half the length of her arm – wobbled with a radius nearly as large as her wrist. Still, she managed to peel the first two carrots without incident and had just picked up a third when Victoria cleared her throat.

'So,' Victoria coughed for a second time. 'Felix has been offered this wonderful business opportunity.'

Letty's lungs quaked. The wobble on the knife grew considerably larger.

'Has he?' She swallowed and tried to keep her voice steady.

'But the thing is, he has to invest a little bit in the company to start. You know how it is, speculate to accumulate and all that? Not that this is speculation. This is an absolutely certain thing.'

'Uh-huh.'

'He's very lucky to be asked, actually. It's highly lucrative.'

'Oh, that's good.' Letty's pulse was clobbering her internal organs. She could feel her heart rate hasten by the second, while the knife was wobbling almost beyond control. At work, she could talk about money and budgets with anyone, but mention it in private and her whole body felt as if it were going into anaphylaxis.

'And it won't hang around,' Victoria continued. 'If he doesn't take the deal by next week, they'll pass it onto someone else. So, it really is a good thing, you see.'

'I see.'

'So, when we say investing, we're talking five to six per cent. Apparently, one year, it even got up to nine per cent.' Numbers. Letty's head began to spin.

'Well that's—'

'We knew you'd be excited.'

'Well, I'm—'

'Getting in on the ground level like this is a chance in a million and it would be short term, of course.'

Letty thought she might be sick.

'—but as a starting figure, we were thinking you might want to invest forty thous— Letty? Letty? Good God, Letty, is that blood? Is that blood? What have you done? You're bleeding, you're bleeding!'

Victoria was predictably useless. 'Well, don't go near the furniture! Get it under the tap! Get it under the tap! No not that one, you might stain the marble.'

It took Letty a few seconds to get herself together. She'd never had a problem with blood, and the cut was only a nick, but it was the shock that caught her unaware. She hadn't even felt it happen.

'What were you thinking?' Victoria snapped, flinching as she watched the blood soak into one of her organic cotton dishcloths.

'It was an accident,' Letty said. 'It's fine. It's almost stopped bleeding. I've got some plasters in my handbag if you can pass it to me.'

Victoria's nose tilted upwards as she took Letty's bag from the chair and placed it on the sink beside her. Letty waited, watching her sister grimace as she pinched the zip between her thumb and fingertips and pulled the bag open.

'They're in there somewhere,' Letty said.

Victoria leant outwards as she reached inside and pulled out Letty's wallet. She turned it over, touching only one torn corner.

'Good God, how can you still use this?'

'It works perfectly well,' Letty said, snatching it back with her good hand.

'Yes, but really, Leticia. It's our possessions that define us. What does this say about you?'

'Just give it here,' Letty said. She plucked the bag out of Victoria's grasp, delved her hand into the inside pocket, and pulled out a strip of plasters.

'Always the girl scout,' Victoria sniffed. 'Wouldn't Mum be proud.'

Once Letty's finger was plastered, and the chopping board and carrots disposed of, Victoria broached the subject of money once more.

'It will be a two-year turnaround at the most,' Victoria said. 'But we'd need the money by next Wednesday.'

'Forty thousand pounds?'

'I know it seems like a lot. But it would be worth it.'

'I'm not sure that we—'

'It would be worth it,' Victoria restated. 'Even if you had to take a small loan against your house to start with.'

'You want me to take out a loan?'

'Who's taking a loan?'

Donald had returned with the same glass he'd taken, although now it was empty. Felix, however, was nowhere to be seen. 'What's that I heard about loans?' he said.

Victoria flushed. 'Actually, I was talking to Leticia about a fantastic investment opportunity.'

'Oh yes?' Donald said. Letty watched as the muscles along his jawline constricted. A short, but intense silence followed.

Victoria shot Letty a hopeful glance. Instinctively, Letty looked at her shoes. Eye contact was her weakness and her sister knew it; a few puppy dog eyes and well-timed sniffs and she'd be handing over her bank account details before she could stop herself. If Victoria wanted money, she'd have to go through Donald. She owed him that much.

That's it. The absolute nerve. We're not coming here again. Not ever.' Donald slammed the car door shut. 'No Christmas cards. No birthdays. We're done. I can't believe the bloody nerve. I honestly can't.'

Letty, by comparison, was ashen. Her skin was blotchy, her eyes red, and the nominal smudge of mascara she'd applied earlier had slipped off her eyelashes and now ran downwards towards her chin.

'She was upset,' Letty said, when she'd managed to stifle her sniffs long enough to get a few good gulps of air. She'd finally stopped shaking, although the entirety of her body felt like it had been put in a washing machine on an extended spin cycle.

'She felt let down.'

Donald snorted.

'Don't you let her come crawling back,' Donald said. 'She will, you know. How you two are from the same gene pool is beyond me.'

'You could have been a little more tactful,' Letty said. Donald offered a glare that told her it would be wisest not to say anymore.

It had all turned very personal very fast. Donald had followed up Victoria's speech by asking when she was planning on paying back the ten thousand they borrowed last year. Victoria had responded that that was always a long-term investment deal, to which Donald had asked why, when rates for cheap boob jobs and tummy tucks were at an all-time low. Victoria had exploded. Plates had been thrown, hummus smeared, and endless insults tossed about, all in front of two rapturously elated eight-year-olds. Then came the attack on Letty.

'Are you going to let him speak to me like that?' Victoria snapped. 'I'm your sister.'

'I ... I ...' Letty's tongue flapped uselessly in her mouth. In truth, she was as dumbfounded by Donald's response as anyone. The last time she'd seen him erupt like that was in 2007. The telephone had rung at a rather inconvenient time and, as such, Donald had been somewhat curt to the double-glazing salesman on the other end, providing more than a few choice words about ringing someone up, unwanted, on a Sunday afternoon. Said salesman then registered Donald and Letty's number on auto-dial for every Internet, pension, and car dealership cold-calling centre between London and New Delhi. Two hundred calls and a new telephone number later, and Donald had made a concerted effort never to speak rudely to a cold-caller again.

'You're a sister when you want to be,' Donald said to Victoria. 'The rest of the time, you're a half-functioning, alcoholic social climber.'

Victoria gasped. 'I raised you,' she wagged her finger in Letty's face, ignoring Donald's comment. 'Who dropped out of college to help pay the bills when Dad left?'

'I—'

'Who went to your parents' evenings when Mum was working the late shift?'

'I didn't—'

'And now, when I try to help you, try to give you an opportunity to better yourself, to move up in life, this is how you repay me.'

Letty could feel the tears pushing their way up the back of her throat. Her chest shook as she tried to hold them down. The attempt was to little avail.

'Don't tell me you don't have money squirrelled away somewhere,' Victoria spat. 'You live in that dingy little house, working in that tacky little shoe shop. You must have paid your mortgage off years ago.'

'I don't—'

'I know what you're like. You're conniving. Spiteful. All the birthday presents we've given you – cameras, an iPad – and what do we get in return? A Christmas cake and yet another cheap polyester scarf.'

'Now hang on,' Donald attempted.

'How much cake do you think we eat?' Victoria continued. 'Normal people don't eat like you, Letty. Honestly. No wonder Dad never got in touch after the funeral. He was probably embarrassed by you. I know I am.'

'That's enough,' Donald said. 'You've said more than enough.'

'I think you ought to leave,' Victoria said as she spun around, grabbed Letty's handbag, and threw it at her. 'And don't come back grovelling,' she added, glugging back yet more wine. 'I don't have a sister anymore. You're dead to me.'

CHAPTER 11

*E*VEN WALTER, with his limited interim experience, had heard of Hector, although until that moment had assumed the man a figure of interim mythology. Reconciling with Hector's actual existence, however, was substantially easier than accepting the premise that he and Pemberton were acquaintances. Or accepting that Pemberton had any acquaintances at all for that matter.

'How do you know he'll even help us?' Walter asked, puffing as he kept up with Pemberton's stride.

'He'll help us,' Pemberton said.

Hector was one of the lifers. Once a mediocre philosopher, inferior mathematician, and useless husband, no one was entirely sure how he'd remained for so long in the interim. Most frequently, when his name cropped up in conversation, it was followed by the line, 'Not that Hector', to which he consistently took great offence. For while this particular Hector was often as scantily clad as his Greek warrior namesake, he lacked quite the physique to carry off a single sheet toga. Not that that stopped him from trying.

'He always used to spend this time of the week playing

golf with a rather flamboyant Mister Mercury,' Pemberton said. 'I assume his schedule is unchanged, although I suspect he has several new protégés under his wing now.'

Once again, Walter was thrust into the incommodious territory of the corridor. Aromas of raw cacao and paprika diffused from the dark green marble flooring. Rather than doors, the inhabitants wandered in and out of coiled vine archways, some of which bore fruit, while others dripped with a kaleidoscope of flowers and butterflies. Walter had had to take several deep, meditative inhalations to help quash the swirling unease in his stomach. Thankfully – apart from one brief frenzy involving a man with floppy hair and round sunglasses – the corridor had been quiet, and as such, Walter had allowed himself to stray a little farther from Pemberton's side. He was plucking up the courage to peer through a particularly well-embellished archway when a man of disproportionate proportions appeared from another doorway to his left.

The gentleman in question was clearly not afraid of trying new fashions or of mixing genres. He stood in front of Walter with his lower half wrapped in a Hawaiian print sarong and his top half clad in an open leather jacket. A bunch of grapes hung from his waistband, occasionally dropping fruit to the ground, and his bare and rather pallid chest was decorated with a giant butterfly tattoo. He strode forward, chest out and shoulders back, a studded dog collar gleaming around his neck. Walter gasped in awe, but before he'd had time to marvel fully at the sartorial masterpiece, Pemberton had leapt in front of the man.

'Hector, old fella.' Pemberton's smile was so strained it mimicked constipation. 'How have you been? It's been decades.'

The man came to an abrupt stop, causing a landslide of

grapes to tumble to his feet. He glanced down at them, bemused, before clocking the figure in front of him. Lifting his gaze, he scanned Pemberton down, then up, then down again. A second later, a look of clarity dawned.

'Ahh, yes, of course. Of course.' Hector spoke with impossibly round vowels. 'Pimpely, isn't it?'

'Pemberton.'

'Of course. Of course. Pemberton, that's right. Sorry, old chap. Forgive me, forgive me. How are things? How is ... um, um ...' He rapped his temples with his knuckles. 'Apologies, apologies. So many names nowadays. Not like the old times, aye?'

Pemberton offered a polite smile then shot a glare to Walter, who hadn't, until that moment, realised that his mouth was open, gawping. He shoved his hands into his pockets and straightened his back out, trying to make himself look less nervous. The swirling in his stomach had intensified since Hector's arrival, and Walter was starting to suspect that this peculiar sensation was not standard corridor nerves at all, but something far closer to reverence.

'Hector,' Pemberton said, breaking Walter's chain of thoughts. 'Forgive the intrusion.'

Hector waved his hands energetically.

'It's no intrusion. No intrusion at all. Truth is, I thought you'd moved on, old chap. I would have sought you out sooner had I known you were still rattling about this place.'

Pemberton's lips twitched.

'Yes, well,' he said. 'I must confess, I have come in the hope of a favour on that matter.'

'A favour? If I can, old chap. If I can. You know me. Always ready to help. Always one to help.'

'I hoped you might say that. You see, due to a series of, ahem, unavoidable incidents,' he threw Walter a glare on the word unavoidable, highlighting the fact he clearly thought they were anything but, 'we have found ourselves in an extending spot of bother. Down below. I was hoping you may be able to rectify this for us. Swiftly.'

Hector took Pemberton by the arm – an act that would have probably caused Walter to lose the limb – and rubbed his shirt reassuringly.

'Things always look worse down there. There's no need to rush. Perhaps we should partake in a little aperitif? You and your friend.' Walter's insides quivered as Hector looked in his direction. 'Then you can tell me all about it.'

'It would have to be quick,' Pemberton said. 'I would like to get this situation dealt with as deftly as possible.'

'Of course, of course,' Hector said, leading Pemberton away through the corridor. 'But one can always think more clearly after an aperitif, can they not?'

The three men had returned to Walter's cottage. Thick shafts of light shone through the shutters creating small, isolated patches of heat on the cold tiled floor. Hector's apparel had transformed into a more fitting three-piece suit, complete with pocket watch and monocle. Although he was disappointed to find that Walter had no form of liquor stashed anywhere in the cottage, he managed to rectify the situation by withdrawing an unopened bottle of Macallan 1946 whisky from his newly acquired leather briefcase, along with three cut glass tumblers and a small jug of ice water. Walter took the glass poured for him, sniffed the drink, and fought back a coughing fit as the fumes filled his lungs. From then on, he took only imitation sips.

'You see,' Pemberton said, rounding up the story thus far, 'the only real option we have is to burn the book in the house, now before she gets back. Otherwise, we may find ourselves in somewhat of a predicament.'

'A predicament indeed,' Hector nodded in agreement. Pemberton sighed with relief.

'So, you'll do it?'

'Do what?'

'Burn down the house.'

'Burn down the house?' Hector released his hand from around the glass at which point the tumbler plummeted three feet to the ground and landed, perfectly upright without so much as a crack. 'Good Lord, man, is that what you were asking me to do?'

'I thought you understood.'

'I can't go around burning down houses. There are rules. Imagine if everyone up here went around setting fire to everything down there that brandished some unwanted name on it. Good Lord. It would be absolute chaos.'

'That's what I said,' Walter chimed in.

Pemberton's narrow face flushed with anger and embarrassment. 'But if we don't destroy it ...'

'I understand. I do, I do, old chap. But you must think logically here. Impulse is as impulse does, after all.'

While Walter wasn't entirely sure he understood the sentiment of Hector's final phrase, he was awash with relief and more than happy to overlook the issue of Hector's functioning alcoholism in favour of his response against common arson.

'What would you suggest?' Walter asked, finally thrusting himself into the conversation. 'There has to be something we can do.'

'Yes. Yes, I'm sure. I'm sure there is,' Hector tapped his thumbs together rapidly as he thought. 'You moved the book, you said?'

'Well, actu—'

'And you managed it easily enough?'

'Not exactly.'

'But nonetheless, you moved it?'

'It did move, but I wouldn't say—'

Hector frowned. 'Did the book move or not?'

'Yes, but—'

'Then semantics are neither here nor there. What matters is that we have a place to start training.'

'Training,' Walter said, and his stomach did a tiny, but most energetic somersault.

*I*n Hillbrook Crescent, the three men crowded into the moderate-sized living room. A thin film of grey cat fur mottled the carpet of an otherwise clean house, while sugary aromas of dates and cocoa powder spiked the air.

It took numerous repetitions before Hector was confident that his newfound students had truly absorbed the significance of his words.

'I will act as a mentor and a guide, but nothing more,' he repeated. 'One cannot interfere with matters that do not concern them in this domain. The consequences, I'm afraid, are not ones that I am willing to embrace. Do you understand?'

'Yes,' Walter said, nodding eagerly. He was intrigued as to what said consequence would entail but decided that it was probably not an appropriate time to ask.

'Good. Now as far as I can see,' Hector continued, 'the idea of relocating the book into a terminal situation, for example a dustbin, is most favourable. Of course, for that to happen, we need to get it along the corridor, through a closed door, and two feet off the ground into a lidded rubbish bin. All before someone arrives home and catches us. But everyone loves a challenge, eh?'

Walter pushed his lips together and tried to conceal his excitement.

With a wide, white-toothed grin, Hector smacked Walter on the shoulder. His monocle wobbled, magnifying his eye to the size of a golf ball.

'Let's get this thing moving, shall we?'

He took a large step back, followed by a healthy glug from a hip flask. All eyes fell on Walter. A nervous fluttering rose up from beneath his sternum.

'Surely, we both should try,' he said. 'After all, Pemberton has as much a connection to the thing as I do. More in fact. He was the one that was thought about, not me.'

'I am not a common poltergeist,' Pemberton said.

'All in good time, my boy. All in good time.' Hector brushed over Pemberton's indignation. 'We don't want to confuse matters. Best if one person gives it a go at a time. Now, if you can give it a little nudge, that would be a most propitious start.'

'Just a nudge?'

'Just a nudge.'

Walter's mouth had become inexplicably dry, particularly inexplicable, he thought, given his lack of physical state and absolute non-requirement for water. He swallowed repeatedly and considered asking Hector for a sip of his flask, although swiftly decided against it.

'Whenever you're ready,' Hector encouraged. 'Let's see what we're working with.'

The fluttering in Walter's abdomen deepened and spread. With a deep breath, he clenched his jaw and focused his sights on the book.

'Move,' he whispered below his breath. 'Move. Move.'

Whether it was having Hector there as moral support, the urgency of the situation, or simply his determination to prove

Pemberton wrong, Walter couldn't say. What he knew for certain though, was that something had changed. He felt confident and self-assured.

'Move,' he said.

His vision pinholed on the faded gilding, slowly at first, then faster and faster. He could see it all, every speck of dust, every grain of the paper, every quark and lepton of every atom that made the book a book. He pushed his mind towards it, surrounding it, willing it with every fibre he'd ever possessed. Was it wobbling? It looked like it could be wobbling. He was almost sure it was. Just a little bit more. One tiny nudge and—

'Stop!' Pemberton leapt between Walter and the book. 'Don't do it. Don't move it!'

'What the ...?' Walter staggered back, his attention truly severed. Pemberton, red with heat, had a look of sheer terror on his face, but a second later, he straightened himself back upright and returned, almost instantly, to his normal, unflustered persona.

'What was that for?' Walter's hands shook with rage. 'I had it. I had it. It was going to move.'

'You don't know that.'

'What in heaven were you thinking? Why did you stop me?'

'I have to say, old chap, that did seem rather uncalled for,' Hector interjected. Hector, who had somehow found himself a leg of ham, was gnawing meat directly from the bone. He coughed up a bit of fat that landed on his chin. He flicked it off with his thumb.

'I had it,' Walter said. 'I would have moved it.'

'Well ... well ...' Pemberton's lips went into a fleeting spasm. 'If it was that simple, you won't have any issues doing it again, will you?'

'No, I will not,' Walter said and got straight into position.

Once again, Walter concentrated all his efforts on the cover. His focus narrowed, the soft fibres of the book pixelating before him.

'Don't forget to put your shoes away.'

'What the—' The second disruption caused Walter's blood to boil at a record-breaking pace. A millisecond later, he was rooted to the spot.

CHAPTER 12

WHILE DONALD went upstairs to change, Letty went straight into the kitchen under the ruse of making a cup of tea. Once there, she opened a cupboard, reached into the back, and withdrew a bag of fun size Mars bars. They were supposedly for her baking supply – rocky road kids' cakes, that type of thing – but very few of the chocolate bars she bought managed to make it that far. After devouring three of the fun-sized bites, she left the tea to brew and went upstairs to change, predictably tripping over Donald's kicked off shoes as she went.

'Are you alright?' Donald said when she appeared in the bedroom. He was halfway through peeling off his shirt. 'I'm sorry I lost my temper, but the way she treats you, like you're some damn cash cow. As if we have money to spare. And when she hasn't worked a day in the last thirty years.'

Letty looked at the ground and mumbled.

Donald grunted. 'What's the time?' he asked, throwing his socks towards the laundry basket, only to have them land a full six inches short.

'Not sure. About a quarter to five?' Letty said. She walked

over and picked up the socks and relocated them to the laundry basket.

'Quarter to five, is that all?'

'It's been a long day.'

Donald scoffed.

'You can say that again.' He squeezed the bridge of his nose as he sat down on the bed. 'I think I might have a little lie-down. You don't mind, do you, love?'

Letty looked behind him at the soft plump pillows piled up on the mattress.

'I think I might join you,' she said.

~

'$\mathcal{T}$his is entirely unproblematic,' Hector said as he took another slug of whisky. 'It may, in fact, be to our advantage.'

'How exactly?' Walter asked.

They sat on the squidgy blue sofas, debating how to proceed.

'They don't even know we're here,' Hector had assured Walter earlier as he strode through into the kitchen and waved a hand in front of the rather overweight middle-aged woman. 'We could strip down to our goolies and dance a jig if we wanted.'

'Please don't,' Pemberton said.

Now that the couple had headed upstairs, Walter was feeling only marginally better. The smell of whisky mingled with the aroma of pear drops as Hector took another large gulp of his drink and puffed out on the exhale.

'Well, let's not waste time,' he said. 'We need to get moving if we're going to get this thing out of sight before they come back down.'

With a nervous sigh, Walter stood up and stepped towards the book.

'Here goes nothing,' he said.

'You can say that again,' Pemberton replied. Walter ignored him.

Taking a firm stance towards the book, Walter began to repeat his early actions. With all his attention honed on the cover, he blocked out the thrumming sound of the car engines on the road outside and the slight rattle of conversation as it drifted down from the second floor. As before, he sunk his efforts into the gold gilding. Or was it the pages he'd focused on earlier? He wasn't quite sure. Shaking his head clear, he took a deep breath and started again. A heat began to build behind his temples, although not like before. This was an unpleasant heat that distracted him from the task. He could feel Pemberton and Hector's eyes boring into the back of his head. 'Focus, Walter,' he said, clenching and unclenching his hands then knocking his fists against his thighs.

'Try closing your eyes,' Hector said. 'I often find, in these situations, closing one's eyes can help tremendously.'

Walter sucked back the urge to reply. He followed the guidance, closing his eyes, only to open them again half a second later.

'It's no good,' he said. 'It's not happening.'

'Patience,' Hector patted his arms with a grubby, greasy hand. 'These things aren't always instant. Particularly when an object has so much sentimentality.'

But they were out of time.

*L*etty stood in the living room doorway, stopped and sniffed. Donald had fallen straight to sleep. Her mind, on the other hand, had refused to settle. Generally, naps were not a habit Letty indulged. They always felt like a good idea at the time, but she knew come nine o'clock she would be wide awake, listening to the clock ticking in the hallway, cursing those thirty minutes of shut-eye. So instead, she'd decided to come downstairs, planning to whip up a batch of scones for Donald to take on the retreat. He almost always complained about the lack of food at these places.

She was deciding whether to make the scones cheese or fruit when the smell hit her. She winced, frowned, and sniffed again.

'Pear drops?' she questioned out loud. She took a step into the living room. The smell didn't strengthen, but it didn't lessen either. Perhaps it was on her, she supposed and sniffed her arm to check. After all, there had been so many sweets at Victoria's, although Letty didn't remember seeing pear drops among them. She took another step into the room then stopped.

Squarely sat, in the centre of the floor, was the poetry book Jean had given her in the shop. Letty glanced around the room searching for a reason or explanation for its position. In finding none, she bent down, picked it up, and opened to a random page at which point she proceeded to read one of the shorter poems aloud.

*W*hat does the sun miss so
That it must leave for such a time,
At such a time?

Does it, too, look on the world of ice
And shudder?
But man cannot make warmth like the sun.
We must wait at her mercy.
Gazing out at the seas
Awaiting the swallows.

*S*he flicked over to another.

*F*or if I had a song to give,
    Of which you'd keep your life and live,
I'd choose not lark or sweet song thrush,
Despite their sounds so rich and lush.

*S*parrow and hawk would both fall foul,
    Instead, my love, I'd give an owl.
For who needs songs when there is sun?
I'll give instead when there is none.

a silence expanded around the room, taking in everything but the sound of her heartbeat. Letty closed the book and looked once more at the cover. Rubbing her finger over the gilding, she strained to make out the name on the front.

'Walter Augustus,' she said out loud.

*I*t felt like a horse kick to the stomach. There was nothing delicate about it. No gentle tug or warming sensation. No prickling on the back of his neck or cold chill running down his spine. It was one almighty wallop that left Walter J. Augustus gasping. He was unable to move, unable to think, unable to see anything other than a hazy half-vision of a chubby middle-aged woman and an old blue book. He wheezed and struggled to stand.

'No!' he screamed, watching the lady's lips move with his name for the second time. And then, without thinking, he pounced.

It was like being catapulted headfirst into a solid brick wall, only to crumble down into a pit of viscous lava before having your head dumped into a bucket of liquid nitrogen and your fingernails removed by way of a thousand fire ants.

The sensation was unlike anything Walter had experienced in life or death. How long it lasted he couldn't say; hours, minutes, less than a second perhaps. It didn't matter. It had lasted too long. Walter opened his eyes then shut them immediately. The pounding at his temples hammered with such a force he feared the possibility of a post-existence cranial fracture. Everything was foggy. Everything hurt. Walter Augustus was feeling pain.

'My goodness. My goodness, my goodness.' Hector hovered over Walter, shaking his jowls as he spoke. 'Young man, are you alright?'

'Argh ...'

'What just happened?' Pemberton asked.

'Am I still alive?' Walter questioned, somewhat ridiculously.

'I can't believe it. I actually can't.' Hector followed his

exclamation with a slap on the shoulder that caused Walter's mouth to twist in pain.

'What a marvellous display. Marvellous display, I tell you. Well, this is fantastic news. Fantastic news indeed.'

Walter was lying flat out on the carpet, staring up at an etched glass light fitting. In his peripherals, he could see the woman rubbing her own head, a confused, disorientated expression on her face. Hector reached down to help him up.

'What happened?' Walter asked, blinking. 'What? Where?'

'Fantastic. Simply fantastic.' Hector clasped his hands together in excitement. 'My, what a talent. You have not done this before, I assume?'

'Done what?'

'Occupancy? Possession? Melded your mind with a living subconscious?'

'What? I ...' Walter rubbed his eyes and pushed in on his forehead with his fingers. Hector's booming voice had somehow doubled in volume and every consonant shot through his skull like a freshly-forged iron nail.

'To master it so quickly. Remarkable. Remarkable.'

'He's hardly mastered it,' Pemberton said. 'Look, he's a wreck.'

'Trust me. With a little bit of practice.'

'Practice? Why on Earth—'

'Sorry, say that to me again?' Walter said, having finally managed to regain some grasp on reality. 'What happened? What did I do?'

'Occupancy, dear boy. You did it. You only damn well did it. Screw moving the book. A little bit of time and you'll have the old girl doing it for you.'

'I ... I ... I did? I mean, I will? I mean ... I mean ...' Walter's head was still too foggy to form a cohesive thought. 'Sorry, I think I need to sit back down.'

'Well don't sit for too long. We've got work to do.'

Walter lowered himself onto his knees. Occupancy? It seemed unlikely, yet at the same time, it made sense. Even now, he wasn't feeling right. Swarms of emotions – memories, sensations, smells even – that weren't his were flitting around in the back of his head. Occupancy though, – he repeated the word several times in his head – that was a thing of the masters. A thing of the greats. The excitement wriggled around his prior-intestinal region, followed immediately by another skull cracking headache. Walter clutched his head as he tried to stem the throbbing. If this was what occupancy involved, then maybe it wasn't a surprise that most of the dead went mad trying to master it. Using Hector's arm as a crutch, he pulled himself back onto his feet.

'If you'll excuse me, gentlemen,' he said. 'I suddenly feel like I need a rest.'

～

*H*eadache was an understatement, and the dizziness that went with it was mind-boggling. She must have stood up too quickly, Letty thought, then glanced at the book in her hand and remembered that she hadn't stood up quickly at all. She'd been standing the whole time. Letty scratched her head and tried to gather her thoughts. It wasn't just the headache making her dizzy, she realised. Her thoughts were awhirl. Images of a clifftop cottage and a man in a leather apron fought their way to the front of her mind. Her sense of smell seemed completely off-kilter too. A familiar sickly scent of sugary sweets was diluted by something different. Something earthy and clean.

'It's been a long day,' she said to herself. 'You need a rest.'

Donald appeared in the doorway, slippers on and his shirt swapped for a comfy polo.

'You alright, love? Who are you talking to?'

'Oh, no one. Sorry love. Go back to sleep.'

'It's fine, I only needed ten minutes.' He paused. 'Are you sure you're alright love? You look quite pale.'

Letty took a moment to readjust to the conversation, pushing the strange images of a man and cliff out of her head.

'Yes dear, quite alright. I think I just stood up too quickly.'

After another moment's pause, Letty ambled over to the book cabinet. She hesitated, studied the cover once more, and then pushed the book on top of one of the rows.

'What's that you got there?'

'Nothing, love. It's nothing.' Her eyes lingered on it a moment longer, unable to assess the feeling of anxiety niggling uncomfortably beneath her skin. Letty shook herself right.

'It's just a book,' she said to herself, turning to her husband and trying to ignore the images of horses running through her head. 'Right, it's time I did some baking.'

∼

*M*ore bizarre than the fact that Walter had slept was the fact that Walter had dreamt.

There was a time shortly after Pemberton's death when nightmares struck repeatedly. He would wake up in cold sweats or worse still, screaming loud enough to wake the children. Then he would reach over for Edi and spend the rest of the night awake, clutching her, fearful some fateful terror may befall them all. The nightmares faded eventually, in both frequency and ferocity, but the memory of them lingered even after death.

All that was centuries ago, however, and as such, Walter had assumed life in the interim came with an absence of dreaming. So, when he awoke in the soft comfy confines of his rocking chair, to the distant squawk of seagulls and the scent of cut grass, he was most alarmed to find the wispy residues of his half-conscious murmurings still drifting around inside his head.

He had been in a village of sorts, with peculiar trees and large-doored shop fronts. There had been people there too, but not people he knew; modern people, with modern clothes and modern colloquialisms. It had been a bizarre place, but not altogether unpleasant. Still, Walter wasn't sure that he'd want to return.

Shrugging the last of the images from his head, he noticed a freshly brewed pot of tea waiting by the stove and moved to fetch himself a teacup.

'Well, what a turn up for the books, eh?'

Walter jumped back into the fireplace.

'What the?'

Hector was slouched in the rocking chair, where only seconds before, Walter had been sitting. His jowly face was sporting a white bushy beard, while his outfit included a deerstalker hat, complete with pipe and slippers, ripped denim jeans and a tie-dyed top.

'I have to say, the more research I've done, the more impressed I am.'

'Sorry,' Walter said, trying to figure out if he'd missed part of the conversation. 'Impressed? With what?'

'With what?' Hector took a puff on his pipe and blew out a perfect smoke ring. 'With you, dear chap.'

'Sorry, with me?'

'With your gift, your talent! Occupancy. Squatter's rights if you will. You're all the talk up here. All the talk. Apparently, the last person who managed it with that little training was a Byzantine monk with a penchant for fine liquor and less fine ladies. And that ended a lot worse, believe me.'

A sugar pot had appeared on Walter's window ledge. He took a spoonful and stirred it into his tea.

'It was an accident,' Walter said, tipping in another heap of sugar. 'And I'm not sure it can be considered actual occupancy. It's not as if I made her do anything.'

'Neither here nor there, here nor there. This needs to be explored. You need to—'

Walter shook his head, stopping Hector mid-stream.

'I'm sorry. I don't think you understand. Whatever happened wasn't deliberate. I don't know if I could repeat it, even if I wanted to.'

Hector puffed out his cheeks. From between his lips, he sent three consecutive smoke rings into the air, each one slotting perfectly through the centre of its predecessor.

'But you do want to?' he said, holding the pipe at arm's length from his lips. 'That is the question. Not if you think you can, but if you know you want to?'

Walter's stomach stirred. Did he want to see into a human soul? To meld a subconscious to his will? Did he want to experience something even the dead thought of as sacred? The thought terrified him, nonetheless, his eyes gave an involuntary glint.

'Good.' Hector grinned back. 'Then we're going to need to get a few things.'

CHAPTER 13

*I*T WAS ONLY after the walk back through the corridor and past several dozen entrance ways that Walter considered the time. He had been so soundly asleep before Hector's arrival he suspected his name could have been yelled out by the entire congregation of Westminster Abbey and he still would not have felt the tugs.

'How long was I asleep?' he asked Hector as they weaved their way through the carved wooden pagodas and cherry blossoms that were currently embellishing the corridor.

'Asleep?' Hector stopped. He squinted. 'You were actually asleep? My goodness. You are full of surprises, aren't you?'

'Yes, I was just wondering how long I've been back up here.'

'How long?'

'Yes.'

'You mean in time?'

'Yes.'

Hector pincered his fingers and pulled on his beard. 'Hmm. I've always been fascinated by the concept myself. Intriguing, isn't it?'

'Sorry?' Walter said.

'For what is time?' Hector continued to mull. 'After all, what could be the briefest whimsical spell for one may be a most lengthy diatribe for another.'

'Sorry, I wanted to know—'

'And who are we, if not our actions, but what are our actions if not simply what time allows?'

'I think you might have—'

'And while unlimited time is the dream, infinite time is,' he gesticulated to the space around him, 'by all indications, the nightmare.'

Hector paused and looked ponderingly into the distance.

'Sorry,' he said, finally re-acknowledging Walter's presence. 'Did you ask something?'

'How long have I been up here?' Walter said.

'Oh, I've no idea. I've been at a hammam,' Hector replied. 'Anyway, we're here now,' he said and stepped through into one of the pagodas.

*W*alter frowned and waited for his eyes to adjust to the light. The room was dim and filled with a dense aroma of leather and tobacco smog, through which he made out the shadows of chairs and a bookcase.

'Where are we?' he asked.

'Just gathering a little material,' Hector said.

Hector's study was set up as an exact replica of the late Sigmund Freud's. A strange looking dental chair sat against the deep heavy desk, where a pair of round glasses lay at a skewed angle. A long couch, swamped in an expensive looking Persian rug took up a large portion of the floor space, the rest of which was covered in books with dubious titles like *Eternity be Dammed* and *A View Out Beyond*. Walter reached his hand out to touch one.

'Probably best leave those alone,' Hector said, moving the book to one side and out of Walter's reach. 'Some pretty nefarious things in some of those. We don't need any more problems, now do we?'

Hector picked up a statue from the desk in front of him.

'As you know, I'm not one to brag, but a couple of these are gifts from the man himself. I helped him out of a spot of bother in the 1970s, you see. That's what I do, see. I help people. Like how I want to help you, in the easiest, most elegant way possible.' He paused and brushed his finger along the curve of the statute, although his eyes remained solely on Walter. 'You know, what you did last night, it really was rather remarkable.'

A sliver of pride flickered in Walter's belly.

'Well, it was mostly luck, really.'

'Don't put yourself down, boy. You've got a natural talent. You think Bluidy Mackenzie managed it all first time?'

'Bluey Mackenzie?'

'The thing is, moving the book does not solve the problem. Who is to say the woman doesn't start spreading your name at any second? First, it's her husband she tells, then the woman at the checkout. Then they tell their work colleagues. It's an exponential disaster waiting to happen. You can see that, can't you? The list of calamities is unending. And we both know that burning down the house is out of the question. But this way, you get to choose. You get to decide exactly what happens to that book. Burn it, bury it. Post it on the Internet for all I care.'

'Internet?'

'What I'm saying is that now you have choices. These are

exciting times. Very exciting indeed. I have to say, in all my years up here, I have never met a man like you.'

Walter tried to stop his face from cracking into a wide, goofy grin as, once again, his pride swelled. Other than discovering the afterlife was real, he was under no doubt that this was the single most exciting thing to happen to him since his death.

'Well then, let's have a looksee here, shall we?' Hector found himself a small footstool, stepped up onto it, and began to pull down various old and heavy looking tomes that he promptly threw into Walter's arms.

'Hmm ... perhaps ... no, no, no ... yes that's for certain.' Hector continued to mutter as he scoured the shelves, piling Walter up as he went. Six books in, Walter was struggling to stand under the weight.

'Maybe I should leave you to this?' Walter said. 'After all, I should probably go keep an eye on the girl.'

'What was that, lad?' Hector peered over his shoulder, a large, black book with a series of ominous looking skulls currently resting in his arms.

'The girl,' Walter repeated. 'I should probably make sure she's not telling people about the book.'

'Good, good, yes. You go, you go. I'll come down once I'm sorted.'

Hector turned back to the shelves, leaving Walter to find a place to drop the heavy pile of books. In the end, he decided the couch was as good a spot as any. The blanket already looked like it had had a fair amount of use.

It was only when Walter left Hector's study, he realised he had no idea where he was going. On their previous visits to the woman's house, Pemberton had done all the guiding and Walter had been content to follow behind, sticking close to his heel and keeping his eye out for any errant looking corridor lurkers. He had not even thought to ask how Pemberton was conducting his navigation or if there was a particular route to take. The butterflies had evaporated from his stomach, leaving behind a tangled mass of knots and coils that showed no signs of loosening any time soon.

Having transformed yet again, the corridor was now set along the top of an infinite mountain range. The cut grass scent was heightened by the crisp air and the scree crunched and slide beneath his feet.

With no real idea of which direction to head, Walter started walking one way, but after two minutes, changed his mind and turned back. A minute later, he double-backed on himself for the third time. The knots and coils tightened; he could be lost up here for weeks, he considered.

Fortunately, the corridor was relatively empty. A man dressed as a one-man-band clashed, strummed and honked in and out of doors, while a woman with waist-length chestnut hair and emerald green eyes appeared to be watching him from a distance. She was most striking, with her long hair and a slight crookedness to her lips. Walter stared at her a fraction longer. By mistake, he caught her gaze. She hurriedly looked down before scurrying away, leaving Walter even tenser than before.

'Bloody corridor,' he said.

It was as he gazed around the vista for some sort of inspiration that his eyes fell upon another young woman, this time with a short bob of platinum blond curls and a bolt of red lips. He was about to avert his gaze when she caught his eye and smiled. A second later, she was walking towards him.

'Darling,' she said. 'You look lost.'

'I ... Umm, I am a little, I guess.' Walter could feel his cheeks reddening. The woman's dress was short and white and the type of thing that he and Edi would have most definitely frowned upon in a previous life. Up here, however, she appeared like an angel.

'You're doing ever so well,' she said and brushed against his shoulder. A smell of expensive perfume rippled in her wake. 'Stop making it all so hard on yourself.' She planted a small kiss in the middle of his cheek then sashayed off and disappeared through one of the doors.

'Mr President?' she called into the ether, her voice echoing in the air around her. 'Mr President, is it your birthday?'

Walter was still swimming in her scent when he felt the tug.

The feeling was small and its location almost impossible to trace, but it was the first sense he'd had since coming back up. Closing his eyes, he put one foot in front of the other and began walking. Progress was slow. He twisted and redirected himself with every small sensation, second-guessing every step he took. But the more steps he took, the stronger the tugs became.

It was as though a metal detector was located in his sternum, leading him exactly the route he needed to go. As he drew closer, the feeling swelled, then tingled, and then came to an abrupt stop outside a steel blue door. Walter smiled. He had done it, all by himself. He was so proud he didn't even look behind to notice that the woman with emerald eyes was back and, once again, watching him.

*P*emberton was sitting on the couch, pear drops in hand, cat around his ankles.

'You're still here?' Walter said.

Pemberton peered at Walter from under half-closed eyelids.

'Somebody had to stay,' he said. 'Sad to say I thought even you would have had a little more decency and common sense than be gone the whole day. Alas, I was wrong.'

'A whole day?'

'And you will be glad to hear that there have been no major calamities since your departure. The woman has not so much as sneezed in the direction of your waffling nonsense book. Do you have any idea how dull spending your time as a ghost in a shoe shop is?'

'I ... umm ... thank you,' Walter said. He hovered awkwardly. As much as he despised his former employer, he would have been more upset to find the woman had been left unattended all day to do whatever she liked with his writings.

'I take it you had time to think through your actions up there?' Pemberton said.

'My actions?'

'What you did to that woman.'

'Oh, you mean the occupancy? Yes, as a matter of fact, Hect—'

'What you could have, why it doesn't bear—'

'Ahh, Walter my boy, there you are. Ready to get started?'

Pemberton stopped mid-flow, his lips still twisted with the acridity of his words.

'So, you're back?' he said to Hector.

'Why, of course.'

Hector's current apparel involved a purple velvet suit, while his beard had now reached chest length. In addition to his clothing, he'd managed to find himself a pair of ankle castanets that clashed musically every time he stepped.

'Come to tell him the news, have you?'

'News?' Pemberton said.

Hector stomped forward, slapping Walter on the back, his hand in impressive unison with the castanets.

'Walter here's going to undergo a little afterlife schooling. Occupancy training.'

'Occupancy?'

'The boy has a talent.'

The pride in Walter's chest wobbled as his gaze fell on his former employer. Pemberton's eyes were solely on Walter. His fingers were held in a perfectly frozen steeple. Even his pear drop filled mouth was unmoving.

'Do you have an idea how dangerous that could be?' Pemberton said. 'Do you not realise how lucky you were before?'

Walter's nerves accelerated.

'It's not like I'm going to be doing anything bad,' he said.

'It's invasion. It's unethical.' Pemberton's voice rose. 'Surely you can't think this is a good idea?'

Walter's mouth was parched. He could feel his blood pressure rising as it pulsed. Over one hundred years dead and no one could get to him quite the way Pemberton did.

'Well?'

Walter pushed his shoulders as far back as he could manage. His days of being bullied were done.

'I think you'll find it is a rather pragmatic solution to our problem,' he said.

'Pragmatic?' Pemberton's left eyebrow slanted up. 'How? You would be invading her mind. Taking her free will.'

'Well ... well ...' Walter could feel his tongue swelling under the scrutiny, the bravado rapidly fading.

'What is it you plan on doing when you're in her head, exactly?' Pemberton pressed.

'Well, we ... we haven't ... I mean ...'

'Come on, I want to hear this.'

Hector coughed.

'Pimberly, I know what you're thinking,' he said, placing a

hand on Pemberton's shoulder. 'But honestly, let's not get ahead of ourselves. A few precautionary measures, that's all we are talking about.'

'Precautionary measures?' Pemberton's words dripped in doubt. 'What is that supposed to mean?'

'Exactly what it says. Walter will go in, remove a few memories—'

'He'll do what?'

'An infinitesimal number,' Hector said. 'She'd squander double what he'll take out on a thrifty barman's gin and tonic.'

Pemberton didn't look convinced.

'What about you?' he said to Walter. 'You are telling me you see no issues with it? With altering a person's subconscious.'

Walter tried to look like he knew this was the plan all along. Removing memories was not something Hector had mentioned during their conversation earlier, however, on brief consideration, it sounded like a good idea.

'Well,' Pemberton insisted. 'I'm waiting.'

Walter took a deep breath in through his nose. The air was sickly sweet and clung to the back of his throat. Beneath his rib cage, his heart bounced around with sporadic beats, half apprehension, half excitement.

'It's the only plan we've got,' he said, 'and I think it's a pretty good one.'

CHAPTER 14

*O*NDAY HAD dragged like only Mondays could. It was damp and drizzly from dusk until dawn, and when Letty finally curled up on the sofa, it was nearly eight in the evening.

'I can't chat long,' Donald said, when he rang to let her know he was there safe and well. 'There's a blind man's treasure hunt before dinner.'

'How's it going?' Letty asked him as she snacked on a post-pudding cake and ice-cream.

'Good, good,' he said. 'You know, same as last time.'

'Are they cars I can hear?' Letty said. 'I thought it was a countryside retreat.'

'Oh, it is. It is. It's ... it's one of the young lads playing a game on his phone. Some racing thing.'

'I thought you were in your room?'

'Well, it's more of a communal place. A dormitory type thing.'

'That's not normal, is it? Are all the managers in one?'

A sharp intake of breath vibrated down the line and Letty

realised that, even with a hundred and fifty miles between them, she was still failing to stick to her no-nagging policy.

'Well,' she said, breaking the silence. 'I should let you go. I'm sure you've got lots of exciting activities to do tonight.'

There was a short pause before Donald spoke.

'Yes. Well, lots of love then. And sleep well.'

'I love you too,' Letty said, but the line had already clicked off.

Soaking in the tub, she mulled over the day. She'd picked out the wrong shoe twice, for two different customers and was barely able to keep her mind focused when Head Office rang, giving her details about this visit and that visit and all these orders she had to get done by this and that deadline. Joyce had been sobbing at the time over an argument with Kevin and the wails rattled through from the storeroom. When Letty finally got off the phone, she scribbled a few dates on the calendar and sent Joyce home. The last thing she needed was someone else's family trauma.

The argument with Victoria had been at the forefront of her mind all day, and her stomach had roiled with guilt. Would it really be that bad, lending her a little more money? But then, if she said *yes* this time, when was it likely to stop? And what if Victoria started asking where the money came from? She could hardly justify taking out a loan when her bank account was bursting at the seams. And then there was Donald, of course. He would want to know where the money had come from, and as much as she wanted to tell him, she needed to give herself a little time to prepare.

The money issues combined with the nervous twitching she felt every time she thought about that little blue book had left Letty mentally exhausted. Even when she finally switched off her bedside lamp and closed her eyes, her mind was still turning over and over. What she needed, she decided, was a proper night's sleep.

~

*W*alter made no attempt to hide his disappointment.

'You said occupancy training. I thought I'd be going back inside her head,' he sulked.

'All in good time, all in good time. You don't run before you can walk, do you? Besides, Pimberly is right. We need to make sure you've got a bit of control while you're in there. You'll be no good to anyone flitting in and out every two seconds. Now have another go. Make that light bulb flicker.'

~

A proper sleep was most definitely out of the question for Letty. One minute it was a flickering light bulb, the next it was the curtains whooshing from a breeze. For a quiet house on a quiet cul-de-sac, there was barely a second's silence. The bangs and the bumps seemed unending, and she knew exactly who was to blame. All night, floorboards creaked, and she could hear the toys flying around the living room as Mister Missy gallivanted about. Twice she decided – for only the third time in as many years – that he was going to sleep outside. She dragged herself out of bed, found her slippers and stumbled into the living room ready to read him the riot act and hurl him out the nearest window. Both times, she found her cat curled up on the sofa, one eye looking lazily up at her from beneath his paw. He was playing her, she was certain, and he hadn't been this annoying since he was a kitten. It must have been having Donald away, she concluded.

Although if the antics continued through the week, Letty strongly suspected her husband would be coming home to a catless house.

Morning was announced with an ear-piercing alarm that jolted Letty straight out from her sleep, although, it was another ten minutes before she finally managed to coerce herself out from under the blankets and into the chill air. Her eyes ached, her back creaked, and her knees and hips felt like they'd been replaced with rusted machine parts. She stumbled downstairs and into the kitchen.

'What on Earth have you been doing?' she said.

Half a dozen fridge magnets sat scattered on the floor, and at least three of them had broken. Next to them was one of Donald's old hiking boots, two of his work shoes – all left feet – and a pair of flip-flops she hadn't seen for three summers past. Mister Missy looked up from the ground and mewed.

'You're on thin ice,' she said.

Before Letty left for work, the rest of the house was given a quick once over; the last thing she wanted was to come home and discover Mister Missy had been using her Calathea pot as a litter tray. In the living room was another stray shoe. Letty tilted her head and studied it. There was something strange about the way the laces were tied; how they flopped in large loops like they'd been tied by a child who did not yet know how to control the tension. She picked it up and went to leave, when her gaze fell on the bookshelf. Letty shuddered. It was inexplicable, but even now, looking at the little antique book made her skin prickle. She took a step towards it, then hesitated and glanced at the shoe in her hand. The shudder deepened.

'Don't you start making something out of nothing,' she said to herself. 'You know what you're like.'

By lunchtime, she was on her knees. Tuesdays were

normally quiet, but while customers were scarce, deliveries were sky high. Forty-five minutes of carrying knee-high winter boots through to the stockroom was enough exercise to see her through the week, and the fumes from the shoe polish did nothing to help her headache. Head Office had called twice to confirm they would be sending trainees over for two hours on Friday, Joyce was still bursting into sporadic fits of tears or swearing, and when twelve thirty came, Letty dropped down onto the only chair in the stock room, closed her eyes, and groaned.

The stock room was not the most pleasant place for a cheese and pickle sandwich – with no windows, endless merchandise and a washroom with an unfeasibly small sink, tucked away in the far corner – but she'd gotten used to it over the years. That day, a pile of sale shoes brought in from the shop floor were stacked up in the corner, and a strong smell of carpet cleaner pervaded the air. Normally, Letty would never have left shoes unsorted, but the thought of rummaging through, trying to find the boxes with matching pairs or assessing which ones had been damaged enough to be reduced even further was too much to deal with before lunch. She would take her break and see to them then. Or perhaps, she'd ask Joyce to do them.

~

*W*alter was ecstatic. Not only was he getting to grips with his newly acquired poltergeist skills, but he'd also spent a full fifteen minutes up in the corridor by himself.

The poltergeist skills were, as yet, rather temperamental, although Hector had been right; it was all just a matter of confidence.

'Have some patience,' he'd said when Walter continued to sulk over his lack of actual occupancy training. 'You might even like it.'

Hector was right. Half an hour in and Walter was hooked. Now, after a whole night honing his craft, he considered himself well on his way to full-fledged poltergeist. Naturally, there were still a few semantics to overcome. So far, he had no difficulty in moving shoes, socks or floorboards and could, on occasion, rotate the odd fridge magnet. This was hit and miss as evidenced by the shards of ceramic that covered the woman's floor. Filament bulbs he could flicker with ease, but LEDs and the strange looking spiral bulbs in the living area were an impossibility. He could move cat food, he discovered, but not human food, decorative bowls but not crockery. He could move door handles, but not the doors themselves and had thus far managed to relocate several magazines but not, most frustratingly, any books. Still, he reasoned, it was only a matter of practice, and if one night could yield such dramatic progress, he would be back tumbling into the girl's subconscious in a matter of hours. That was Walter's plan at least.

∾

*C*hocolate and diet coke were what Letty required. She bought four of each at the newsagents on the corner with the intention of saving one for the walk back home and one for the evening. By the time she'd returned to the shop, two chocolate bars had been demolished and she was two-thirds through the second can of drink.

Joyce was mid-conversation with a man at the time. Letty glanced down at his feet – genuine leather, with contrasting stitching and metallic bridge – and deduced that he'd not come to Shoes 4 Yous for the discount loafers.

'Ahh, here she is,' Joyce said. 'Letty, this man wants to talk to you about making a cake. For his mother.'

'Oh great,' she said. 'Let me take my coat off and I'll be right with you.'

In the storeroom, Letty whipped off her coat, then placed the unfinished can on a shelf above the mountain of unsorted shoes. She stopped and yawned before heading back out onto the shop floor.

'So,' she said, in her best saleswoman voice. 'What is it I can do for you?' she said.

Twenty minutes later, she had another customer on the cake list.

'I could pay a professional,' the man said for the third time.

'I understand,' Letty said.

'But apparently, you know what you're doing. Besides, the decent people were fully booked. You were the last resort.'

'Oh.'

'You did my friends' engagement cake. Clarissa and George?'

'Oh yes.' Letty recalled the cake with a smile. She had been so proud of its sugar spun flowers and lace design pipe work. The bride-to-be had sent her a wonderful thank you note.

'Well, I don't want anything like that,' the man said. 'Far too fussy. I want clean cut. But not too rigid. She's an old woman.'

'So, something classic?' Letty said. 'A few flowers and balloons? Or hearts perhaps?'

'Oh, God no. Did you not hear me? She's an old woman, not a teenager. I don't even know why we're throwing the damn party. She won't remember it in a week.'

Letty's smiled pinched. 'I'm sure she'll appreciate it all the same.'

The man grunted.

Letty picked up a piece of paper and began to scribble down a quick sketch of something she thought he would like.

'And don't go overboard on the colours either,' the man said as she was drawing. 'There's nothing tackier than a gaudy cake.'

'Subtle colours,' Letty spoke as she wrote.

'I didn't say they had to be subtle, just not gaudy.' The man sighed and shook his head.

It took another fifteen minutes and two and a half sides of A4 paper before the red-headed businessman finally left. 'I won't pay for something that's not up to scratch,' he said on the way out. Letty grimaced.

'Well hopefully, you'll all like it,' she said. 'See you on Friday.' She offered a wave, but he was already back on his phone and marching out the door. Letty dropped her hand and yawned.

'I don't know why you don't do it as a job. You could pack up this and open a bakery. If I could bake like you that's definitely what I'd do. You'd earn a heap.'

Letty chuckled. 'Maybe one day.'

'You could. Seriously. My friends started their own shop. It sells, like, incense and sarongs and these natural herbs and stuff from Thailand.'

'I'm not sure that's quite my thing.' Letty said.

'I know, but what I'm saying is, our friends a' well young. And a bit stupid, and they can run a shop. You're way older.'

'Thanks.'

'You know what I mean. You've way more experience than them. You'd be good at it.'

Letty sighed. 'Maybe one day,' she repeated, the words feeling as distant as they always did. 'I'm fine here for now.'

'Well, I think you're a fool.'

Letty laughed. 'And on those kind words, I'm going to go sort out the stockroom. Yell if it gets busy.'

Joyce raised her hands and indicated the emptiness around them.

'I think I'll be fine.'

In the stockroom Letty swallowed the last dregs of her drink, threw the can in the bin, and then turned to tackle the mountain of unsorted, discounted shoes. She stopped, blinked once and rubbed her eyes. When she removed her hands, nothing had changed.

'Joyce,' Letty said, poking her head around the doorframe and into the shop. 'Did you sort those shoes out in the stockroom?'

'What, the big pile?'

'Yes.'

'No.'

Letty sucked on her bottom lip and turned back to the stockroom. Each shoe had been straightened up and arranged in size from smallest to largest.

'Are you sure?' she said, her head back on the shop floor. 'You didn't just straighten them up or anything?'

Joyce shook her head. 'No. Why would I do that? They've only got to go back in their boxes, right?'

'Right,' Letty mumbled.

She stepped back inside the stockroom and closed the door. Her stomach lurched. Letty grabbed her handbag from the shelf, pulled out her wallet, and checked inside. Her lungs gasped with relief. All notes and cards were still in place. Joyce's bag was on the top shelf. Letty reached up, pulled it down, and had a speedier glance inside. A brand-new phone sat on the top. If someone was going to come into the stock room and steal things that would have surely been the first choice. Definitely before straightening up reduced price shoes.

Still struggling with the unease that lingered inside, Letty plucked a shoe off the floor. It was from last season, faux suede and had a tiny scratch on the heel. She placed it in her palm and turned it over. Then, at last, she noted the source of her discomfort. The laces on the shoes were tied into a bow, but loosely, with large drooping loops.

'Like a child that can't control the tension,' she said out loud.

CHAPTER 15

'I SAID YOU should have stopped.'

A large vein protruded out of Pemberton's forehead as he spat. The two men were alone. The woman had just finished spending twenty minutes boxing up Walter's neatly arranged shoes and had left the stock room three shades paler than when she'd arrived.

'It's fine,' Walter said. 'She has no idea it was me.'

'You don't know that,' Pemberton said.

'I'd have felt it, wouldn't I? We're fine. There's barely been a single tug all day.'

Walter grinned widely then looked sideways and prayed that Pemberton would not see the bright red tinge blossoming on his cheeks.

The comment had not been an outright lie. Obviously, the woman had thought of him in the living room after breakfast when she was looking up at the bookshelf. That one had been painfully strong, truth be told, but after that, they'd all been far subtler. He had flitted through her mind on her leisurely stroll down to work and as she munched on her cheese and pickle sandwich at lunch. There had been a few other flickerings too, but nothing to raise the alarm about. Not until now. Now it was taking all of Walter's control not to clutch his stomach and yell out in pain.

'Why don't you go upstairs?' he said, desperate to get Pemberton gone before he noticed something was awry. 'I'm fine here watching her.'

Pemberton's eyes narrowed.

'I'm fine staying,' he said.

Walter gulped.

'Honestly, take some time for yourself. After all, you watched her all day yesterday.'

Pemberton's gaze didn't falter. Walter could feel the perspiration beading on his neck as he held the gaze with as much resolve as he could muster.

'What are you up to, Augustus?'

'Up to? Nothing,' Walter winced as another tug dug sharply into his diaphragm. 'I thought you might like a little time that's all. Like I said, you were down here all day yesterday.'

Pemberton did not so much as blink. Walter continued in desperation.

'Besides, I was thinking, you know, with you just back, perhaps there were a few people you might like to visit. Or somewhere you might want to go again. You know, while you've got the chance.'

A muscle along Pemberton's jawline twitched.

'Of course,' Walter carried on, sensing a lead. 'If you don't want to, I wouldn't mind getting in a little upside time. After all, the woman may well have forgotten us in a week. I, for one, don't want to regret wasting my last few days before moving on.'

Pemberton ran his tongue along his top teeth while Walter gritted his.

'I will be gone for thirty minutes at most.'

～

*J*oyce was wearing a pair of children's shoes on her fingers and making them walk around like little puppets.

'I hate days like this,' she said. 'It's too quiet.'

'Everyone's probably having a rest after the holidays,' Letty said.

'I suppose.' Joyce made her shoe puppets jump from one shelf to the next.

Outside was more like autumn than the end of summer. It was as if the clouds were aware that holidays had ended and had decided to react appropriately. Leaves skipped up the high street, taunted by the same wind that caused the door to rattle on its hinges. A customer came in and wandered over to the women's shoes. Joyce removed her shoe puppets, Letty smiled and offered her professional and well-versed greeting.

'Do let me know if there's anything I can help you with.'

The woman grunted. Thirty seconds later, she left.

Letty drummed her fingers against the counter as she tried to stop her stream of thoughts. She opened her mouth to speak and then closed it again, repeating this action several times.

There was a logical explanation, she thought. There had to be. So some shoes had moved; that didn't mean anything. And as for the smell of pear drops, she'd never heard of a ghost with a confectionery addiction before.

'Everything alright?' Joyce said.

'Just tired,' Letty said. She shifted her weight from one foot to the other.

'Do you believe in ghosts?' Letty said, breaking the silence far more suddenly than she anticipated. A strong gust of wind caused the door to shake.

'Ghosts?' Joyce put down the shoes. 'Definitely.'

'You do?'

'"Course. My aunt was haunted once.'

'Really?'

'Yup, by the ghost of Robbie Williams.'

Joyce studied her colleague for some trace of humour. Her face was entirely straight.

'Robbie Williams?'

'Yeah. Followed her everywhere for days. She went and saw one of those women about it and everything. What d'ya call them?'

'Mediums?'

'Maybe. Anyway. She said it was Robbie Williams.'

'Robbie Williams? The singer?' Letty said.

'I don't know if he sings as well, but he's in all them films. The funny ones. Except that one with Matt Damon. He ain't very funny in that one.'

'You mean Robin Williams?'

'Ain't they the same person?'

Letty took a deep breath. She knew she would be on dubious ground with her next question, but nothing ventured nothing gained.

'Joyce, have you read much poetry?'

Joyce shrugged. 'A bit at school. You know. Wilfred Owen, Siegfried Sassoon, that type of thing. "*Bent double, like old beggars under sacks, Knock-kneed, coughing like hags, we cursed through sludge*". Why? You think there's a poet haunting you?'

'No, no,' Letty said hurriedly, her jaw still hanging open from Joyce's recital. 'Nothing like that at all. I saw a book; that was all. I wondered if I should get it.'

'Oh.'

'For a friend. They like poetry. Only I hadn't heard of the poet before, so I didn't know if it's any good.'

'Dunno. I might have heard of him I suppose. What's the name?'

'It's fine. I'm sure you won't have heard of him.'

'You never know. I'm great at pub quizzes.'

Letty paused for an intake of breath. 'It's Walter,' she said slowly. 'Walter Au—'

A gust of wind shot through the shop floor strong enough to send several shoes flying from the shelves. Letty jumped back, her heart rate rocketing. She looked towards the entrance. The glass continued to tremble as the door swung back and forth.

'Bloody hell that wind's strong,' Joyce said, moving towards the door and picking up the tossed shoes in the process.

Letty stayed rooted to the spot. Her pulse hammered in her veins, her muscles rigid. Even after a minute, she could barely manage to find the strength to speak.

'Well that was weird,' Joyce said as she ambled back down the shop and rested her elbows on the counter. 'Anyways. What were you saying? A poet guy, right? What was his name?'

Letty shook her head. 'Oh, it doesn't matter,' she said, her voice quivering. 'I can't quite remember it all exactly. Actually, I don't think I'm going to buy it, after all.'

Joyce hummed and went back to making finger puppets from children's shoes.

'Probably a good idea. Most poetry is crap, anyway.'

~

'What did you do?'

The voice made Walter jump backwards against one of the mirrors.

'Well?' Pemberton said again. 'What did you do?'

Walter squinted.

'Oh,' he said. 'You mean the door?'

'Yes, I mean the door.'

Walter's puffed out his chest, giving a slight shimmy to his shoulders. The act rather resembled a proud rooster.

'I thought you'd be impressed by that.'

'Impressed?'

'Thinking on my feet. Not to mention moving an entire door that size. I never thought I'd manage it – it's massive – but I just thought about what Hector had said.'

Walter's eyes met Pemberton. His smile dissolved.

Pemberton was livid. His eyes bulged from his head like a beetle's, and his fists, clenched into tight little balls, quivered at his sides.

'Aren't you pleased?' Walter said.

'Pleased? Pleased?' Pemberton repeated, sending specks of saliva flying. 'This is a disaster.'

'What? No.' Walter shook his head. 'She didn't say my name. She specifically chose not to say my name.'

'Because you terrified her.'

'Because she doesn't want people to know. This is a good thing.'

Pemberton sucked a lungful of air in through his nose. Then, in a movement most uncharacteristic to the man Walter knew, threw his arms up in dismay.

'What is the point?' he said to the sky. 'What *is* the point?'

He paused, turned, and looked at Walter. His bottom lip trembled ever so slightly.

'Tell me you won't go ahead with this occupancy nonsense, please,' Pemberton said. 'It's not safe. Not for you.' There was an earnestness to his voice that Walter couldn't remember having heard before. It almost sounded heartfelt. But Pemberton didn't do heartfelt, Walter remembered. Pemberton was the man who chastised the living Walter for every little mistake he'd ever made. A man who refused to listen to his opinions, who ridiculed his desires, and who burnt his books. No, the Pemberton Walter knew did not do heartfelt.

'I'll do whatever needs doing,' Walter said determinedly.

*O*nce Pemberton had gone, Walter took a moment to ponder the situation. The way he saw it, nothing was any worse than before. True, the woman may now have a slight inkling that she was being haunted – judging from the tugs he was feeling at least – but she hadn't told anyone. In fact, she'd done the complete opposite. She had, in his mind, proven that she was not going to brandish the name of Walter Augustus over every hill and dale; thus, the slight poltergeistical act had, he reasoned, improved the situation.

She looked exhausted, he thought, with bags under her eyes and a slight limp to her walk that Walter recognised all too well as knee problems. His stomach squirmed. A twenty-forty-hour poltergeist was probably the last thing she needed. He would keep it to a minimum, he decided. No more messing around, only absolute necessities from this point on. And occupancy training of course, but hopefully, that wouldn't be too stressful.

He stayed by her side during the walk back home, even heading into the corner shop when she went in to purchase yet more chocolate. The wind was blustery, and Walter watched on with a nostalgic yearn as she battled against it. He had forgotten about good old blustery days. He had forgotten about storms and thunder and rain so heavy it shook the thatch from the cottage roof. Walter chuckled to himself. Perhaps he would go back upstairs to find rain dripping through a crack in the timbers. That would no doubt be the interim's idea of a joke.

It was outside the house, while the woman was finding her keys, that Walter caught sight of someone watching them from a distance. The person had attempted a disguise, wearing dark glasses and a thick coat, although judging by the way the jacket cinched in at the waist, it had to be a woman. Walter made a move to inspect, but no sooner had he shifted his footing than she'd gone.

Hector was waiting for him in the living room. He had on a leopard print leotard, sequined tights and golf visor, and was puffing on a cigarette down long tortoiseshell holder.

'So,' Hector said, taking a puff. 'Another busy afternoon I hear.'

'Well—'

'Do you know something? You are impressing a lot of people, believe me. A lot of people indeed.'

The compliment helped lessen the swirling sense of doubt Walter had been experiencing since Pemberton's departure.

'I wasn't lying when I said about these talents of yours,' Hector continued. 'When I think of all that time you've spent holed up in your little cottage when you could have been ... well ...' He gave a full-bodied judder. 'I think you may prove yourself more useful than you ever imagined.'

Walter mused. There was no denying that Hector was right; he'd wasted his time in the interim. Endless years spent staring at the same dozen seagulls on a loop. Hour after hour wishing the next one by. Who knows, had he paid more attention to the book and its whereabouts, they may never have ended up in this situation; Betty moving house, spring cleaning, there must have been hundreds of opportunities throughout the years when he could have destroyed it – or perhaps have made Betty do it. All of them were gone now.

'Let's not dwell on the past,' Hector said, slapping Walter on the shoulder. For one ghastly moment, Walter thought he'd been voicing his musings out loud, but Hector smiled in his typically absent-minded manner.

'Now, I've got to rush,' he said, tipping his visor disturbingly close to Walter's face. 'Playing lawn tennis with Adolf, this evening. I know he's got a bad rep and he's a terrible cheat, but for some reason, I can't resist the old charmer. Must be something to do with the accent.'

He stood up and strode towards the door.

'But tonight,' he said, turning back to Walter, 'I'd like to start some real practice.'

'You mean ...' Walter was barely able to say the words for fear Hector would take them back.

'Yes,' Hector said. 'Tonight, Walter Augustus, we start the occupancy.'

CHAPTER 16

*L*ETTY'S CONVERSATION with Donald had been painfully short.

'So how did it go?' Letty said when he finally picked up his phone. 'Any more obstacle courses tonight?'

'What?'

'The obstacles course? You did one last night, didn't you?'

'Oh, yes. It was fine. Fine. Wet.'

'Oh. Well, I hope it was still fun.' Her voice came out with a forced joviality. 'And what are you doing tonight?'

'Tonight? Why would I be doing anything?'

'I thought they put on evening activities?'

A pause followed. She could envisage Donald down the other end of the phone, removing his glasses and polishing the lenses.

'Donald?'

His throat clearance rumbled down the line.

'To be honest, I ought to be going, love. It's food in a minute. I don't want to be late.'

'Oh, okay.'

'But I'll be home soon. We can talk properly then.'

'Oh, alright then. Speak soon.'

'I love you.'

'You t—' The phone rang dead before she finished. All in all, the conversation left Letty deflated.

There were three cakes on her to do list; none of them were imminent, the most urgent being the lemon sponge that today's businessman wanted to pick up from the shop on Friday. Still, she spent half an hour faffing, checking her ingredients, making a shopping list and then, just because she felt like she ought to use up the browning contents of the fruit bowl, whipped up a banana cake. After which she licked out the leftover batter from the bowl, finishing every last morsel, and stubbornly ignoring how sick it was making her feel.

While the banana cake baked, she ran the vacuum over the house and rearranged the clothes in the spare room, after which her knees had had enough. When neither cleaning or baking managed to settle her, she turned to the television. The only programmes on were an exposé of the American election and a reality show on how to con buyers into paying more for your house. Even in her state of extreme loneliness, boredom and anxiety, Letty couldn't bring herself to watch more than five minutes of either.

Letty's eyes wandered for something else to do and, after scanning the contents of the bookshelf, landed on the little blue book. The hairs on her skin prickled. She chewed her lip, wavered, and then in a change of direction lowered her gaze to one of the drawers. A solid swarm of butterflies engulfed her as she walked over and pulled on the little brass handle.

As Victoria had accused, the iPad was still in its box with the cellophane wrapper torn only at one side. Letty pulled the box out of the drawer and sat back down on the sofa.

Apparently, modern technology was intuitive – the twins had had their own iPad's since they were three, and Letty had seen children younger still toddling into the store with their faces glued to a screen – but to her, it may as well have been alien technology. The shiny black glass glistened with her reflection; the smell of plastic and polished metal harsh beneath her nose. She rotated the device in her hands, in search of an on switch. Two minutes later, she located a small button on the side. She pressed down and waited. A minute later, she tried again. Still nothing.

Frustrated, Letty muttered, put the device on the arm of the chair and returned to the box. Her hand delved inside and pulled out a small cable, a pair of white headphones, and a disconnected plug. If she was expected to start wiring a plug before the thing worked, she may as well give up now, she thought.

It was not until she'd torn the sides of the box apart and shaken the remaining cardboard to within a fraction of its original pulpish form that Letty conceded that there was nothing more to help her in her plight. No manual, no instructions, not even a leaflet explaining what the buttons did or how you were supposed to get the thing charged.

Letty looked at the plug and cocked her head. No wires on a plug when she was a child meant that something was broken, but wireless was all the rage nowadays. She remembered Donald setting up wireless around the house last year to access the cricket, and Joyce was always saying how her family stole next door's to save buying their own. This, she decided, probably worked the same way.

With a fair amount of hesitation, Letty rose from the sofa. Still second-guessing herself, she plugged the white plug in next to the standard lamp and placed the iPad on the table beside it. She stared at the two items, then changed her mind and propped the iPad up against the socket. Distance made a difference, she knew that much, and if it didn't work, she would ask Joyce about it in the morning. Joyce loved it when Letty showed her age.

Letty was running through tomorrow's to-do list in her head when the doorbell rang. She expelled an irritated sigh. The only person who came by unexpectedly at seven-thirty on a Tuesday was their neighbour, Mike, who had an unfortunate habit of locking himself out in his towel and, as such, had resorted to leaving a spare key at Letty and Donald's. The last time he'd locked himself out, he had only a flannel and a loofa for coverage. Letty went into the kitchen and picked the key off the hook.

'Just coming,' she called and then opened the door as little as necessary. 'Here you go.'

'Would you mind if I come in? I won't stay long.'

Letty froze. Mike's key dangled from her fingers, and the smell of banana cake drifted out from inside the house. After half a minute, her jaw tightened. Desperately, she racked her brains for something cutting to say, but Letty could not do cutting, and she didn't get angry; she got upset. Even now, she could feel the tears battling their way up through her throat.

'I'll put the kettle on,' she said.

In the kitchen, Victoria hovered.

'You can go and sit down. I'll bring the drinks through,' Letty said.

'I'm fine waiting for you,' Victoria said.

What followed was an awkward silence that lasted through the entire tea making process. While Letty busied herself finding matching mugs, Victoria's tongue darted in and out of her mouth in a manner that would imply she was about to start speaking. However, no actual attempt at conversation took place until they were sitting down on opposite sides of the living room, their cups of tea haemorrhaging heat in the silence.

The tightness around Letty's neck intensified.

'So—'

'Let me get a—'

'I was, sorry,' Victoria said. 'What were you about to say?'

Letty reddened. 'Oh, I was going to say we need some coasters.'

'Oh yes, of course.'

Letty got to her feet and moved to the bookshelf. A stack of old cork coasters was hidden behind a dilapidated copy of *Jane Eyre*. Letty kept her eyes down, deliberately avoiding looking at the book on the shelf above.

'Thank you,' Victoria said as Letty placed the coaster next to her.

Yet another silence ensued. The heat around Letty's neck was starting to itch. Victoria was keeping her cards unusually close to her chest. If she was planning on giving Letty a well-deserved apology, then the build-up was getting ridiculous.

'So,' Victoria said, finally putting her mug down and leaning into Letty. 'I suppose I should get to the point. I wondered if now that you've had a bit of time to calm down you might have reconsidered our offer?'

Letty choked on her drink. 'Sorry?' she spluttered.

'I know that Sunday was rather intense. I forget how sensitive you get when you've been baking your cakes. Just like when you were a kid really, isn't it? Do you remember that time you refused to come out of your bedroom because someone said the cat cake you baked looked like a deranged werewolf?'

Letty's faced thundered. Yes, she did remember that, and she remembered exactly who had said it.

Victoria continued. 'You didn't need to get so worried,

though. The children loved them. I wish you could have seen their faces, but never mind. Maybe next year.'

'Maybe,' Letty said, her teeth grinding against the ceramic of the mug. Victoria, sensing the need for a rethink, reached for her handbag and pulled out a small rectangular package. She thrust the item in Letty's direction.

'Here, go on, open it.'

Letty looked at it quizzically. 'What's it for?'

'Just a gift. Can't I buy my baby sister a gift now and then? Now, go on, open it.'

Letty hesitated.

'Go on. Take it.'

The dainty package was patterned with small brown and green polka dots and infused with aromas of bergamot and grapefruit.

'Thank you,' Letty said and tentatively began to peel back the tape from one side. 'But I don't know why you would think I need a present.'

Victoria was beaming. 'I saw it this morning in the store, and after what you'd said, well I knew you'd like it. Even if it isn't your normal type of thing.'

Letty removed the wrapping. The paper was followed by a box, which was, in turn, followed by a slim cloth bag. When she reached the concluding item, she stared at the gift inside, certain her mouth was hanging open, but not quite able to shut it.

'Oh ... Well this is ... It's ... it's so very thoughtful of you,' she said.

Victoria glowed. 'I knew you'd love it. And don't think you have to save it for best either. It's strong enough that you can use it every day. You will use it, won't you?'

'I ... I'm sure.'

'Where's your old wallet?' Victoria scanned around the room. 'We can swap all your cards and things over now.'

'You don't have to do that,' Letty said, hurriedly trying to replace the wrapping and cover up the monstrosity.

'Go and get it for me. The sooner we get rid of that ghastly tattered thing you carry about, the better. Go on. What are you waiting for?' Letty hesitated.

What Letty held in her hand appeared to be the end result of a fight between a crocodile and a particularly aggressive sewing machine that had taken place in a paint processing plant. The textured skin had been dyed a multitude of neon colours before being sewn together, folded and zipped down the middle. It exuded a scent of rotting leather, department stores, and polyethene, but before she could object, Victoria was out in the hallway, snatching her old and trusted purse from her handbag.

'This is a ridiculous number of cards,' Victoria commented as she began emptying Letty's old purse. 'Why on Earth do you have so many?'

Letty tensed.

'They're mostly old ones,' she lied and let her sister carry on with the decanting.

'Then you should get rid of them. You never know, someone could steal your identity. It wouldn't be hard with this many cards lying around. And I suspect your PIN numbers and passwords are all the same too, aren't they?'

'No,' Letty lied again.

'Well. Go through it. The last thing I want is this purse to get all warped and misshapen because you were too lazy to throw things out.'

Letty looked at her feet and mumbled. She was trying to think of some way to respond, when the oven timer pinged in the kitchen.

'I'll go get that,' she said and leapt to her feet.

Much to Letty's dread, Victoria decided she would wait until the cake had cooled so that she could try a slice.

'Besides,' she said. 'We didn't get to finish our conversation.'

'We didn't?'

Victoria miraculously managed to tut, sigh, and groan simultaneously.

'Look, I know the money might seem like a lot at the minute but think what you could do with the returns. A nice holiday. A wardrobe update. I'm not saying it'll be early retirement money, but who knows? Stranger things have happened.'

Letty cleared her throat, although Victoria was nowhere near finished.

'Now, I know borrowing money against the house can seem scary, but it's what people do nowadays. Honestly. You go into the bank tomorrow and they will be throwing money at you. I'm telling you.'

'I'm not sure—'

'And before you start on about Mum's inheritance, I told you. That's in a long-term investment situation. That's how you earn money nowadays. There are no quick fixes. This business venture with Felix though, this is an entirely different thing. Entirely different,' she hurriedly added.

Letty was still not sure how she was supposed to respond but was certain that she needed to say something before Victoria took all her cards and went to the bank herself.

'Now, I know you'll need to talk things through with Donald, and at a time when he's feeling a little more ... receptive. But I've spoken to Felix, and he reckons he can get you until Monday. That's it, though. He's had to work very hard to get that for you. You don't want to miss this chance.'

Letty dropped her chin, expecting Victoria to interrupt her once again. When she didn't, she found herself stuttering to find something to say. 'Well ...'

Victoria was on her feet.

'I know you're not stupid, Leticia. I do. And I'm sure you'll make the right decision about this.'

Letty squirmed. 'Umm ... well, I guess. I suppose I can talk to Donald.'

From the size of Victoria's grin, she'd said the right thing.

'Thank you,' she said. 'You won't regret it.'

It was in standing up from the sofa and moving to the door that Victoria caught sight of the iPad, dropped down by the side of the armchair. A small, repressed smile twitched at the corners of her mouth, and familiar tightness built around Letty's chest. Letty held her breath and waited for the ridicule. Instead, Victoria bent down and picked up the device.

'Do you want me to show you how to put in on charge before I go?' Victoria said.

Letty opened her mouth to offer some sort of indignant retort and then closed it again.

'Yes, please,' she said. 'I'm not sure the wireless is working.'

CHAPTER 17

'ARE YOU SURE she's ready?' Walter said. 'Shouldn't we wait until she's in bed or something?'

The excitement had given way to nerves. In his head, Walter had imagined it being more of a step-by-step process, perhaps with a demonstration, or group warm-up activity. It did not help matters that the cat was staring at him from the neighbouring cushion.

'Relax,' Hector said for the umpteenth time. 'Do exactly what you did last time.'

'I know.'

'Only try to stay there a little longer.'

'Okay.' Walter took another deep breath.

'And have a bit of rummage around if you can. Try to find some bearings, feelings, memories that kind of thing.'

'I understand.'

'It's important you only observe at this stage though. And don't forget to—'

'Sorry,' Walter said. 'Would you mind? I need a bit of quiet.'

'Of course. Of course.' Hector paused. He puckered his

lips and shuffled his feet a half step to the right. 'But if you can try to make sure that you take note of what you're seeing. And don't just—'

'Will you be quiet?' Pemberton said. 'You'll be lucky if you don't scramble the woman's brain at this rate.'

'That can't happen, can it?' Walter said, his eyes wide.

'No, no,' Hector assured him. 'Of course, it depends how you define scramble ... But no, no. Not at this level. Remember. Just observing.'

Walter's insides turned. He brushed his hands on the seat of his trousers and attempted to reconfigure his thoughts. He wanted to do this, he reminded himself. This was his call.

'Just do—'

'What I did last time. I know.'

Only Walter didn't know what he'd done last time. That was the problem. He had walked into the woman and somehow – apparently – merged their existential spirits.

'Anytime you're ready,' Hector said.

Walter studied his target one last time. Her arm was slung over the edge of the sofa, and her bottom lip wobbled as she let out a slow but consistent snore. He closed his eyes and lifted his foot. A second later, it hit the ground in front of him.

'It's no good,' he said. 'It's that cat. It's hard enough that she's lying down, but the cat, it's throwing everything off balance.'

'The cat?' Hector said. He marched over to the now sleeping feline and clapped his hands. 'Oi. Hiss, off with you.' The cat remained sleeping. 'Come on! I said get off! Off, I say.' Hector waved his hands above, around, and within the cat. Walter watched on, somewhat embarrassed for the man.

'Not that I agree with what you're doing in the slightest,' Pemberton said, moving forwards and steering Hector out of the way. 'But the last thing I want is a dead cat on my conscience, along with everything else.'

Crouching down on all fours, Pemberton approached the cat, pursing his lips and emitting a high-pitched squeak.

'Here, Kitty, Kitty,' he said in a voice far too soft to be his own. 'There's a good boy. Come on now. Wakey, wakey.' The cat's left eye slid open. 'That's a boy. Come on now. Off you come.'

Mister Missy's right eye opened to a slit. He yawned, exposing endless needle-like teeth, then rose onto all fours. A second later, he sauntered off the seat and onto the floor by Pemberton's feet. Walter watched agog as Pemberton ran his hand over the back of the purring tom.

'How? What? When did you learn to do that?' Walter asked.

Pemberton sniffed. 'Perhaps it's simply that my enigmatic animal skills travelled with me from my previous life,' he said.

Walter wasn't sure how to respond.

Still confused by what he'd just witnessed, Walter turned once more to the woman. There were no excuses now that cat was gone; his path was clear, and any thinking and over-analysing was a waste of time. He focused his attention, took a deep breath, and walked.

The tumbling was instant. Walter's head whirled, as he hurtled downwards then upwards then side to side. He could sense it all, the tiredness, the confusion – the effects of his little display from the shop that afternoon – and a mixture of emotions linked to her sister. He was in the woman, at one with her subconscious. All her memories were within his reach, a hair's breadth away from his fingertips.

And then, they weren't. All of a sudden, he was tumbling

in a different direction, upwards and outwards, and any second now ...

Thud. Walter landed with a thump against the floor.

'Ugh,' he groaned. The room was spinning. His ears rang, his vision had blurred, and while he was aware it wasn't entirely likely, it felt like he might have grown an extra limb. Slowly, he righted himself to a sitting position. Pemberton and Hector's jaws hung open.

'Did I do it?' he asked.

'Did you do it?' Hector clasped his hands and bounced on the spot, spilling the liquor from a tumbler that had somehow appeared in his hand. 'I can't believe it. Really. Not that I doubted you at all, but by Jove, you really did it. You really did it. How was it? How do you feel?'

Walter put a hand to his head. 'Dizzy,' he said. 'I feel dizzy.'

'Anything else?'

'No, I'm fine, I think.' Walter gave himself the once over, although it was difficult to decipher any possible peculiarities when his heart was skipping like a bug on hot coals. It wasn't just luck. Hector was right; Walter Augustus had a talent and was well on track to becoming a fully possessive spirit.

'Feel like you can go again?' Hector said.

Walter nodded. 'Definitely.' He moved to stand up, only to stumble back towards the wall. 'Perhaps we should wait a bit,' he said, recalling the twelve-hour nap he'd needed after his last similar event.

'Of course, of course. Take as much time as you need,' Hector said. 'Although obviously, not too long. We are on a tight timeframe.' Walter staggered across the living room and flopped down beside the sofa.

Hector mused.

'If you're going to have a little sit down, I might pop

upstairs for a minute,' he said. 'But don't do anything else until I get back. You hear me? By Jove, wait until the boys hear about this one.'

Walter grunted his reply. He felt substantially better than last time, but he still felt damn awful. His ears were still ringing, his eyes stung, and every muscle from his eyelids to his little toe twitched uncontrollably. Other than that, he was on cloud nine. He lowered his head in his hands then lowered it again onto his knees.

'One more minute,' he told himself. His eyelids grew heavier by the second.

'It isn't some game, you know.'

Walter was startled back awake. Pemberton was standing over him, his sour face even greyer than normal.

'Sorry,' Walter said. 'Did you say something?'

'I said this isn't some game. What you do here. It has consequences.'

'I never said—'

'You think this whole afterlife is about you. You and your book. You and your wife. There are other people's lives at stake here, too. Other people's eternities.'

'I know that.'

'Really?'

'Of course, I do.' Walter could feel the blood starting to pound in his ears, but he refused to rise to it, not this time.

Pemberton turned on his heel as if to leave and then paused. He twisted his neck back around to Walter.

'I need to get back too,' he said. 'I can't stay in the interim. It's not meant for people like me. It's not meant for people who've seen ...' Pemberton stopped and left his sentence hanging unfinished in the air and prickling the hair on the back of Walter's neck. His expression had changed. His eyes glistened in the dark.

'People aren't meant to come back,' Pemberton said. 'They're not. And now I'm here. And I shouldn't be.' He paused. Walter waited. It was a length of time before he spoke again.

'I don't think what you're doing is right,' Pemberton said slowly. 'I think it's fundamentally wrong. Invading minds. That's a power we are not meant to have.'

'I didn't—'

'But if you are sure that you know what you are doing there, and if you're certain that you won't hurt the girl—'

'I won't—'

'—then I will trust you,' Pemberton said. 'I will trust you, Walter Augustus, with my soul and hers. I will trust you to do whatever it is you think needs to be done so that we can all move on from this.'

Walter's throat swelled in a way that made it difficult to breathe, and he found himself looking at the ceiling and blinking rapidly.

'Thank you,' he choked out.

'Now, don't you dare screw it up,' Pemberton said.

*B*y 9.30 p.m. – and a total of eight occupancies later – Walter had gained a modicum of control. For starters, he had mastered the initial tumble, so it was more like a very fast slide, head first down a helter-skelter as opposed to being chucked off a cliff, naked, into a raging storm. The last few times he'd managed to stay there long enough to have a little bit of a poke about. The human subconscious, it turned out, was nothing like Walter had imagined.

'This is excellent going. Truly remarkable,' Hector said. 'We should get some people down here to see it. I know a lot of people who would be very impressed. Oh my, how old Mr Johnson would love to see this. Always been trying to master occupancy. Get a bit of soul back, I suppose. Not surprising really, given that incident down at the crossroads.'

'I'm still miles off,' Walter said. 'I'm sure no one would want to hear what I've got to say.' He shook his head in modesty, while internally imagining the crowd *oohing* and *ahhing* at his tales. Walter Augustus: Master of minds.

'What you need to do, according to this,' Hector tapped at the dirty great book he'd brought down with them, 'is find the Athenaeum.'

'Athy-what?'

'The Athenaeum. It's where the memories are stored. Now, if you can find where it's located and can get inside it, well, then you'll be at the heart of her subconscious. You can dig out all those memories you don't want her to remember.'

'Like when you slammed the door and terrified her,' Pemberton interjected.

'And, poof. Gone. Just like that.'

'Just like that?' Walter questioned.

'Well, I have a little more work to do on the minutiae of the situation. But, pretty much, from what I can tell. You'll have to get them all though; you don't want to leave any stragglers hanging around in there. Once we've rid her of the memories, it should give us a bit of time to work out how to dispose of the book. Then you're home and dry.'

As Walter took some time to think, his thoughts were subtly infiltrated by the flutterings of doubt.

'But what if that's too late?' he said. 'What if I'm already too deep in there? Too many memories, too many links, I can't just wipe her whole memory clean. Can I?' Without realising it, he'd directed the question to Pemberton.

There was no pear drop in his old boss' mouth and the

lack of suction made his cheeks appear unusually plump. He held Walter's gaze.

'You wanted to do this,' he said. 'So, do it right. For all of us. No half attempts. Do it properly.'

Something new and unexpected stirred in Walter's abdomen. It struck in his chest and spread out through his rib cage and beyond, solidarity. He could do this, he told himself. And he would do this. Not only for him, but for all of them. With a newfound sense of urgency and confidence, Walter prepared himself for round nine with the girl's subconscious.

'Maybe I can give it one more go, before we call it a night,' he said and stepped forward, ready to try again. He looked at Hector. 'A library, you say?'

'Of sorts.'

'Then that's what I'll find.'

Walter had the start down to a tee. He locked his gaze, focused, and breathed. Within seconds, the room swam around him. Images were sharpening his senses heightening. Clenching his fists, he prepared for what was to come. Then, milliseconds away from the tumble, something hard yanked him back.

Walter gasped. The force struck half an inch beneath his sternum, pulling him back into the room. His eyes pinged open. It hit again.

'I have to go,' he said.

'What?' Hector spat the drink out of his mouth, spraying Walter in whisky-fuelled spittle. 'You can't go now. The Athenaeum. We need the Athenaeum.'

'I have to go. I'm sorry. I shouldn't be long.'

'But ... But you're doing so well.'

'And I'll keep going. I'll get there. I'm sorry. I'm really sorry. I will be as quick as I can. I promise.'

He turned to Pemberton to offer an apology. Walter's stomach dropped. Pemberton had gone, and a cold chill of disappointment blistered in his wake.

Walter's insides were a mess, and his head was worse. Letting people down was never something he enjoyed, but he wasn't leaving out of choice, and it wasn't like he was going to be long, ten minutes he suspected. There was always the odd one that took longer, but this wasn't going to be one of those cases. This was straightforward. No *umming* and *ahhing* and certainly no returning from the light. Ten minutes and he would get back to the woman and her occupancy.

Walter sprinted through the corridor, the tugs in his chest lessening with every step. He needed to get there before it happened. Over a hundred years dead, and he hadn't missed a relative's passing yet. He was damned if this was going to be the first one. He followed the tug to its source, twisted the carved oak door handle, and slid silently into the room beyond.

'Sorry. Ouch.'

'Shh!'

'Oh, excuse me. Sorry, I—'

'Do you mind?'

'Shh!'

The room was crowded, packed to the walls with people of all ages and generations. At the front, a young woman and man waited, a small child bouncing on their knee. Behind them, people chatted excitedly, peering over one another's shoulders. Walter pulled in his shoulders as he muscled his way into the room and found a place close to the back.

'You close?' said a woman next to him. She was wearing a sequined dress and held between her fingertips a small hand-rolled cigarette. Ordinarily, her attire would have been entirely out of place in such a sterile hospital environment, but given the miscellany of personage, she fit in as well as anyone else.

'Distant relative.' Walter said.

'Me too! What side?'

'Mother's,' Walter said.

'Ahh, I'm on the other one. But you know what they say. You're only two bloodlines away from Genghis Khan's clan up here.'

'Is that what they say?'

'Apparently so.' She took a puff on her cigarette. 'I don't think it will be long. Apparently, they've already glimpsed her once or twice.'

'Really? It could be any second then,' Walter agreed. He was relieved that he hadn't spent any more time arguing the toss with Hector.

It was during his moment of contemplation that the shuffling increased. The crowd bent and stretched, pulling themselves onto tiptoes. Walter sank farther back against the wall.

'Don't you want to watch?' the lady asked.

'I've seen it enough times,' Walter said and beckoned her into the space in front of him.

'So have I,' she confessed. 'But it never gets old, does it?'

'No, I guess not.'

Walter hung back as the whoops of joy flooded the room. His heart was heavy and yet light, and a single teardrop ran a course down his cheek.

'I'm sorry, Edi,' he whispered, hoping that somewhere, somehow she could hear him. 'I should be with you now.'

'Am I ...? Am I ...?' A confused voice spoke from the front of the room. Walter edged his way back to the door.

'Are you not staying?' the lady in the sequins asked. 'I'm sure she'll want to meet you. You remember what it's like.'

'I will,' said Walter. 'I'll come back in a little while. Give her a little time.'

'Oh, well perhaps, I'll catch you later?'

'Perhaps.'

Through the crowds, Walter glimpsed the girl. Her hair was no longer grey but burning mahogany. Her skin smooth, her eyes clear.

'Mum, Dad? Is that really you?' she said. 'I am ...? Where am I? Is this ...?'

'You're okay, Betty. You're better than okay,' the man beside her said and then he hugged his daughter for the first time in decades.

CHAPTER 18

$\mathcal{I}$T WAS THE second day that Letty had risen with a blazing headache, although the headache was nothing compared to bizarre dreams she'd had while sleeping. She'd been sitting on a cliff edge writing poetry in a little blue notebook. Every time she finished the book, she would get up to leave, only to have a bearded man hand her another one and tell her to keep writing. At the start, it had felt like a bit of a joke, but then the man's face grew dark and the sea grew rough, and no matter how fast she wrote, it wasn't good enough.

'Sounds like stress,' Donald said over the phone.

'I'm tired; that's all,' Letty insisted. 'What is it you're doing today?'

'More of the same,' Donald said. 'More of the same.'

'Well, you better go and have a good breakfast then,' said Letty. 'And don't worry about me. I'm fine.'

In the living room, she stared up at the bookshelf and the small blue slither of spine.

'I know. I'm being ridiculous,' she said to Mister Missy. 'It's not haunted. Houses are haunted. Books can't be haunted.' Mister Missy mewed, but the niggling continued all through breakfast and on route to the shop.

'Have you ever heard of a book being haunted?' Letty said to Joyce as they dusted under the shelves during a quiet spell.

'You mean like in Harry Potter?'

'Is there a haunted book in that?'

'Kinda. Well, it's ain't haunted exactly. More possessed. But that's kinda the same thing, ain't it?'

'Possessed?' Letty said. Somehow that sounded worse.

When closing time came, Letty walked back up the high street and grabbed a large portion of fish and chips for dinner. At the corner shop, she picked up some cat food and a family-sized bar of Dairy Milk to see her through the rest of the week. One row a day. She was going to be sensible. That was the plan at least, but after her second phone call of the day to Donald, all plans were forgotten.

'Honestly, Letty, what do you want me to tell you?' Donald said when Letty had enquired about the day. 'It was the same as last year, the same as the year before. There's nothing new to say.'

'What about the food?'

'What about it? It's food. We eat it.'

'But you're having a nice time?'

'No, no Letty, I'm not. And your constant questioning isn't helping.'

Letty stifled her breath and attempted to hold back the tears. In thirty-odd years, she could count the number of times Donald had snapped at her on one hand. The silence lingered down the line, the sting of his words resonating in Letty's chest.

'Well, I should get on with some baking,' she stammered when the silence had gotten too much to bear. Donald's reply was a stuttering mumble, and Letty hung up the phone, fearing he might say something else she didn't want to hear. It was, Letty realised as her hand shook on the receiver, the first time she could remember him ending a telephone conversation without saying I love you.

Letty's mind was a train wreck. Perhaps he'd found out about the money and the lying, she thought. Or perhaps the thought of retiring in three years and having to spend all his days with her was giving him second thoughts about their marriage. There was no denying she'd let herself go on cakes and pies. Donald could easily get another woman, one with a degree, or grownup children even. He may have missed out on being a father because of her body, but perhaps he was still clinging to the chance of being a grandfather.

Unable to focus – and knowing there was no point baking in her current state – she turned on *Emmerdale* and demolished the family-sized chocolate bar. Letty always did her worst baking when she was upset, and she had the distinct impression that even her best might not be good enough for this particular customer. During the advert break, she lumbered into the kitchen and demolished the rest of the banana cake, and it was only when she was about to open her cupboards in hope of finding some out of date, plastic tasting cooking chocolate that she stopped herself.

'Get yourself together,' she said, then shut the cupboard door and wandered back into the living room. What she needed, she decided after ten minutes of channel hopping, was a distraction. Something to keep her mind busy, so that she did not start worrying about Donald or Victoria and make her way through the entire week's groceries stress eating. She cast her eyes across the room, where it landed on a small, rectangular object. Her insides danced nervously.

Letty's pulse knocked in her chest as she picked it up. It was lighter than she remembered, although it carried an undeniable mental weight that caused her throat to dry and her hands to tremble ever so slightly. She pulled out the charger, then sprung back as it lit up with life.

'Oh!' she said, startled.

Enter password, it said. Letty swallowed a lungful of air. Password. She remembered Felix telling her to enter a password when she first got it. Letty hesitated. By the looks of things, it was a six-digit code; that meant she would have used the long version of her mother's birthday. Zero, eight, zero, six, thirty-six. She typed. There was a moment's pause, then, UNLOCKED, flashed on the screen.

A sense of pride rose through her belly. It instantly evaporated; now she'd turned the thing on, it was the small matter of working out what to do with it.

On Boxing Day – upon receiving the gift – Felix, Victoria and the twins had given her an iPad crash course, but nine months was a long time to remember something. Letty's eyes were drawn down the screen to a small white square labelled music. She tapped it and a short list of songs appeared. With wobbling breaths, she pressed the first one on the list.

Letty leapt from the chair as a blast of sound shot out from nowhere; the silver sheet of metal flew from her hands, landing with a small bounce on the carpet. Letty fell to her knees and grabbed the device. Her pulse raced as she turned it over and over, desperately searching for some way to stop the sound. Her fingers knocked a tiny divot in the side, and the volume dropped by a smidgen. She found the divot and did it again. With a sigh of relief, she continued to press the button until the sound had stopped altogether.

With her pulse still substantially above a resting pace, Letty studied the screen for a less traumatic icon to start with.

'Photos,' she said to herself and tapped the little flower icon.

You have no photos the screen said. Letty pouted then saw another one of interest. A small round sun nestled behind a white cloud. She tapped *Weather*.

A black screen instructed her to type a city or postcode. 'East –leigh –lee –ch,' Letty said, sounding out each syllable as she typed. There were several mistypes before the device finally accepted her answer. A moment later, the screen filled. Letty bounced around excitedly. *8°C. Cloudy. Possible showers.*

'That sounds about right,' Letty said, then, quite content with talking out loud to the cat, said, 'Let's see what it's like in London.' She typed the capital city into the screen. A moment later, it blinked. *8°C. Cloudy. Showers likely.*

'Hmm,' she said.

Letty spent the next ten minutes searching through the various capital cities and places of interest she could think of before the novelty wore off. Even so, a lingering satisfaction of having learnt something new remained. Clicking back to the home screen, she saw a small colourful icon, labelled beneath in tiny writing it said, Internet. Letty's insides quivered. What harm could come from just looking? Feeling like a small ant's nest had taken up residence in her abdomen, she clicked on it.

'What would you like to know?' The screen said. Letty stared at the wording. What did she want to know? She wanted to know how to say *no* to her sister. She wanted to know why her husband was so grumpy at the minute and how to tell him she was hiding over a half a million pounds in various bank accounts. She wanted to know why Opal Fruits had changed their name to Starbursts all those years ago and exactly how much Creme Eggs had shrunk in the last decade, but none of those questions seemed Internet worthy. Looking up from the screen, she glanced around the

153

room. Her eyes stopped. There was something else she wanted to know.

Whether the adrenaline came from the use of the Internet or the question she was typing was indiscernible. All the same, Letty's hand quivered as she began to type. When she'd finished, she looked at the words, read them through to herself and pressed okay.

At first glance, Letty assumed she'd clicked on the wrong page, as adverts for second hand cars, online dating, and holidays in Corfu flashed up on her screen. A few clicks later, however had emptied the page and in place of the adverts was one glaring title: Are you being haunted?

The page consisted of a twenty-question multiple-choice quiz that would evidently tell her if she was indeed being stalked by some post-physical being. Her heart fluttered as she began to read.

The initial question was – in Letty's opinion, fairly disturbing – *Do you feel like you are being watched? Yes, No* or *Maybe* being the available answer options. Letty lifted her head. Her eyes met with Mister Missy, who had positioned himself directly in front of her and was staring up intently from the mat.

'Maybe,' Letty said and tapped the appropriate option.

Do you ever hear sounds in your house at night? the second question asked. Letty looked at Mister Missy again. 'Yes,' she said, shooting him a glare as she selected her answer.

The next questions went through how old her house was, whether she'd ever seen anyone watching her while she slept – she would be sleeping with the light on after that question – or if she'd ever seen objects in the house move unexpectedly. Initially, she selected *No* for both questions before changing the one about moving objects to *Maybe*. After all, the shoes and the door had both been at work. Fifteen questions later and she was done. She scrolled up – an accidental act, but one she was rather thrilled to have discovered – then submitted her answers.

A small wheel formed, disappeared then reformed as Letty waited for the verdict. Her pulse grew steadily faster, increasing with every spin on the wheel, and the colony of ants in her stomach was rapidly joined by a rather large swarm of wasps. Finally, the wheel stopped. Letty had her answer.

It's all in your head the screen said.

The sigh of relief was audible. Of course, she wasn't being haunted. Ghost stories at her age. It was a ridiculous notion. Clearly, she was under more stress than she thought. On the positive side, Letty considered, her fear of the Internet appeared to be, at least mildly, abated. Mister Missy jumped up beside her. She stroked his fur and laughed.

'Silly Mummy.'

With a newfound assurance, Letty strode over to the bookcase, picked up the book, and held it in her hands. There was nothing to be afraid of. It was just like any other book. Paper and words and nothing more.

The cover was supple, the yellowing pages crisp to turn, and it smelled musty and dank, like flowers left too long in a vase. Inside, the musty smell lessened and tangs of ink, straw and wood burning stoves held dominance. She flicked through until she found a reasonably short poem and started to read.

Better days I never knew,
Since I laid eyes and lips on you,
And whilst sweet tastes have touched my tongue,
Sweeter than you I know are none.

I will not lie, I will not cheat,
You are my soul, you are my sweet.
You are my air, my stars, my breath.
My love holds true in life and death.

*I*t was pretty, Letty thought, and much easier to understand than the poems with fifty hidden meanings that she'd been forced to dissect throughout school. She skimmed through to another one. This time, she said the words out loud as she read.

'*D*rift between daydreams I no longer do.
   Each hour is a daydream when held close to you.
Come winter, or summer, or storms on the sea,
I'll brace all bad weather. I'll cling on to thee.
So let the horse whinny, and let the winds roar,
My heart will not falter, no not anymore.
And when the time comes for all weather to cease,
Together, my love, we will rest in our peace.'

*L*etty closed the book and ran her fingers over the speckled cover.

'Walter Augustus,' she said. 'I think I quite like you.'

~

*W*alter had been returning from Betty's passing over, and the enthusiasm and determination to free himself from interim binds was as strong as it had ever been. He would find the Athenaeum, he would rid the woman of these memories, and he would be reunited with his wife and children. His resolve was certain. He stepped into the comfy surrounds of Letty's living room, repeating a speech he'd prepared for his peers. Two steps in, however, and Letty's voice caught him off-guard. His ears pricked. The words were painfully familiar, yet they still took the longest moment to place.

'What the ...'

Pemberton turned towards him, his long face saddled with sadness. 'I'm sorry,' he said to Walter. 'I truly am.'

CHAPTER 19

*L*ETTY WAS hooked. With some, she only read the first line before deciding they definitely weren't her type of thing, while others she re-read two, three, four times before she moved on. Those that she enjoyed the most she read to Mister Missy or marked the page with a slither of chocolate paper wrapper. When the book was done, she flicked back to the front.

'To E.M. Pemberton,' she read. 'For his guidance.'

The non-descriptive dedication was a little saddening. Letty had been hoping for the first name of the woman he'd written so passionately about. Emily, she thought, studying the dedication, perhaps it was an Emily. She would love to know more about her, she thought, about them both.

Then, with an unexpected moment of inspiration, Letty put down the book, picked up the iPad, and began to type.

alter fell to his knees, too weak to scream, too numb to cry. This was it, the final severing of his hope.

'This is not good,' Hector muttered beside him. 'Not good at all.'

'I ... I ...' Walter stammered. 'I won't be able to get rid of all those thoughts. She'll ... she'll never forget me now. She marked the pages. Did you see that? She marked the pages. This is it. I'll be stuck here until she dies.'

'We've got a little bit more of an issue than that,' Hector said.

'Like what?'

'Like that.'

~

alter Augustus offered 8.8 million results. Even Letty, with her limited knowledge of the Internet, knew there was slim chance that she would find her Walter Augustus in the first five minutes of looking with the odds stacked that high. Biting down on her bottom lip, she rethought her strategy. If the shop's system had taught her anything, it was to be specific in your searches. Searching womens shoes, for example, when what you're actually after is a pair of memory foam, slip-ons would lead you to hundreds of unwanted pairs of stilettos, hiking boots, and kitten heels.

She tried again. *Walter Augustus poet.* Less than half a million hits; a substantial drop. The first Walter on her screen was Australian. There was nothing in the poems to say that her Walter was not Australian, but Letty was convinced otherwise. The second one, Walter Augustus Shirley, looked more promising; it was certainly the right era, and the gentleman was British. She clicked the link "Memoirs of Lords". The title did not seem to fit the image of a man who wrote about cold nights, leaking roofs and stone hearths, but she scanned through a couple of his poems to be sure.

Back on the search engine, she clicked in the bar and started her search differently. Poems, she wrote, by *Walter Augustu* – Letty tapped the S again. Nothing happened. She wiped her finger and pushed with a little more force. Still nothing.

'That's odd,' she said, then deleted the surname and started again. *Poems by Walter Augu* – This time, she only got as far as the second U before the letters stopped.

Deleting the entire thing, Letty held down her finger to form an extended series of *Ss*. There was no problem with that; in fact, each letter in the alphabet seemed to be in perfect working order when tested individually or when writing any other word. She tried typing the name fast. She tried typing slowly. She tried typing capital letters and letters with full stops and spaces and hyphens and dashes between them. It made no difference. Every time she reached that final U, if not before, the computer stopped writing. A cold draught blew and sent tingles down her spine. Whoever Walter Augustus was, he was even less of a fan of the Internet than she was.

~

'What do you think you're doing?' Pemberton bellowed. 'Stop it. Stop it now. You're drawing more attention to yourself.'

Walter was shaking. 'What is that thing? Why does it know so much?'

'What is it? What do you mean *what is it*? It's the Internet.'

'The what?'

'The Internet.' Pemberton lowered his voice and shook his head. 'God help us all.'

The woman had stopped typing now, but Pemberton was right. Walter had drawn more attention to himself. He could feel his name bouncing around her thoughts like an echo chamber.

'I don't understand. What is the Internet?' Walter asked. 'Why were all those people on there?'

'Because that's what happens now,' Hector said. 'Devastatingly inevitable.'

'I don't understand.'

'It's how people get trapped. Five minutes of fame. Less for some. And that's it. Once your name is on that thing, eternity in the interim awaits. There is no escape.'

Walter gulped. The room felt hot and stuffy and extremely short on air.

'Am I on it? Are we?' he directed the question to Pemberton.

Hector shook his head. 'You'd know if you were on it,' he said. A sad glint shone beneath his monocle. It was all there in his eyes.

'You are?' Walter said. 'You're on it?'

It was the first time Hector had looked his age – or at least somewhere in that region. His skin sagged, his shoulders hunched, and it was almost as if a grey cloud hung directly above his head, despite his grass skirt and the stuffed parrot on his shoulder.

'Four thousand, seven hundred and eighty-seven entries,' he said. 'Six fake profile pages. An average of nine hundred and twenty-two clicks per day. Oh yes, I'm on there,' he said bitterly.

Walter shuddered. 'So you're ...'

'Trapped,' Pemberton finished for him.

Hector's face tightened. 'That's me. Destined to spend all eternity roaming the interim with reality television stars and dogs who drive jet skis with their tails.'

'I'm ... I'm ...' Walter couldn't finish. He didn't know what he was, sorry? devastated? heartbroken? He turned to Pemberton but his elder could offer no solace either.

'Oh, cheer up you two,' Hector said, dispelling the heavy grey cloud. 'It's not as if it's all bad company. Freddy Mercury, Madam Curie, da Vinci. I've been holding out for David Attenborough for a decade now. Sometimes, I wonder if that man has learnt something on all his travels, if you know what I mean?' Hector chuckled. The others did not.

'You never know,' Hector spoke slowly. 'Maybe somehow, I'll find a way to see the other side. One day.'

Walter still couldn't speak. Nothing made any sense. He was numb, yet every nerve from his toes to his chest blazed with a searing pain.

'No,' Walter said, finally breaking the silence and lifting his gaze to meet the others. 'It's not going to happen. I'm not going to let it happen to me. To us.'

Pemberton sniffed. 'There's nothing you can do. If the woman decides to—'

'She won't,' Walter interrupted. 'She won't decide to do any of it.'

'How are you going to stop her?'

'The only way I know how.'

'Surely you can give us a little more information than that,' Hector said as Walter struggled to regain his balance. 'Are you sure?'

They had started work the minute the woman had fallen asleep. With this latest development and additional urgency driving the situation, Walter had found his arrival in the woman's subconscious much more smoothly than on his previous attempts. He had managed to navigate himself through Letty's subconscious several times and – despite the constantly changing nature of the place – was beginning to get some form of bearings. He wiped his brow on the sleeve of his shirt and sat down, breathless.

'It is. I'm sure of it. I've found the Athenaeum.'

Hector could barely stand still.

'Well, don't keep it to yourself! Tell us everything. Is it as big as they say?"

'It's huge,' Walter said. 'Humongous. It's like a massive library, only too big to see the ceiling. And there were birds in it. And thousands of little boxes on shelves.'

'And that's where the memories are?'

'I suppose so. I didn't look.'

Hector stopped bouncing.

'What do you mean you didn't look? How are you going to find out which ones you need to get rid of if you don't look?'

It was Walter's turn to frown.

'I just need a little more time to make sure I know what I'm doing,' he said.

Hector pouted.

'He's right to be cautious,' Pemberton spoke for the first time since Walter's latest return. 'The last thing he wants to do is find he's in a place and can't get out.'

'Oh, that won't happen, not with his talent.'

Walter squirmed. As much as he admired Hector's faith in him, he was beginning to appreciate the magnitude of the job. When he said the Athenaeum was big, what he meant to say was huge, colossal, like another version of the interim corridor, stuck inside the mind of this one, dumpy middle-aged woman. The last thing he wanted to do was start picking things up and messing around in there.

'You need to start picking things up and messing around in there,' Hector said.

Pemberton coughed.

'With caution, of course,' Hector added. 'Otherwise, we're not even going to know if it's possible for you to get rid of these memories.'

Walter stiffened.

'You said it was possible. That's why we're doing this. Because you said it was possible.'

'Ahh yes, well in theory, dear boy, a great many things are possible. Reforestation, genuine politicians. But in reality ... Who knows?'

Hector paused. 'Why not have one more quick look. See if you can't weasel out a little bit more about the place before she wakes up.'

Walter looked to Pemberton. His old blacksmithing teacher gave one short, stiff nod.

'Okay then,' Walter said. 'Time to get going.'

Walter landed in the woman's subconscious with barely a bump and took less than a minute to gather himself. The scent was one of spring flowers and old stone cottages, with sounds of birds and gurgling water.

The overall layout of Letty's subconscious mind was one of a small village, with a large, shallow river running through the middle and an array of crooked, leafy trees lining a cobbled path. The light was neither day nor night, with the sky a deep luminous purple. Like the interim, the temperature was interminably pleasant. Wasting no time, Walter crossed a small stone bridge. On a former visit, the bridge had been made of glass, and he'd paddled in the river, managing to catch fish with his bare hands, but there was no time for that now. There was a job to get done, and he was there to do it. With his mind full of Hector's last words to him, he followed the curve of the river past various shops and houses until he came to a stop in front of a small, thatched cottage. Walter closed his eyes and twisted the door handle.

The inside was at least a thousand times bigger than the outside implied, with a large open entrance area on the ground floor and stairs that spiralled upwards towards an open sky. The scent of afternoon rain and chocolate chips encased him, while up in the sky, silhouettes of small birds danced against a backdrop of blue. From the distance came the threat of a storm and the rumble of thunder, although currently, all Walter felt was a gentle mist of rain that lightly dampened his skin.

He stepped past a set of neatly arranged armchairs, running his fingers across the leather. These were new. Last time, there had been a garden, growing beans on vines and tomatoes in glasshouses. The time before that, it had been a child's nursery. Now, a coffee table sat with a half-finished slice of cake and a cup of tea on top. The sponge, Walter noticed, looked fresh, the tea still steaming.

Walter hesitated.

'Hello?' he said. 'Is anybody there?' An intense silenced filled the space around him. Walter held his breath and waited. He had the distinct feeling that someone was watching him. A minute later, he shrugged it off and headed up the spiral staircase, towards the library.

The majority of items on the shelves resembled shoe boxes, some a little bigger and some considerably smaller. As to how many containers there were, that was anyone's guess. Hundreds of thousands? Millions more likely. With no idea what he was supposed to do, Walter picked an aisle, walked towards it, and began to browse. A few moments later Walter stopped, lowered one of the boxes off the shelf, and opened the lid.

The box was weightless and, on first inspection, appeared to be empty. With plenty more to investigate, Walter was about to replace the lid when something glinted in the bottom. He squinted, tilted the box a little then reached in. The item in question – something flat and thin – gave a little between his fingers. As carefully as he could, he lifted it out. His hand and pulse trembled as he moved towards the light to get a better view.

Despite the half-light, the item was easily identifiable as a photograph and the image recognisable as a set of keys. They were hanging up vertically, dangling down in the centre of a little teak box. They could be for anything, Walter thought, although they were far thinner and lighter looking than the keys of his day.

Walter was busy studying the small rectangular image when something pulled at his attention. He tried to ignore it, but it struck again and again, like a light flashing in the periphery of his vision. Clutching the photograph, he abandoned the box and drifted up the steps. Around him, winds bolstered, and the once silent birds began to squawk as they dived. However, at that moment, Walter was entirely oblivious to everything else in the Athenaeum.

There was nothing for the naked eye to see, but something akin to a tug was pulling him, dragging him up from the sternum. He was almost positive he could have fought against it had he tried, but he didn't try. He didn't want to.

'I might have heard of him, I suppose. What did you say the name was?'

'It's Walter. Walter Au—'

Whether the voices were inside his head or inside the

room, he couldn't tell, but they were on replay over and over. Two women, one asking a question, the other replying with his name. Every step Walter's legs trembled a little more. He reached the next floor, stopped and steadied himself against the wood.

Despite the thousands of boxes, Walter knew which one it was. It beckoned him, one un-extraordinary box somehow calling out. His hands quaked as he lifted the lid and retrieved a second photograph.

Walter studied the picture. The sepia tone of the print was the same as the photograph in his other hand, although this photo was taken on a shoe shop floor. Two women were talking, one young, one older. Behind them, a door was holding back the wind.

Walter backed away from the shelves, still staring at the image, aware that this was exactly what he'd been looking for, a memory that needed destroying. There was no movement to it, yet he could see it all, hear it all, and feel it all as if the event were unfurling in front of him there and then. The scent of shoe polish spiralled up in the air. The bang of the door shook the women time and again. If he was ever to be free, then eradicating every trace of him was the only choice.

Walter was pondering this eradication when a bolt of lightning struck the floor above. He gasped. The wind that followed screeched, strong enough to push him back against the shelves and slam his shoulder into the wood.

'Argh!' he said, reaching for his shoulder. Another blast hit him. Walter grappled for support. Still clutching the images, he pulled himself up to standing when a third gust struck, knocking the photographs out of his hand.

'No!' Walter shouted. He twisted down, but it was the wrong direction; the photographs were spiralling up, up and away.

CHAPTER 20

I T HAD NOT been a good morning. The combination of the previous evening's visit from Victoria, excess sugar, and the undeniable unease of the mysterious disappearing name on the iPad, had been compounded by yet another disastrous night's sleep. All night, Letty had tossed and turned, and when she did finally drift off, the dreams were worse than had she eaten a four-person fondue with cheese dippers by herself. It was all foggy now, but there were some bits that had stuck. Like standing at the bottom of a massive staircase watching a man peering into little boxes on the endless shelves, taking whatever he wanted as he went.

In her dream, those boxes were hers, and somehow the man was defiling her. When she finally plucked up the courage to climb the staircase and approach him, a gust of wind had blown her from her spot and sent her tumbling down the staircase, battering her shoulder. Her stomach churned inexplicably at the memory. What's more, now that she'd woken, her shoulder throbbed. As much as Letty dismissed dreams as the leftover ramblings of an over-tired mind, she was certain that the pain was in the exact same place as where the bannister had struck her when she fell in her dream.

Adding to the stress of the day was the issue of the car keys. Outside, the August drizzle looked set to harden, and with Donald away, the last thing Letty wanted was to get caught in some torrential downpour, unable to get home. She thought she'd left her keys in the kitchen, but having scoured the room from top to bottom, she failed to find them. Next, she'd searched her coat pockets and the bowl by the door where Donald had a tendency to dump things. Eventually, after removing the cushions off of the sofa and armchairs, emptying her handbag twice, and even having a quick rifle through the rubbish bin, she located them in – of all places – the key box by the door. Letty scratched her head. She had no recollection of placing them there, yet there they were.

Letty's stomach turned. The Internet may have said this stuff with Walter was all in her head, but she wasn't so sure. Keys and computers were a step up from moving shoes. If Letty really was as haunted as she was starting to think, then maybe she should be concerned about what his next upgrade might be.

In the shop, Joyce was threading laces into a delivery of boy's trainers.

'You sure you're alright?' she asked Letty for the twelfth time. 'You look rough.'

'Just tired,' Letty said. 'I'll be fine when Donald gets back. I've got a few things on my mind; that's all.'

'You should talk to someone about it, then,' Joyce told her, putting a laced trainer aside and picking up another, unlaced one. 'My Aunt was keeping this thing about m' nephew, and anyway, she didn't tell anyone, and she got an ulcer.'

'Like a stomach one?'

'Yeah, only it wasn't there. And anyway, it burst.'

'The ulcer?'

'Yup.'

'That's terrible.'

'She had to have stitches and everything. And the doctor said it was all because she wasn't talking about stuff. It all built up. Apparently, he's seen people die from it before.'

'From not talking about things?'

'Uh-hu. Scary, ain't it? 't's why I won't keep quiet about stuff if you tell me it.'

Although Letty was somewhat unconvinced over the legitimacy of Joyce's claim, she couldn't help but feel that talking to someone would have its benefits. In the three days since Donald's departure, her main sources of conversation had been Mister Missy and Joyce – neither of which had much to offer in the way of intelligent response. Throw in Victoria's unexpected visit, the constant anxiety over her ever increasing savings and this thing with the book, and she reasoned she had enough to keep any well-qualified therapist in the black for several months. When lunchtime came, she decided to seize the opportunity.

'Are you alright if I take a little bit longer today? I want to pop and see a friend,' she said to Joyce, taking her sandwich from the back room and dropping it into her bag. 'Then if you want to go a bit early, we can call it square.'

Joyce shrugged. 'Fine with me. Going out with the girls tonight. Thought they might like to come to mine for a bit of pre-lash.'

'Great. Well, I'll try not to be too long,' Letty said, then pulled on her coat and hurried out the door.

The morning's precipitation continued at an inoffensive pace, and after briefly considering her options, Letty decided to walk up the hill to Jean's. Taking the car would save time, but no doubt she would struggle to find a space when she was up there and probably lose her current one when she came back down. As long as the rain didn't get much harder, she would be fine.

Letty spent the walk up the hill in a state of deliberation. Jean had little patience when it came to Letty's sister, so steering clear of Victoria talk was probably a good idea. Any comments about ghosts would have her friend reeling with laughter, so it was likely best to keep those to herself too. Besides, Letty mused as she walked, all the thoughts about ghosts, the noises and seeing things were symptomatic of something else. Symptomatic of the stress. As such, Letty decided to tell Jean about the money. She wasn't going to tell her the true extent of it, only that she had a few savings and wasn't sure how to tell Donald. Hopefully, that would be enough.

Letty was halfway up the hill when the weather changed. Without warning, the light, misty drizzle became large dollops of rain that pelted down onto her coat and sprung up on the pavement around her. She cast her gaze back down the road, where a sea of multi-coloured umbrellas was popping up below. There were two options; she could race back down to the shop now and get soaked, or head forward to Jean's and hope the rain lessened off while she was inside. If it didn't, there was still a definite possibility that Jean had a towel or two in the store that she could use, not to mention an umbrella. Lowering her head, Letty drove herself forward against the wind, forcing herself the remaining way up the hill.

Every step, the rain-soaked deeper into her clothes. First, it was just the hems of her trousers, then it was up to her knees and soon her feet squelched in her shoes. Water ran in gullies off her hands and face as Letty picked up her pace to as close to a sprint as she dared, before coming to an abrupt stop outside Jean's shop.

Letty's heart sank. 'Back in five minutes,' the sign said.

With her coat draped over her head as a hood, Letty scanned the road from one end to the other. The sound of the storm was deafening, and the rain now so heavy that the people on the other side of the road had dissolved into nothing more than small smudges of colour. The soles of her shoes were soaked through, and even with her coat over her head, drops of rain were trickling their way down the back of her neck. Both the Chinese and the kebab shop were closed, and the small newsagents had a crowd of people under its canopy, suggesting that inside was already full. Letty glanced around again, searching for any kind of refuge when her eye caught sight of a small flashing sign.

'It's better than catching pneumonia,' she said.

Paint peeled from the walls, accenting the aroma of stale kebabs and chilli sauce as Letty took her first step into the stairwell of Mystic Moiras.

Letty had never believed in things like psychics or mystics, but then until a week ago, she'd never believed that a pile of shoes could straighten themselves out or a computer delete words it did not want to write. When the stairs ended, she pushed the white wooden door and stepped through.

'Hello?' she said.

The one bed flat had been decorated with an array of fittings and features designed to convey a more mystical appearance, including several lava lamps, with rising blobs of red, glowing wax and a fibre optic feather-like structure. Two of the walls were adorned with a variety of tie-dye scarves and sarongs, and the scent of kebabs and chilli was now blended with a precise perfume of incense, coffee, and cheap apple cider. In the corner a plump lady with platinum blonde hair was staring at a television.

'If you're here for Steve, I don't know when he'll be back. Better off asking that skank over on Albany Road.'

'No, I'm here for Moira.'

'Oh.' The woman looked up from the television, eyes wide. 'You are? Shit. Hold on. I'll just be a sec.'

A mad dash around the flat followed as the woman began removing empty cider cans and takeaway wrappers while simultaneously lighting some of the two-dozen candles that were littered around the place. The entire time, she was swearing to herself in what sounded to Letty like an Essex accent. When she was done tidying, she switched off the television and darted through a door by the kitchenette. 'I'll be two minutes,' she said.

When she returned, the platinum blonde hair had been swept up and disguised under the wrap of a multi-coloured scarf. A thick rimming of kohl eyeliner had been added to her makeup.

'My daughter. Sit. Please sit.' She beckoned Letty over to small a table, her voice having dropped an octave and adopted a Spanish accent. Letty hesitated before lowering herself onto one of the chairs having spotted a puddle of bean juice coagulating on the table top. Noting Letty's gaze, the woman leaned forward and mopped up the spillage with the sleeve of her jumper.

'You 'ave troubles from *zee* spirit world, do you not?' The Spanish-Essex twang was hard to hear past, but Letty tried.

'I—'

'I can help. I can. But first, you must cross my palms.'

'Cross your palms?'

'With silver. The spirits will accept no reading until a payment has been made.'

'Oh,' Letty said. Another fluttering of misgivings rose through her intestines. 'How much is it?'

'Fiver for a quick read of the cards. Tenner if you want the whole hog.'

Letty reached in her hand bag and felt around for a purse. It took a second to remember that it was the thing that felt like a dead toad, which Victoria had gifted her. She pulled it out of her bag and opened it up. A small stab of pain radiated from the sore spot on her shoulder.

'Woah, that's well nice, that is,' Moira said. 'Bet that was expensive.'

'It was a gift,' Letty said. Then finding only one ten and one twenty-pound note in her bag, pulled out the smaller ten-pound note. She handed it across the table to Moira, who deposited it in her ample cleavage with barely a glance.

'The reading may now begin,' she said.

CHAPTER 21

'THERE'S NO possibility that this will actually work, is there?' Walter said. His eyes were glued to the woman with a bedsheet wrapped around her cranium. Walter had been drained by his trips to the Athenaeum the previous night, and as such, Pemberton had been on duty watching Letty that morning. When she'd deviated from her normal lunchtime routine, he'd come up to the interim to gather the others. He needn't have bothered on Walter's behalf, though. The tugs had become so intense, he was heading back down himself. Now that he was sitting in the dank and weirdly furnished apartment, they'd only gotten worse. As had his nerves.

'Those cards won't actually tell her anything, will they?' he repeated. Hector and Pemberton scoffed in unison.

'Tarot cards, Augustus,' Pemberton sneered with derision. 'Really?'

'Good God, boy, she has as much chance at connecting to us through those as through the back of a cereal box.' Hector slapped him on the back. Walter flinched. Something had been up with his shoulder all morning. It wasn't hurting as such, but there was definitely something off about it. Like it was recovering from the longest bout of pins and needles.

Hector noticed his reaction.

'Everything okay?' he said. 'Last night wasn't too rough on you?'

'No, it was fine. I'm fine,' Walter said and turned his attention to the table. His chest tightened. Letty was rubbing the exact same spot on her arm. Pemberton's eyes narrowed towards him. Walter swallowed.

'So, the cards. They're just ... well, what are they then?' Walter said, trying to distract from his shoulder.

'Cards,' Hector assured him. 'An Amazon purchase if I'm not incorrect. No, the lines to this place are pretty well sealed from things like this. Pentagram, crystal balls. All a lot of hocus-pocus. Excluding Ouija boards, of course.'

'Ouija boards are real?'

Hector frowned at him. 'Of course, they're real. Have you never heard of the Call Centre?'

'The *Call Centre*? What's that?'

Pemberton let out a deep and onerous sigh. Walter ignored it.

While they'd been speaking, a set of cards had been placed face down on the table.

'I hope it'll be a good show,' Hector said. 'I do like it when they make it a good one.'

Letty perched on the edge of her seat, her heart thumping as she waited for the cards. She had shuffled them – at the woman's request – for what seemed like an unfeasibly long time. Once she'd returned them, she'd waited while the woman placed them down in front of her in a manner slower than an arthritic tortoise. Letty's stomach fizzled as Mystic Moira reached down, finally ready to turn the first card.

'Hierophant,' she shouted, causing Letty to jump from her seat. Moira closed her eyes and let out a long hum.

Letty glanced at her watch. The second hand ticked loudly.

'Hierophant,' Moira said again, keeping her eyes closed.

'Is that good?' Letty said, now suspecting that the difference between a five-pound and a ten-pound reading was the amount of time you spent shuffling the cards and the number of times the same word was repeated at you.

Moira's eyes snapped open wide. Her head cocked.

'The Hierophant,' she said, relishing her accent, 'is zee most mystical of all cards.'

'Really?' Letty said, her stomach twisting further. 'What does it mean?'

'A great many things, my sister, a great many things.'

Letty's jaw tightened.

The woman turned her next card and was thankfully quicker to speak this time.

'The Empress. A powerful card. A powerful card indeed.'

She hovered her hands a few centimetres above the table, then locked eyes with Letty.

'You are confused, sister. The cards tell me that you are confused, but ...' she pointed her fingers uncomfortably close to Letty's eyes, 'your confusions will pass. The cards tell me they shall pass.'

She shut her eyes again. Letty was feeling increasingly awkward. She was torn between absolute certainty that the whole thing was a load of mumbo jumbo, and that she should walk out then and there, and the desperate urge to stay, just in case. She shuffled in her seat.

'Wait,' the woman grabbed her by the elbow. 'There is more. I see a spirit. A spirit is near you. He is watching you.'

Letty's skin prickled.

'The spirit,' Letty said, 'is it a good spirit, do you know? Friendly?'

The tarot reader closed her eyes and shook her head. 'I cannot see. I cannot see him clearly enough.'

'Does it want me to do something?' Letty said.

'He needs your help. The spirit. He needs your help. He needs ... he needs ...'

The change was instantaneous. One minute she was sitting at the table, her hands languishing over the cards; a second later, she'd dropped Letty's arm and was on her feet, rocking back and forth while emitting a most disturbing moan.

Letty cowered in her seat, cringing at the scene unfolding.

'Is everything alright?' she asked tentatively. The moaning grew to a new apex. Mystic Moira's eyes rolled back and forth.

'I think perhaps I ought to go,' Letty said.

After enduring a further minute of disconcerting noises, Letty stood to leave.

'Wait, wait.' Moira grabbed her by the wrist. 'He is here. He is here with you now. He is entering me. He is entering me!'

It was mortifying. The noise emitted was the type of moan that, had it happened during some scene on a television show she was watching with Donald, Letty would have been forced to make her excuses and head to the kitchen for a cup of tea and not return until it was most definitely over. Letty reached for her bag, but the woman had too good a grasp on her wrist. 'He is entering my mind with his spirit,' she yelled again. 'He is inside me! The spirit is inside me!'

*W*alter was equally mortified.

'Is one of you doing this?' he demanded. 'You need to stop it. Whoever's doing this needs to stop it now. Do you hear me? Please, stop it. Stop it.' He took the woman by the shoulder and attempted to shake her, but his actions were futile. She had now taken to convulsions. Her chest and arms flailed out in front of her as she continued to garble gibberish. Letty, understandably, looked terrified by the whole event, while Pemberton appeared truly disgusted. However, Hector was wearing an expression of great amusement.

'I don't understand,' Walter said. 'Has she been occupied? Is there someone else? Is another spirit doing this? How do we stop it? How do we stop her?'

Hector laughed. 'Stop her? She is mid-flow.'

'Mid-flow?'

'Why it appears, that our lady here has found herself a histrione.'

'Pardon?'

'A histrione, a trouper. An actress of the highest calibre if you will. Don't worry. She'll stop soon. They always do. Time to get onto the real hogwash.'

As if she'd heard him, the woman stopped her moving and placed both her hands back on the table. She pushed her head forward.

'The spirit world is watching over you,' she said to Letty, her voice dramatically quiet. 'I cannot say why, or who, but they are watching you.'

Whether an actress or not, it was good enough to send prickles running down the length of Walter's spine. And – he could tell without seeing – Letty's too.

'Do you have a name?' Letty said.

'A name?'

'For the spirit that's watching me?'

The woman closed her eyes, a frown deepened on her forehead.

'There's a man. I can see a man. But he is not of this time.'

'No?' Letty's voice came out with a quiver.

'He's ...' With her eyes still closed, Moira reached her arm out towards Letty, before dropping it with a moan. 'He is gone. I am sorry. He came here for you. But he will not speak to me. Spirits are strange. They have their own fears too.'

Walter shuddered.

'I'm afraid time's up,' the woman said, her voice miraculously changing back into its east Essex accent. 'Normally, I'd keep going, but I've got a regular in ten, and he likes me to dress a little differently for it.'

'It's finished?' Letty said.

'I can book you in for a regular slot if you fancy?'

'No. It's fine. It's fine.'

Walter watched on as Letty hurriedly stumbled to her feet.

'Well, crisis averted,' Hector said, rolling up his sleeves. 'No magical clairvoyant is going to be spreading your name over hill and vale. At least not today, anyway.'

Walter sighed in relief. 'It's definitely over?'

'Well, yes, yes. Now don't forget we've got a lot of work to do tonight, now we know how those photograph thingamajiggies work. I'll see you back at the house for say, ten o'clock? Assuming no major calamities beforehand. You don't mind me not staying, do you? Only Cleopatra is having one of her brunches, and I would so hate to miss it. After all, she does have rather the temper, and I have said that I'll attend.'

'You go,' Walter assured him. 'I'll stay with the woman

now.' Then he turned to Pemberton and said, 'You should go upstairs too, have a break. I'll take over.'

'Thank you,' Pemberton replied. Walter's jaw nearly hit the ground.

With both men had gone and Letty was busy pulling on her coat, Walter stood mesmerised by the blobs of molten wax that rose and fell in the orange coloured lamps. They were remarkable things, he thought, like a single feather caught in the heat of the furnace. He could have watched it forever, only something made him turn back around.

~

*M*ystic Moira's headscarf had now been removed as she held the door open, ready for Letty to leave. From the stairwell, the scent of refried meat wafted upwards. Birds chirping indicating the end of the storm.

'Well, um ... thank you,' Letty said as she moved to go.

'Have a good afternoon,' Moira said and squeezed her shoulder in response. Three seconds later and the squeeze was still in place. Letty smiled tightly and wiggled her arm as a hint, but the grip only tightened. More money was the first thought that came to Letty's mind.

'Sorry, can you—'

'There are strange dealings afoot here,' Moira said. Her voice was breathy and weak as if it had travelled miles to be there. Her eyes unfocused. 'Strange things are happening to you.'

'Sorry, could you—'

'You want a name,' she said,

'Yes, but it doesn't matter.' Letty's pulse was beginning to quicken. 'I can come another time.'

'Walter.'

'Pardon?' Letty choked on the cold air that filled her lungs.

'Walter Augustus,' Moira said again. 'That is the name you wanted to hear, isn't it? Walter, Walter, Walter.'

CHAPTER 22

*L*ETTY BOLTED down the stairs. Outside, the rain had stopped, although there was barely time to notice. She turned left and pushed through the yellow door beside her.

Jean was standing on a small step ladder arranging a display of hats along the top of a clothes rack.

'Letty? This is a nice surprise,' she said.

Letty slumped, catching herself on the inside pane of the door.

'Letty? Is everything alright? My goodness, you look as white as a sheet.' Jean stepped down off the ladder and gathered Letty up. 'You sit down,' she said, lowering her into one of the vintage leather armchairs. 'I'll go put the kettle on.'

Letty's hands and feet shook, and her chest felt as though she'd spent a full morning taste-testing different buttercream recipes.

'Here we go,' Jean said, reappearing and handing Letty a steaming mug. 'Get that down. I managed to find some digestives out back too. They might be a bit soft, but I'm sure they'll do for dunking.'

Letty took a biscuit and dunked it into her tea. It was only while it was resting there she remembered the cheese sandwich in her bag. Perhaps upstairs had been a hunger hallucination. She wasn't sure if that was a real thing, but it sounded plausible – like mirages caused by thirst in the desert. She lifted the biscuit back out of the mug. The bottom half fell back in with a plop.

'Never mind. Take another one,' Jean said. 'And tell me what's going on. You didn't come up here before, did you? Only I had to shut up shop for a bit. Margo over at Save The Children got into a bit of a pickle with a faux-fur mink coat. Then I got caught in that bloomin' downpour.'

Letty took another biscuit. 'It wasn't a problem.'

'So?' Jean's eyes were unblinking in anticipation, her lips curled down with concern. 'It's not Donald, is it? Everything's alright with him?'

'He's fine,' Letty said, not wanting to add her marital issues to the load.

'Then what is it?'

'It's ... it's ...' Letty's thoughts swirled with everything that had happened in the last week, wondering if there was a way to put it into words. She felt disconnected from her body, like it wasn't solely hers anymore. She was emotional and paranoid, and no matter what, she couldn't shake the feeling that this Walter Augustus was somehow behind it. There was no way to explain what was really going on without coming across as a complete loon. As liberal as Jean was, she wasn't going to sit there and accept that Letty was being haunted by a ghost that she'd picked up and carried home from this very shop.

'You know you can tell me anything, don't you?' Jean said.

'Of course. It's only ... well ... it's just Victoria,' Letty said.

Jean's eyes rolled.

'What has she done this time?' she said.

$\sim$

I'm sure you were seeing things,' Hector said. 'After all, you did say you'd been staring at the lava lamp for a rather long time.'

'I wasn't seeing things,' Walter insisted. 'And even if I was that wouldn't affect my hearing.'

He had raced straight back up to the interim and had stumbled on Hector almost instantly. Dressed in a red leather catsuit, complete with whip, he'd been most miffed by Walter's insistence that he come back downstairs immediately.

'She said my name. You realise that, don't you?'

'But it's Cleopatra,' Hector said. 'Do you know how difficult it is to get an invite to these things? I'll be one minute. I'll just show my face.'

'Really?'

'Five minutes tops.'

Out in the corridor, the music of lutes and lyres drifted to Walter's ears as he awaited Hector's return. He took a moment, closed his eyes, and felt around between his innards. Something had changed since last night and his escapade in the Athenaeum. It was difficult to put his finger on it, but his body – or lack thereof – felt as if it had taken on a more physical counterpart. The tiredness he felt was draining into his muscles, and every now and then, he would be struck with a waft of emotion that would catch at the back of his throat and leave his eyes blinking. What's more, the woman was feeling it too. He could tell. However, this current concern of Walter's had since been overridden by an altogether more confusing issue.

'It makes no sense,' Walter said out loud to himself. Currently, he was experiencing tugs aplenty, from his kidneys to his cochleas. Barely a minute went by before he popped back into the forefront of Letty's thoughts, and with such intensity that, half an hour ago, it would have sent him running. But that wasn't what had him fretting. Surely, Walter considered, the other woman – this Mystic Moira – should be thinking about him too. At least a small amount. She had, after all, said his name out loud several times. But there was nothing, not a trace. Not even a faded glimmer of a trace.

'Why aren't you thinking about me?' he said. A man, sauntering down the corridor with a monkey on a leash, stopped, turned, and eyed Walter suspiciously. Walter grinned apologetically.

Mid-grin, Walter noticed the person behind the monkey. He frowned. In a blink her head went down, but the flash of her green eyes was too bright to forget. Walter took another step towards the woman. His pulse accelerated. There were billions of people up in the interim. Probably more. So why was it that he kept seeing the same woman with her luminous green eyes? She turned on her heel, but Walter quickened after her.

'Wait,' he called out. 'I want to talk to you.' The woman weaved in and out of the crowds. 'You're following me. Why are you following me? Stop, stop!'

A hand clasped his shoulder and stopped him in his tracks.

'Something happen, old chap?'

True to his word, Hector had returned after only a couple of minutes. Red wine sloshed around a goblet in his hand.

Walter glanced back down the corridor.

'I, I ... there was a woman ...'

Hector chortled. 'There always is, my lad. There always is.'

'No, it's not like that.'

Walter scoured between the doorways and the figures, but Hector, with his hand still holding his shoulder, steered him the other way.

'There'll be plenty of time for that later,' he said. 'Now let's get to the bottom of our little actress, shall we?'

Walter glanced behind him. There was no sign of the woman. After less than a minute searching, he turned back to Hector.

'Do you mind if we go downstairs? I don't feel comfortable discussing it here.'

'Of course, of course, after you,' he said. 'Unless you want to fetch Pimberly first?'

'That would probably be a good idea.'

Two minutes into his search for Pemberton, Walter had realised that he had no idea where to start. He attempted to follow the tugs the way he did with Letty, but with his body so overwhelmed with Letty's current ruminations, he could barely pinpoint a single atom of his employer, and as such, he quickly ceased trying.

'*W*ell, if what you're saying is true, then the only answer is that she was occupied. And advanced stuff, making her talk like that. Very tricky.'

The pair had reconvened in a small bric-a-brac shop, where Letty sat on a red chair, dissolving biscuits in weak tea.

'But why?' Walter said. 'Why would someone do that?'

'Why indeed?'

'I mean what would they gain?'

'Who knows,' Hector said as he unzipped the catsuit a

little then stretched the fabric to allow some air circulation. 'Do you have any adversaries that you know of?'

'Adversaries?"

'Opponents? Foes? Devious archenemies determined to chase you from one side of the afterlife to the next?'

'I know what an adversary is,' Walter said. 'And no, I don't. Not unless someone has a problem with well-meaning spirits who stick to their own corner of the interim and never come out unless under duress.'

'You never know,' Hector said. 'Perhaps it was an accident then.'

Walter watched the women continue their conversation, Letty devouring biscuit after biscuit as she went.

'The way she repeated it. It wasn't an accident. They wanted to scare her. Scare Letty. And they wanted me to be ... to be—'

'Wanted you to be what, Augustus?'

Pemberton's bag of pear drops was out in his hand.

'Please don't tell me you've gone and screwed something else up?'

Walter studied his old employer. The bag of sweets was new, barely touched, and his shirt was clean pressed. His face sported a smile, but his eyes were dark, and a smudge of dirt marked his chin. Walter stiffened.

'Where have you been?' Walter said. 'I looked, but I couldn't find you.'

'Well, that's hardly surprising, given the limitations of your skills,' Pemberton scoffed.

Walter's jaw clenched. The last day or so, it had felt like he and Pemberton were finally making progress, but that comment stung like they'd moved back a century and a half.

'Answer the question?' Walter said. 'Where have you been?'

'I struggle to see why that's of any relevance.'

'It's of a lot of relevance, actually, when somebody is deliberately jeopardizing my chances of moving on.'

'Jeopardizing your chances? Why? What happened?'

'Tell me where you were first.'

'No,' Pemberton said.

Walter stepped back. His left hand had begun to twitch.

'It was you,' he said. 'You did this.'

'I did what?'

'You don't want to move on. You like it here. You like being able to berate me day in and day out.'

'I can assure you—'

Heat was rising to Walter's cheeks.

'You stopped me. The first time I tried to move the book. You stopped me. Why?'

'Why?'

'Yes, why. Why did you do that?'

'I, I—'

Walter struck the air with his fist.

'Tell me!'

Pemberton blanched.

'Fine, fine. You want to know why I stopped you? I'll tell you. I was scared. I was scared of what might happen.'

Walter snorted. 'You're lying.'

'No, I'm not. Hector said it was dangerous to interfere with things that didn't concern you. That woman hadn't thought of you. It was me. I should have been the one to move the book, but I didn't want to. I was scared.' Walter refused even to blink at the comment.

'I don't believe you,' he said.

'Well, it's the truth.'

Walter pressed his tongue to the roof of his mouth as he shook his head.

'You don't have anyone waiting for you,' Walter was pacing as he spoke. 'Why would you care if I do? Or perhaps that's the point. Perhaps, because you have to live a lonely and miserable post-existence, you think I should do the same.'

'Now hang on there, lad.'

'Keep out of this, Hector. This has nothing to do with you.'

'Hector's right,' Pemberton said, his voice quiet and calm. 'You should stop now, before you say something you regret.'

'Regret? I'll tell you what I regret. Ever thinking you were trying to help me. Every turn, you've been there, waiting for a chance like this. Waiting for the opportunity to turn up and send me down the river.'

'Send you down the river? Me? I'm not the one who caused the cat to send the book flying. I am not the one who startled the poor woman with your slamming door and moving shoe parlour tricks.'

'No, but you—'

'And I suppose I somehow made you do that bloody ridiculous act with the computer?'

'No but—'

'If anyone is to blame for your confinement to this menial excuse for an afterlife, I can assure you, it is entirely your own doing.'

'It's you.' Walter slammed his fist into a nearby door, only to have it pass straight through.

His pulse was racing and rapid, but his mind – for the first time in nearly a week – was exceptionally clear. He tried to control his physicalities as he spoke.

'It's you. I know it's you,' he said. 'I saw that thing with the cat, remember. I know you can do more than you let on.'

Pemberton paused. His lips narrowed.

'That's really what you think?' he said.

'That's exactly what I think.' He could feel it in the depth of his bowels; he was right. Someone was deliberately trying to ruin his chances of ever moving on, and there was only one person it could be.

'Thank you for making your feelings so clear,' Pemberton said before turning to Hector. 'Do you have an opinion on this? Do you think I would deliberately jeopardize my own chance to return up there?'

Hector's jowls wobbled as he half-nodded and half-shook his head.

'I ... well ... of course, I wouldn't. But well, if it all adds up ...'

'Honestly? After ... after everything bef—'

'Yes, well, things have moved on a lot since then. And it's really not my place to interfere.'

'That would be a first,' Pemberton said. He inhaled deeply through the nose, let the air out the same way and then directed his gaze back to Walter.

'Well, if that's the way you feel. You'll have no more interference from me.'

'Good,' Walter spat with a voice he didn't know he possessed. 'I'll see you in hell.'

'If the last five days are anything to go by, I think I'm already there,' Pemberton said, then turned and left.

CHAPTER 23

TALKING WITH Jean had done little to relieve the problems; however, Letty considered it was probably due to the fact that she'd refused to disclose what the actual problems were. There were moments in the conversation, lulls and pauses, where she considered coming clean, telling her about the encounter with Mystic Moira upstairs, the shoes, the fact that everywhere she turned she was now thinking about some bloody, headless, ghoul, haunting her from beyond the grave, But the moment never seemed quite right. It was closing in on the end of Letty's lunch break when the telephone rang.

'Hang on,' Jean said. 'I'll be two minutes. Just let me see who it is.'

Letty went to speak, but Jean was already behind the counter, picking up the vintage Bakelite. Letty drummed her fingers against her thigh. One minute passed and then another. She glanced at her watch. Joyce would be fine at the store, and it wasn't like she hadn't had the odd extended lunch break in the past. She'd once met a friend at the local Wetherspoons for lunch and didn't come back for three days.

Still, Letty didn't like to leave her waiting. After another two minutes, she stood up, gathered her coat from the back of the chair, and tried to catch Jean's eye. After one minute of trying, Letty decided she'd ring her later to apologise and proceeded to the door. In the final glance back into the store, with her foot hovering and ready to go, Letty caught sight of something in the corner of the room that made her stomach jolt.

It sat amid a pile of boxes at the far side of the shop to Jean. The cardboard edges had split on the corners, and the top and sides were covered with a thick film of dust. Letty edged over, tugged it a little way out of the pile, and brushed the top with her fingers. Her heart rate hastened at the moon and stars packaging with its calligraphic typeface.

Letty snatched her hand back. It was ridiculous. No one did Ouija boards except for fifteen-year-old girls and scam artists. But then she'd read accounts in magazines before; a man had contacted his dead sister through a board, and it had told him where he could find her will. Letty was slightly sceptical when she read that all the money had been left to the brother in question, but if the lawyers had decided there was no foul play, then who was she to judge? Letty went back to the box and lifted the lid. Inside, lay a beige playing board folded in two, with a teardrop-shaped counter placed on the top.

In one movement, she swept up the box and tucked it under her arm while reaching into her bag for her wallet.

'I've got to dash,' she called over to Jean and then raced out the door flinging the twenty-pound note on the counter. Her pulse flew, and her breathing was utterly erratic, and it was only when she was halfway down the hill that she realised she hadn't checked the price. Horrified she may have underpaid Jean, Letty brushed the remaining dust off the top of the box and looked for a price tag.

'Three pounds,' she read. That was one way to get rid of her excess money, she thought.

$\mathcal{L}$etty felt ridiculous. It had just gone 6.00 p.m. and she'd been home now for nearly an hour. The simple refrain of a nearby chiffchaff floated in from the garden, while inside the house, aromas of rising sponge cakes filled the air. The dimmed lighting had helped with the ambience, as had shutting all the doors and closing the curtains, but it was still daylight outside. On the positive side, the extra light helped with the nerves a little.

The entire afternoon, Letty had deliberated her purchase.

'That's awesome,' Joyce said when Letty tried to hide it from her at closing time. 'My friend Kiara used one to talk to her horse. It was dead, obviously. It knew everything. Like this time when she went riding in a storm, and she was wearing a really tight thong, and it kept rubbing and—'

'Oh, it's not for me,' Letty said. 'It's for my nephew.'

Joyce – unlike Kiara – stopped mid-flow. 'Isn't he like six?'

'Nine,' Letty said. 'But he's very advanced.'

Now she was at home with the thing and her heart was already doing ten to the dozen. The walk home had involved a detour into the Spar for a bag of mini Mars bars. Half the pack was already gone. With the cake for the businessman's mother rising in the oven, Letty knew it was now or never. She grabbed a couple more Mars bars for support and muttered a silent prayer to anyone that might have been listening.

≈

alter was a wreck. Immediately after Pemberton's departure, he'd become torn, suddenly worried that he'd made the wrong call with regards to his former employer, but just as his conscience was beginning to get the better of him, events took a new turn and presented him with something far more worrying than a sulky ex-farrier.

'Maybe it's a fake,' he said to Hector, hopefully. 'Maybe it won't come through to here at all.'

'A fake Ouija board? No, not a chance, I'm afraid, old chap. It's all the French's fault. I'm sure of it. Don't get yourself all flustered. We can make it work.'

'Make it work? How?'

'Well,' Hector paused and scratched his eyebrow. 'Remember in the shoe shop, when you slammed the door?'

'Only vaguely,' Walter gibed.

'Well, when she didn't say your name then, you thought it was a good sign.'

Walter frowned. 'I don't see how that helps us now.'

'Maybe all she needs is a little encouragement. A chance to see that staying quiet is to her advantage. All it would take is a few ghoulie words and, poof, no more talking.'

'Ghoulie words?' Walter said sceptically.

'You know.' Hector waved his arms above his head, demonstrating precisely what a ghoul in a red leather catsuit would look like. '*Let my soul rest,*' he warbled in his best ghost voice. '*Never speak my name.* Something like that. Of course, you won't have the advantage of sound, but you get the idea?'

Walter did. 'It could work,' he said after a minute pondering. 'It could actually work. It might mean there would be no more need for the occupancy at all.'

Hector choked. 'No more need for occupancy?'

'Not if she's going to keep quiet.'

'But ... but ... the book,' Hector continued to stutter. 'We still need to get rid of the book. And who is to say she'll stick to her word? No, the occupancy is still very much a necessity. Very much. Besides, you're getting so good. Why would you stop?'

'It's just an idea,' Walter said.

In truth, the thing with the car keys had left Walter shaken. If a simple slip up on his part resulted in a woman hopelessly searching her house for thirty minutes, what damage might a more substantial hiccup cause? If there was a way to solve his problem without invading the woman's mind again, then he was all for it.

'Well, that's all for discussion later,' Hector said, having returned to his previous, non-stuttering state. 'Let's get inside, shall we?'

'Inside?' Walter said.

*A*ffectionately termed the *Call Centre,* this small armpit of post-existence acted in much the same way as casinos and amusement arcades did on Earth and attracted – if possible – an even less desirable clientele. While he'd only learnt about the place's existence in the last twenty-four hours, Walter realised immediately that this was of no great loss.

The door of the entrance was notably different to the others on the corridor on account of a small, rectangular welcome mat placed outside. Inside, the lights were dim and red-tinted, and the aroma was one of slightly soiled linen and over-cooked eggs.

In the entrance stood slot machines. Brightly coloured with flashing lights, they blared out bells and rings and canned applause. Walter jumped back as one machine, trumpeting a fanfare, emptied its innards besides him. Hundreds of shiny gold coins cascaded out onto the ground.

'Watch out!'

'Move!'

'Get outta the way!'

Walter was jostled from side to side as hordes of afterlifers scrambled around, grappling for the money. A few seconds later, a fistfight broke out between a Nomadic Mongolian and a cheerleader.

'What do they need money for?' Walter said as he watched, confused.

'What do any of us need anything for?' Hector answered. 'It makes them feel good.'

'That can't make anyone feel good,' he said, watching the cheerleader land a solid left hook to the Mongolian's jaw.

Walter kept close to Hector as they edged past the fight. Beyond the slot machines were various arrays of table games, from roulette and craps to baccarat and blackjack. Farther back sat a series of low tables, with even dimmer lights, and even more sullen looking patrons.

'That's where we're heading,' Hector said.

Walter felt a definite constriction around his bowels.

'How do we know which table it's going to be?' Walter said, scanning from one side of the room to the next.

'We don't. So, we'll need to be fast. Keep your eyes peeled. It could be anywhere.'

'That's good to know.'

The tables varied in occupancy from only a couple of people to nearly a dozen. All ages, races, and genders were present, and a couple of them possessed dress codes even more curious than Hector's, including a woman dressed only in fruit and a man riding a llama. Walter could hear the

197

blood pumping in his ear. He closed his eyes in the hope of blocking out some of the tugs and emotions that had plagued his stomach all day.

'So, you'll need to tell us when, and we'll both have to spot where,' Hector said. 'Then I'll make sure you've got the all-clear to go.'

'I don't know how I'm going to—' Walter stopped as a sharp tug pulled behind his belly button, followed by another, then another, each one strong enough to cause a gasp.

'She's doing it,' Walter said. 'It's happening now.'

'You're sure?'

'Positive.'

Hector's eyes widened as they whipped across the room.

'That one over there. Go!' Walter sprinted across the room without a second glance.

At the head of the table was a slender woman with frame-less glasses and pink lipstick. In the centre was a yellowing Ouija board. Two other men were sitting down, one with a decidedly orange skin tone and cheap blonde toupee, the other with a live rat on his shoulder.

'Time to get going, gentlemen,' Hector said, pulling out the chair that the rat man was sitting on.

'What the ...?'

'Double booking, I'm afraid. Don't worry; you'll be compensated. If you'd like to come this way.'

'But—'

'No time for questions, please, if you'll just step over here, you can see what we have on offer.'

While Hector proceeded to pull a bag of tricks from the inside of his catsuit, he nodded Walter towards the board.

'Now, I have some beautiful cut glass teapots,' Hector spoke to the rat man. 'No? Not your thing? How about this then? A solid gold die. Yes, you feel the weight of it. I have it on good advice that this is the exact replica of ...'

A solid lump built in Walter's throat as he approached the table. Beside the board sat two round speakers.

'Hello?'

Walter jumped back as a familiar voice echoed out of them. 'Excuse me? Is anyone there?'

Letty's voice was shaking. A twinge of sympathy twisted through Walter's chest. He could picture her perfectly, chomping down on a chocolate bar, cat by her side. Of all the people for him to haunt, an ageing shoe saleswoman was surely no one's ideal. Still, this could hopefully end all that. 'Stay calm,' he told himself and pulled out a seat to sit on.

'Hello?' Letty said again. 'Is anyone there?'

Walter swallowed and moved his hand towards the planchette.

'License and registration please.'

Walter looked up, startled. His hand had been stopped around four inches from its target by another hand that sported fuchsia pink nails of an impressive, yet garish, length.

'I said license and registration.'

The croupier met Walter's eyes only briefly before lifting her own into an exaggerated roll.

'You can't play until you have a License and Registration,' she said and then took the planchette and dumped it on the corner of the board where the word YES was written in large, bold letters.

Walter stuttered. 'I need to be here. This person. She's trying to contact me.'

'They're always trying to contact someone, sweetie. Doesn't change the rules. If you don't have your license and registration, you can't play.'

The lump in Walter's throat had returned at double its former size.

'Well, well, where do I get them?'

'Registration is over there.' She pointed to a small wooden booth with three empty windows and bored looking staff. A man was walking up as Walter watched. He spoke a few words to the person behind the booth, waited a moment, then received a piece of paper back through the window. Walter sighed, and his chest released a little of the accumulated tension. It didn't seem to take that long at all. He could make a run for it and leave Hector to keep watch for a minute.

'And licensing happens over there.'

Walter's stomach sank. The queue to the licensing table snaked twice around the back of the room. Some of the people near the back had set up camp with sleeping bags and campfires.

'That part takes a little longer,' the woman admitted.

Walter shuddered. Every noise, from the clanging of the slot machines to the voices on the other tables, cut straight through him. Letty's voice continued to crackle through the speaker.

'Walter?' she said. 'Am I speaking to a Walter?'

Walter's eyes locked on the croupier. Her pink nails were still firmly attached to the planchette, although it was now floating in the middle of the letters, equidistant from the YES and NO.

'Is that Walter? Walter Augustus?' Letty said again.

'Please,' Walter pleaded to the pink-lipped croupier with all he had. He could feel his eyes welling with tears. If she said 'no' now, it could ruin everything. The woman wouldn't think anything of passing around his name. He would end up on the Internet, the television. He would be trapped forever.

Walter needed this chance. He needed a proper conversation with her.

'Please,' he said again.

The croupier pressed her lips together.

'This is all you get,' she said and swept the planchette over to YES for a second time. 'That's it, though. You can't sit at a table without a license and registration. It's more than my job's worth.'

Walter leapt up from his seat. 'Thank you, thank you,' he said, then raced across the room, only to double back, jump up at the table, and kiss her on the cheek.

Hector, while still bartering with the toupee and the rat man, was currently juggling the glass teapot and gold die with a bemused looking albino guinea pig.

'Well that was fast, old chap,' he said.

'No, I haven't done it. She's still on.'

'What do you mean?'

'I don't have a license. I'm not allowed to speak to her.' Hector caught the teapot and die in his hands, leaving the guinea pig to fall to the ground with a splat.

'What do you mean, you don't have a license? Do you not think that was something you should have mentioned before?'

'I didn't know.'

'Well, don't you—'

'We don't have time. I need you to come and do it for me. Quickly, before someone else takes the table.'

'Well, I haven't—'

'Now!' Walter said.

Leaving the guinea pig at the mercy of the large rat, Walter and Hector raced back to the table. Panting, Walter pulled out the chairs, while Hector rummaged around inside his leather outfit for the necessary documents.

'You,' the croupier said on seeing Walter's return. 'What the heck do you think—'

'License and registration,' Walter panted. 'I know. He's got it. He's got it.'

'It's all right here,' Hector said and produced a small papyrus scroll. The woman picked it up and scanned it over. 'You Hector?'

Hector nodded.

'Okay, you're good to play.' She turned to Walter. 'You need to leave.'

'What?'

'I told you earlier. You can't sit at a table. Not without a litt—'

'But I'm not going to touch it. I swear. I just have to be here. Please. It's a matter of life and death.'

She laughed. 'Yeah, because no one ever says that.'

Walter turned to Hector. He felt sick. Every cell from his stomach up seemed to be dissolving as he stood there.

'Please,' he tried again.

The pink lips pouted while her petite nostrils flared to double their previous size.

'You're going to have to leave,' she said. 'Or I'm going to have to make you.'

CHAPTER 24

*L*ETTY NEEDED another Mars bar. She'd braved the iPad and Google for the second time and – after three thorough read-throughs of a Wiki-how Ouija – had now placed her hands on the planchette to begin.

At first, there had been nothing, and the only movement came from the fact that she was unable to stop herself trembling, but after her third question, Letty gasped. Doubting her own sanity, the small wooden counter glided from the middle of the board over to the YES, taking her hands with it.

'Good Lord,' Letty said. It was one thing thinking that your shoes are moving or that something other than the wind is making your doors slam; it was another to watch something happen that broke the laws of physics.

Letty tried to swallow. She coughed to clear her throat and steadied herself for the next question.

'Walter?' she said. 'Am I speaking to a Walter?'

Her pulse pounded. The evening's pale sun snuck in through a gap in the bottom of the curtains, causing a sliver of light to run all the way up the carpet towards her knees. Her stomach turned over on itself. The last response had happened much quicker. Maybe it had been her, after all. Maybe somehow, without knowing, she'd pushed it.

'Is that Walter? Walter Augustus?' Letty said again, her voice more confident as she spoke. There was another long pause. 'It's all in your head,' Letty said, quoting what the Internet quiz had told her only one day before. She sighed, ready to take her hands away, when without warning, the planchette swung away once more.

YES, it said. The air collapsed in her lungs.

It took several minutes of deep breaths before Letty could manage to look at the board again. She felt sick. Incredibly sick. Beyond that, any concrete description of sensation or emotions was beyond her. Was she scared? Yes, absolutely terrified, but at the same time relieved. She was not insane. Unless, she mused, this was another symptom of the insanity.

It was two minutes before her pulse had lowered itself to a level at which she felt brave enough for her next attempt. Taking her lead from Mystic Moira she formed another question.

'Do you need my help?' she said.

The planchette quivered beneath her fingers.

$\sim$

*W*alter wasn't entirely sure what he'd expected the woman to say, probably something basic and naive, like was her grandmother there or were angels real – a fact he had absolutely no evidence for or against – but she'd come straight in with the big stuff.

He was back in the house, sitting beside Letty and her mountain of Mars bar wrappers. After a brief discussion in the Call Centre, they'd decided this was the best option. Hector would keep watch from up top, making sure that no one else came to the table, while Walter would control the planchette from down by the actual board.

'What if I can't do it?' he said. 'I still can't move the book.'

'You'll be fine,' Hector said. 'Be succinct. Get your answers across in as few words as possible. You know what the living are like when it comes to wasting time. They don't realise there's enough over this side to drive you insane.'

Walter nodded, said his farewells, and then sprinted back through the corridor to Letty.

'Do you need my help?' Letty said again.

Walter took a deep breath, focused on the planchette, and willed it to move. It was far easier than he'd expected. So easy that it flew across the board, stopping just short of the carpet. He reined it back a little and drew it over to the YES. Then, remembering what Hector said about not wasting time, moved it again, this time to the letters.

'S-T-U-,' Letty repeated each of the letters as he touched them.

'Stuck?' Letty said, piecing the word together. 'You're stuck?'

Walter shivered with excitement. YES. He slid the planchette across the board once again, this time without so much as a second thought.

The next pause caused his adrenaline to kick up a notch.

'Is it to do with the book?' Letty said. Walter leapt up so high that his head disappeared into the lampshade. The glass tinkled softly. Beside him, the woman smiled nervously. She could feel it too, Walter thought. There was a connection. Maybe this wouldn't be too hard after all.

*L*etty couldn't believe how calm she was being. She was having a conversation, a real – albeit through a Ouija board – conversation with a ghost, and apart from the moment when the planchette almost flew across the room, it had been completely civilised. Even the draught that caused the lights to shake had a gentleness about it. And so much for the Internet being the font of all knowledge; she didn't even have to touch the counter anymore. Letty thought back over the incidents. None of them had been violent, she considered; in fact, some of them – like the shoe tidying – had been positively helpful. He certainly did a better job at it than Donald. While it seemed bizarre even to herself, Letty had developed a slight affection for the disembodied spirit over the last few minutes.

'How can I help?' she asked.

The planchette slid back to the rows of letters. Letty read as it went.

'F-O-R, for... forgo? Forge? Forge? Forget? Forget? Forget!' She bounced with excitement. 'You want me to forget something? Is that what you want?'

YES, the board told her.

'You want me to forget. Forget what? Forget the book? Is that what you want? For me to forget about the book?'

YES.

The planchette rose up into the air and bounced back down on the board.

Letty squealed.

S-O-R-R-Y, the board spelt out.

Letty laughed out loud. If she was going insane, at least this was an enjoyable way to do it.

While Letty was genuinely enjoying this interaction, now that she had him here, there were so many questions she wanted to ask. Like where was he born, who was the lady he wrote his poems about, and was her mother up there with him?

'Okay,' Letty reassured him. 'I'll forget you. I can do that. I mean. I'm not sure how exactly. It's a bit like when someone asks you not to think about purple elephants.' The planchette quivered. 'But yes. Okay. I'll do it. I'll try.'

She reached out and touched the planchette.

'Is that all you wanted me to do?' she said. The board remained motionless. Seconds ticked by. Letty held her breath, suddenly concerned that Walter may have been under some form of time limit.

'Are you still there?' she asked.

The planchette trembled between her fingers. It was a slow quiver, a wobble, as though the reply wasn't entirely sure it wanted to answer the question. It shifted one way, then the other, then back. Letty repeated her previous question.

'Is there anything else I can do for you?'

A long pause caused Letty's heart to hammer, and when the planchette eventually did start to move, it did not, as Letty expected, move to the top YES or NO, but instead down to the letters. It glided from the centre of the board towards the left-hand side, right to the start of the alphabet. Letty began to read.

'D-I-E. Die?' she read, a cold chill running down her spine. 'Die? You want me to die?'

YES.

~

'*N*o, no, no! Stop! Stop it!'

Walter's metaphysical heart was battering the inside of his chest. It was as though there were a hundred

207

other pairs of hands all dragging the planchette away from him.

DIE, DIE, DIE. The board continued to spell out the same three letter word.

Letty's face was white. Her eyes brimmed with tears, and her hand trembled as it gripped the planchette, her bones shining white through her knuckles as her wrist was whipped back and forth between the letters.

'Let go!' he screamed at her. 'Let go of it!'

Just as he was thinking things couldn't get any worse, Walter's jaw dropped.

'What the ...?'

Along one side of the board, the paint began to lift off in a series of thin parallel lines.

'No! What's going on? Stop it!'

Long, jagged claw marks, dragged their way through the cardboard as if, Walter realised, something was trying to get through from the other side. Faster and faster, they mauled at the board, getting closer to the woman's hand with every strike.

'Let go! Please, please!' Walter pleaded with Letty. 'You need to stop it now. You need to let go.'

He swiped for the board, but his hand passed through without so much as a glance. He tried a second time and a third. His breath was ragged to the point of pain.

'Let go,' Walter yelled at her. 'Let the bloody thing go.' The woman was crying now, screaming as the board refused to stop. 'Let go! It will break the connection!' Walter screamed, but the more it moved, the tighter she gripped. Her nails dug into the plastic planchette.

'Ahhh!' Walter screamed at the ceiling, before collapsing onto his knees. 'What am I supposed to do?' he spoke into the air as if it could answer. 'What am I supposed to do?'

The voice he heard was soft but firm. It came through the air as if it had drifted in on a breeze, and for the tiniest of moments, it caused all the chaos to melt away.

'Make her drop it,' the voice said. 'You have to make her drop it.'

'But how?' Walter said, fairly certain that he was talking to himself during a moment of absolute insanity.

'Make her drop it,' the voice said again.

By now, Letty's eyes were wild with terror, while the planchette continued to swivel madly out of control.

'Make her.'

Then inspiration hit.

Walter focused all his attention on Letty and tried to ignore everything else going on around him.

'You can do it,' said the voice that may or may not have been his own imagination. 'You can do this.'

Walter took one long step forward. It was with a twist and a tumble and a thump that he landed.

The sky was grey, and the waves on the stream were angry and foaming and more suited to a raging ocean than a small village. Shielding his face against the rain that thrashed down around him, he raced over the bridge into the thatched cottage.

'Letty!' He screamed up into the vast cavern of the Athenaeum. 'Letty! Let go. Please! Please.' He wind-milled around, searching for some sort of help. 'You need to let go of the planchette. That's the gateway. That's the key. Please let go. Let it go, and this will all stop.'

Something flickered in the shadows.

'Letty?' Walter stopped and lowered his voice. 'Letty, please. I don't want to hurt you.'

He took a step back trying to prove his good intentions.

Slowly, a shape moved towards the edge of the shadows, although not quite far enough to come into the light.

'Please. Come out where I can see you.'

'You shouldn't be here,' she said. Her voice trembled.

'I know. I know,' Walter said. 'I just need you to let go of that thing. You let go and you break the connection. They won't be able to get through.'

In the distance, Walter could hear screaming. Echoes of screaming, terrified and lonely.

'What are they?' Letty asked.

'I don't know. Please come out, so I can see you,' Walter said again.

The immediate silence made the distant screams sound infinitely louder as the time elongated around him. Finally, the figure stepped out into the light.

'Letty?' Walter said.

She nodded.

In front of him stood a girl of eight or nine with waist-length hair. While her skin and stature were the perfect reflection of youth, her eyes had a depth of someone much older. She bit her lip and gripped nervously at the hem of her skirt.

'You've been here before,' she said. 'I've seen you. Snooping about.'

'I have. And I'm sorry. But please listen. I need you to trust me now. I need you to let go of that thing.'

'And if I don't?'

'Then I don't know what will happen,' Walter said honestly.

Another scream cut through the thunder. The girl jumped back and cowered.

'I don't like it,' she said. 'I'm scared.'

'Please,' Walter begged. 'You have to listen to me.'

The girl's eyes narrowed. 'I don't like you,' she said. 'You stole things. I want you to go away.'

'I will. I promise. I'll leave you alone. You'll never see me again. But right now, I need you to let go of that thing you're holding. Do you understand? You have to let go of it.'

The girl remained motionless, lips sealed, and feet planted to the spot. Then slowly, her head began to tilt into a nod. Walter's lungs expelled a gasp of relief. Young Letty smiled. The smile was small but lingered on her lips, then it tightened and twisted. Her eyes widened. A moment later, she screamed.

CHAPTER 25

*I*T HAD BEEN twenty minutes, and Letty had still not moved. Around her, motes of dust glinted in the half-light. She could hear her own breath, her heart rattling in her ears. She could hear the rain outside, although when it had started, she had no idea.

It had told her to die; that was the single thought that went around and around in her head. The board had told her to die, and it had tried to do the job. She glanced down at her arm. Whatever else may have been in her head, these were not. With a tentative hand, she reached down and touched her reddened flesh and winced. A stifled sob crackled in her throat.

The cuts were not long; an inch and a half at most. She had had far worse scratches from Mister Missy in her time, but these scratches were not from any cat. They were from no place she could explain. She sat there for another five minutes, watching as the droplets of blood grew and then flattened, then turned from red to brown. Then, using the chair to help her, she stood and stumbled out of the room.

'Don't go in there,' she said as the cat appeared at the foot of the stairs. Her mind and body and voice felt detached, as if she'd been dismantled and put her back together in the wrong order. 'I don't think it's safe. Please don't go in there.'

In the kitchen, a smell of burnt cake rose from the oven.

'Oh lord!'

The return to her senses was immediate. She shook her head clear, blinked, and sprinted across the room for her oven gloves, opening the oven door to a face full of hot air.

'Damn it.' She pulled out the cake, dropped it down on the counter and wafted away the steam with her hand, ignoring the sting of her arm as it hit her newly pierced skin. 'Just what I need.'

The top and edges were long past golden, bordering on more of a chocolate colour. She would let it cool for half an hour and see how things looked after that, she decided. After all, she couldn't go back in the living room. Not on her own.

~

*W*alter slammed against the cobblestones. A moment later, he lifted himself to his feet and scanned the corridor. His head was spinning. Never had he been thrown with such force from the depth of Letty's subconscious. Still, there was no time to mope. A quick close of his eyes told him which direction he needed to run.

So intent was he on getting back to the Call Centre that he spared no thoughts to the gangs of bikers with their leather jackets and multiple piercings that only a week ago would have caused him to cower. He pushed past a crowd of Morris dancers, his knees still trembling, not with fear of the corridor for once, but of something far more concerning.

He had felt pain. Real, actual pain. It was the girl who had screamed, but at that moment Walter had felt it, something cold and sharp and raw against his skin. He was still sprinting when he glanced down at his arm and froze.

'What the ...?'

The sounds of the corridor muted around him and the warmth evaporated from the air. Walter reached out his hand and took hold of a nearby doorway. It was all he could do to stop himself from crumbling to the ground.

The wounds were not deep, but the fact they were there at all was enough to turn Walter's stomach. He touched the skin with his fingertips and winced at the tenderness. Pain in the interim? He needed answers and fast.

Shaking himself back to sense, Walter started back on his route to the Call Centre. He sped past brightly tiled doorways, then raced past the slot machines towards the back tables of the Call Centre.

'What the hell happened?' he said as he came careening towards Hector. 'What the hell did you do?'

'You,' the pink-lipped croupier blocked his path. 'I told you, you can't sit down at a table without—'

'I'm not sitting down!' Walter yelled. The woman stopped mid-sentence.

'Well, look. Look at me,' Walter said. 'Am I sitting down? Am I?'

The woman pulled her jaw up until her teeth locked in place.

'If you don't leave now,' she said. 'I'll get security.'

'Well, then you go and get them,' Walter said and took one large sidestep around her so that he was face to face with Hector. 'What the hell happened?' he repeated. 'You were meant to leave it alone. What happened?'

Hector wore the same red catsuit, although the zip had been pulled down to the waist, and several tears had appeared in the fabric. His face was also adorned with similarly sized scratches, and beneath his left eye, a purple bruise had started blooming. Walter's anger changed to shock.

'What happened?' he said again, placing his hand on Hector's shoulder.

Hector shook his head, sniffed, and retrieved a hankie from out of the crotch of his catsuit.

'I'm frightfully sorry, old chap. I couldn't fight them off. There was nothing I could do. Nothing.'

'Fight who off?'

'Them, the others.' Hector waved his hand and loosely indicated the entire room. 'One of them got in a tiz about the gold dice. My fault really, I told him it had once belonged to the last Tsar of Russia. How was I meant to know he was a Bolshevik? Anyway, then another joined in and then ...' Hector's breathing became more erratic. 'And the rat ... and the guinea pig. Oh, the poor, poor guinea pig ...' Hector buried his head in Walter's shoulder as he erupted into tears. Walter patted him awkwardly. Across the room, the croupier was talking to two large men, with less than amiable expressions on their faces. Walter paled.

The board was a wreck, ravaged to tatters with pieces of cardboard ripped from every corner, the letters and words barely visible in the carnage. Beside it, the rat's owner was rubbing a large gold dice on the top of his scalp, while behind him, the rat was chewing on something that looked suspiciously like guinea pig fur.

Hector snivelled. 'I'm sorry; it all went a bit wrong.'

'Just a little,' Walter said and dropped down into a seat.

The two men sat in a snivel-filled hush.

'How's the girl?' Hector said.

'How do you think?' Walter replied with a shrug.

They sighed simultaneously. Hector's eyes fell on Walter's arm.

'Is that? What is that?'

Walter pressed the skin with his finger. It pricked with pain.

'I know,' Walter said. 'Strange, isn't it? I don't know how it happened. Through the board, I think,' Walter said. Hector's lips twitched.

'My, my, my.'

Walter shook his head. There had been a brief moment – during his conversion with the woman – when he had honestly thought everything would turn out right. The woman had agreed to forget him, and he'd even thought he could persuade her to burn the book too – had they had time to discuss it. There would have been no need for anything else. No years spent stalking her, no rummaging around in her subconscious to pick it clean of any bits he didn't want in there. Nothing like that would have been needed. Across the room, the pink-nailed croupier was marching in his direction, fingers pointing squarely at him, an army of four at her side. Let them take him, Walter thought. He didn't care anymore. He would be up here forever anyway. Perhaps there was an interim jail, he considered. Maybe that would offer a nice change of scenery for a few years.

'Come on,' Hector said, hoisting him up out of the chair.

'What? Where?'

'We need to do some preparation.'

'What for?'

'It's not over until the fat lady sings,' Hector said, and Walter knew better than to ask.

~

*I*n the thirty-two years since leaving home, Letty could count on her fingers and toes the number of times she'd dialled that particular number. Every time there had been a reason: a birth, a death, a particularly important anniversary, but tonight there was no reason. At least not one that she could give.

Victoria arrived at the door with a large bottle of red wine.

'I have to say, I wasn't expecting this.' She thrust herself into the corridor and then into the kitchen. 'Three times in one week, but I'm so glad you called. I take it you've spoken to Donald?'

'To Donald?'

'About the money? That is why you asked me to come over, isn't it?'

Letty winced.

'Well, I thought that perhaps—'

'To be honest, it's not the most convenient time, but if you need a little more assurance then it will all be worth it.' Victoria dumped her bag on the kitchen table and began opening the kitchen cabinets until she found the one with the wine glasses. She pulled down the biggest two. 'You sounded strange on the phone. Your voice had that horrid wobble, like it used to when we were kids. You know the one? When you go all high-pitched and squeaky.'

'I'm sure I wasn't,' Letty said. 'And that was the voice I got when I had asthma.' She was regretting making the call already.

'Well, I was a little bit worried something was wrong. Felix had only just walked in from work, and there's been an outbreak of head lice at the children's school. The last thing I need is more drama to deal with.'

'Oh. Well, there's no drama here. I was just ringing for, you know, a catch up.' Victoria's left eyebrow rose by half an inch.

Letty had already managed to pack away and dispose of the Ouija board. It was a speedy hold-your-breath-until-it's-over type affair, in which she'd whisked into the living room, grabbed the remains of the scratched and scraped board, thrown it all into a black bin bag and tossed it outside. As the door slammed shut, she collapsed with relief until she realised that the bin-men wouldn't collect it until a week on Thursday. That meant leaving the death-threatening Ouija board beneath her kitchen window for a full thirteen days. At that point, Letty stepped out into the rain, grabbed the bag, and strode down two streets to the nearest public bin. Most impressively, she managed to keep the plastic bin bag at a full arm's distance the entire time.

In truth, she probably had sounded a little desperate on the phone to Victoria. The cake had been salvaged, although some ruthless trimming and spectacular pipe work had been required. However, even fondant icing hadn't been enough to distract her from the niggling in her gut or the constant need to keep checking over her shoulder. After finishing the cake, she'd fed Mister Missy, doubled checked the locks, and tried every cookery channel that their television had to offer. She'd finished the bag of Mars bars and polished off a full carton of ready-made custard. Only after the discovery that even food couldn't help settle her nerves, she'd phoned Victoria.

'So, what is it you wanted to know?' Victoria said as she opened the bottle. She poured herself a substantial glass then tilted the remainder to Letty. Letty shook her head.

'Oh, I wanted to make sure I'd gotten a few more details, you know, before I talk to Donald about it.'

Victoria grunted. 'It's an investment opportunity, with Felix's full approval. What more do you need to know?'

A strained pause followed. Victoria sipped her drink then scanned across the room, rolling her eyes as she went.

'So, how are the twins?' Letty said, breaking the silence and hopefully putting them in a more neutral conversational standpoint.

'Fine, fine. Starting rehearsals for the Christmas concert.'

'In September?'

Victoria's eyes rolled again. 'This is private school, Leticia. It's not some two-bit school play where the children dress up like lobsters and power rangers. They perform professional standard concerts.'

'Oh.'

'And this year, Damien's in the orchestra.'

'Really?' Letty was genuinely impressed by this revelation. As far as she was aware, Damien had never shown any previous inclinations towards musical prowess. 'That's fantastic. What's he playing?'

Victoria puffed out her chest with pride. 'The timpani. The teacher said he has a great aptitude for hitting things.'

Letty decided she needed a glass of wine after all. She reached across the table for the bottle.

'What did you do to your arm?' Victoria said.

Letty froze.

'Sorry?'

'Your arm? That scratch?'

'Oh ...' Letty looked at the mark. Her throat tightened.

The cut was deeper than she'd first thought, and a thin layer of blood had crusted over on the surface. When it had happened, she thought she'd seen two or three marks, like a cat scratch, but had not looked close enough to find out. For the last hour, she'd managed to avoid thinking about it at all, but now that her attention had been drawn to it, it throbbed and stung simultaneously.

'It was ... It was ...' She struggled to find an explanation, when from outside the room came a soft purr. 'Oh, it was the cat. Just a silly accident really.'

Victoria tutted. 'It's why I'll never have pets with children. You can't trust them. Honestly. One of Dakota's classmates was nearly trampled to death at a gymkhana. I mean, some of these animals. They cost a fortune to keep and have so little respect.' Victoria pondered her own statement. 'Well, you really should clean it up. It looks horrible, and it's turning me off my wine.'

Letty looked back at her arm. She had to say she agreed.

'Where's your handbag?' Victoria said. 'I assume you've still got all those plasters floating around in it.'

'It's in the living room,' Letty said without thinking.

'Good, I could do with a sit down.'

'I'M NOT SURE it's a good idea,' Walter said as he struggled to keep up with Hector's pace. 'To be honest, I'm wondering if messing around in there was ever a good idea.'

'I need books,' Hector said as he marched through the corridor.

'Did you hear me—'

'Now. This evening,' Hector insisted. 'This is it. If we're going to do it, it has to be tonight.'

'Do it?'

'The woman's mind. The Athenaeum.'

'But maybe ...' Walter paused.

'Yes?'

'Well, I was thinking. Maybe it would be better if I didn't go in again. I mean, we could just let her remember me. I'm sure she won't say anything to anyone. Not after this evening. And if she does, then maybe I'm just ... maybe I just ...'

Hector's sudden halt caused Walter to bang straight into him.

'Now,' Hector said, 'there's no need for rash decisions. We need to look through all our options. After all, we don't want to make matters worse.'

'I'm not sure we can,' Walter said. Hector ignored him.

'Listen. I'll go get those books, and there's a few other errands I need to see to. Shall we reconvene at yours in a couple of hours?'

'A couple of hours?'

Walter found himself rather put out by the sudden talk of abandonment. Over the last week, he'd spent very little time on his own. The idea of not having someone to talk to in his hour of need was rather disorientating.

'What am I meant to do while I wait?' he said.

'Make some tea? Visit someone?' Hector was already marching away as he spoke.

Walter stayed put, watching Hector disappear into the horizon, before grudgingly trudging away.

There was only one person in the interim Walter could possibly consider visiting and, although a large part of him was tempted to go on the hunt, it took him only a minute to decide against it. Pemberton may not have been involved in the Ouija incident, but that didn't put him in the all-clear as far as Walter was concerned. There were still too many unresolved issues with regards to his former employer.

He padded down the corridor, past small doorways made of whitewashed stone, completely ignorant of the soft waves that lapped at his feet. When he reached the doorway he knew was his, he stepped through into his cottage room and promptly dropped down into his chair.

The light was muted in the cottage and, for the first time Walter could remember, the room felt cold. It wasn't freezing, but a few degrees below comfortable; cold enough to raise goose bumps on his arms. He removed the blanket from the back of his chair and draped it over his body, then shifted his bottom around and repositioned the blanket to his knees. Half a minute later, he shifted it again. Another thirty seconds and he threw the blanket off, stood up, and ambled over to the window. A gust of cold air shook the window panes.

'I wish you were here,' he said. 'I wish you could tell me what I'm supposed to do.' He paused and waited. Something stirred around his kidney, and he thought for the first time about the voice he'd heard in Letty's house. At the time, he was too preoccupied to pay it much mind, but now that he thought back on it, he could have sworn it was Edi's. There was something about the lightness of it, the compassion in the tone. His nerves flittered. The smell of laundry was so strong it hurt his nostrils, and a deep ache spread out from just below his clavicle.

'Tell me what to do,' he said, desperately hoping to hear the voice again. 'Please, if you're there, let me know.' He glanced at the window, praying it might rattle again. Or that a bird might land on the window ledge, or maybe, just maybe, Edi might walk in the door behind him, a basket of vegetables under her arm, ready to tell him he was fussing over nothing.

'Am I being selfish?' he said. 'Is it selfish that I want to see you again? That I don't want to stay trapped here for all eternity?' Once again, his questions were met without response. He groaned and fell back into his chair.

'Maybe I should give up,' he said.

'*Maybe* you should tell me *exactly* what is going on.'

Walter jumped out of his seat.

'What the ...? Who are you?'

'I asked first. Now start talking.'

Walter was stunned into silence. Partly due to the fact that, for the first time in nearly two centuries, there was a woman in his house that was neither his wife nor a relative, and partly because of said woman's eyes. A layman would have called them green, but these were not a typical green, Walter mused. These were peridot green, like two semi-precious stones, and no matter how Walter tried, he couldn't seem to draw his attention away from them. They glittered and gleamed as if lit from behind, and even when scowling – as they currently were – they were the most mesmerising pair of eyes Walter could ever recall seeing.

The owner of the eyes was a slight framed woman, standing with her hands on her hips. Her hair came down past her shoulders and swayed, despite the lack of breeze. A scent of peonies and plumeria flowed from the air around her. Walter inhaled the aroma as deeply as he could.

'You,' he said finally finding his voice. 'I've seen you before. You've been watching me.'

'And you've been doing a lot more than watching. Now I want to know why.'

'I ... I ...'

'Don't you try to deny it. I want to know exactly what you want with my daughter.'

'Your daughter?'

'And you better pick your words carefully. I might look small, but believe me, you don't want to get between me and my girls.'

'Your girls? What are you on about?'

It clicked like a brass padlock.

'You're the woman's mother. You're Letty's mother?'

'Aye. Now get talking,' the woman said. 'While you've still got teeth in your mouth.'

Patricia Spence – or Trish as she apparently liked to be called – was an impressive woman, Walter decided. Even as she berated him – throwing around obscenities like a fisherman's wife – she had about her a certain degree of elegance. Her long hair had never so much as a strand out of place, and when she listened, her eyes never wavered from his, although they did continue to narrow as he spoke.

'So, that's everything?' Trish said. 'There's nothing else I need to know?'

'Nothing,' Walter said. 'I swear.'

Trish sat back on the window ledge and pressed her lips into a long, thin line.

Walter had told Trish everything, from Pemberton's arrival and his first encounter with Letty in her living room, to the numerous shoe incidents, and all the way through to the unfortunate episode with the Ouija board.

'She bought the thing,' Walter pressed as he spoke. 'Honestly, had I not intervened when I did, things could have ended up much worse.'

'How exactly?' Trish said.

'Well ...' Walter attempted to substantiate his response. 'It doesn't matter, anyway. I'm done. I'm finished with it.'

'Now you listen here. If you touch so much as a hair on my daughter's head, I'll have you wishing you had never been born, let alone died. You hear me?' Trish wiped her hands on the seat of her trousers.

'I hear you,' Walter said. 'I'm done—'

'You're done with it. No more shoes, no more occupancy.'

'I understand.'

'Nothing. You hear me? You even think about—'

'I understand.'

'If you—'

'Are you capable of listening?' Walter's voice came out far

louder than he'd anticipated. He blushed as Trish's tirade came to a sudden stop.

'What I meant to say is, I agree. I will not be occupying your daughter's mind at any point in the near or distant future.'

'Well good,' Trish huffed.

A natural silence fell between the pair.

The scent of plumeria had grown stronger, and Walter wondered if it was, in fact, a natural aroma secreted from the woman, the way that horses often smelt of the hay they ate. He was desperate to step closer and absorb more of the aroma, but he suspected that even modern women, like Trish, had boundaries with that type of thing.

'I've got this lot to get us started.' Hector's head was barely visible behind the mountain of books laden on his arms. 'But to be honest, I was hoping I could have had a quick word with Kath Batts; after all, she has rather more hands-on experience than ... oh my. You have company.'

He dropped the pile on floor and swaggered over to Trish. 'And who might you be?' he asked, stretching out his hand from beneath a sequined trench coat.

'This is Trish,' Walter said. 'Letty's Mother.'

'What a pleasure. What a pleasure indeed. Hector Robernious. You may have heard of me.' Trish kept her hand firmly by her side. 'No?'

'Trish is Letty's mother,' Walter repeated.

'Letty?' Hector's eyebrows rose questioningly.

'Letty, you know. *Letty*, Letty.'

'I'm sorry, you know I'm terrible at names. Letty ...Tyler?'

'Letty.' Trish's face had turned a flaming red. 'As in my baby girl you've been terrorising for the last week. You know, the one who's head you've been jumping in and out of?'

'Baby girl?' Hector's face still drew a blank. 'Oh, the

chubby book woman! So sorry. Yes, of course, of course. I can see it now. Yes, I can see it. You're her mother. Of course, you are. Of course. You've exactly the same ...' he paused and scanned his eyes up and down as he tried to see a feature to complete his sentence. '...knuckles,' he decided.

Trish's face was stone.

'I know who you are. And I know what you've been doing. And like I was telling your little friend, this stops now.'

'And,' Walter lunged forward, 'I was just telling her that I agree. It's gone too far.' He turned to Trish. 'Honestly, if I'd ever thought things would have gone this far. I just wanted her to forget. I just wanted to see ...' His cheeks flushed crimson. 'Like I said, we'll find another way. No more occupancy.'

Hector's bulbous bottom lip withdrew under his teeth. During an elongated second, he studied first Trish, then Walter and then, slowly, he shook his head.

'I understand. I completely understand,' he said.

'You do?' Walter blurted out.

'Of course, I do. Walter, this woman is her mother.' He turned to Trish. 'From now on, you can make all the decisions regarding your daughter. After all, who are we to go poking about in the inner mechanics of one of the universe's most precious creations? Whatever our fates, we will play no more part in your daughter's life. I hand over the baton.'

'You do?' Walter and Trish spoke in unison.

'Of course.'

'But ... but ...' Walter stuttered, amazed by his mentor's sudden change of heart.

'But nothing,' Hector said. 'It is the right thing to do. The only thing to do.'

Trish's hands reached up and clasped his. 'Thank you,' she said. 'Thank you.'

'Of course,' Hector said. 'Of course.'

'I know that you're worried,' she said to Walter. 'But Letty's a good girl. She might not even talk to anyone.'

'I know. I won't do it.'

The realisation of what this decision truly meant began to sink in. He would not be leaving here. Not anytime soon; possibly not ever. Walter sank into his chair. He felt like a balloon that had been popped with an iron poker, then shredded, ingested by a large dog and excreted out, only to be incinerated and have its ashes blown out across a sewage plantation.

Across the room, Hector let out a heavy lungful of air.

'It is a shame, of course, that Walter will not get to do the necessary. But you and your daughter will be together soon; that must be a comfort.'

Walter's ear pricked. Beside him, Trish stiffened.

'What do you mean, be together soon?'

'Together. Reunited. Once more to be clutched to the bosom of maternal magnificence.'

'Where? Here?' Trish frowned. Walter followed suit.

'Well, where else are you going to be reunited?' Hector said. 'If you intended on going the resurrection route, I'm sorry to say but you signed the wrong deal.'

'Wait,' Trish held up her hands. 'Hold up. You mean Letty? My Letty, she's going to ... going to ... no. She can't.' Trish scoffed at the idea. 'You don't mean that.'

Hector shook his head solemnly. 'It is the demon, I'm afraid. The mark of the damned'

'What are you on about? What demon, what mark?'

'From the Ouija board.'

'But, I don't understand.'

Walter stood up and stepped forward.

'I'm afraid I'm a bit lost too,' he felt it necessary to confess.

With a loud exhale, Hector lowered himself into Walter's rocking chair. He crossed his legs and placed a hand on the pile of books beside him.

'It's what I was coming to tell you. The situation is one we never anticipated. And it's not very good listening, I'm afraid.'

CHAPTER 27

*V*ICTORIA SAT in the centre of the sofa, her mustard yellow handbag by her feet.

'You can't invite someone over and spend the whole time in the kitchen,' she said. 'Really, sometimes I wonder how we come from the same gene pool.'

Letty inched into the room. The air in the room felt damp and heady, and she could feel the tension returning to her shoulders. Clutching her handbag, she edged forwards.

'Well, I'm glad to see you're using the iPad,' Victoria said. 'Have you got past the home screen yet?' She gave a little chuckle, then without a moment's pause, picked it up and tapped in their mother's date of birth. The screen pinged to life.

'Leticia, you should really be more secure with your passwords. It's just me now, but anyone could come in here and steal everything. Like all those old bank cards you keep. It's a good job you don't have anything to steal. You're a walking advertisement for identity theft.'

'I like my password. And it's easy to remember,' Letty said, taking back the device before Victoria saw the how-to guide on Ouija boards that was open on the screen. She placed it on the arm of the chair then looked for a place to sit. Mister Missy was on the armchair, and the small ottoman by the bookshelf was far too close to the little blue book for her liking. Even the floor was a non-option, given the evening's events.

Victoria huffed. 'If you're going to spend the entire evening hovering over my shoulder, I'd rather we were still in the kitchen.'

Letty swallowed. 'I just need to see to my arm,' she said. 'I'll sit down in a minute.' She dropped her handbag on the floor then began rummaging inside for the plasters. Two seconds later, Victoria's hands swiped something from under Letty's fingertips.

'Oh, I am so glad to see you're using this,' she said and pawed over the hideous crocodile skin purse. 'I wasn't sure you were going to.'

Letty smiled graciously. 'Of course,' she said, wondering if Victoria had genuinely forgotten the incident in which she forcefully relocated the entire contents of Letty's old purse only days ago.

'Well, if you like it that much, I can always see if they've got the bag for you for Christmas. It is hideously expensive, but I suppose if you're going to use it, it would be worth it. You never know, with your return on this investment with Felix, you could maybe buy it for yourself.'

'The purse is fine,' Letty said. 'I'd hate to overdo it.'

'Well, I'm not saying it would be everyday wear, but there are definitely situations when—'

'And I still have to talk to Donald.'

'Of course, but I'm saying you should treat yourself once in a while. It does us good.'

Victoria's explanation of when a crocodile skin handbag

and matching purse were anything but a walking display of crassness was cut short by a shrill, sharp ring.

'That must be Felix. Oh God, I hope everything's alright. I told him not to let the twins near the blender again.' She searched for the buzzing phone, emptying the contents of her handbag over the floor and the sofa as she went. 'If they got their hands on his credit card again, I swear I'll – Yes? Felix? What is it?' She pressed the phone to her ear. 'Well, did you give it to him? What do you mean, no? You can't not give it to him. What do you mean, why? Do you listen to nothing I say? No! Don't touch it. Don't touch anything. Stay where you are. I'm coming home now.'

Victoria was packing up her things before she'd hung up the phone. She tossed lipsticks and pocket mirrors indiscriminately into the centre compartment, then picked up her crocodile skin wallet and slung her bag over her shoulder.

'I'm sorry,' she said. 'I'd better go. But we'll catch up again soon. And talk to Donald as soon as he gets back.'

'I'll try,' Letty mumbled as her sister air kissed her cheeks goodbye.

~

'It was the scratch,' Hector said as he passed his hip flask to Trish. She downed a substantial glug then passed it to Walter, who hesitated, sniffed, and then swallowed. After all, he reasoned, it couldn't make him feel any sicker.

'An injury sustained from a spirit is most rare, most rare indeed,' Hector said. 'I have to confess, I have only borne witness to one other such event which was during the sixteen-hundreds. And well, yes, the less said about that the better. But mark my words, a spirit who does something like this has dark intentions. Very dark intentions indeed.'

'No, not Letty,' said Trish. 'I don't believe it. I mean, you don't know for certain, do you? You don't have any actual proof?'

'Proof?' Hector's nostrils flared. 'I will show you proof.' He reached over to Walter and grabbed his arm. 'This here. This is your proof.'

The mark was clearly visible and had now adopted a silverish tinge. Trish's mouth dropped.

'You see,' Hector said. 'Whatever or whoever did this is dark. Dark and old. To have power over the dead? To injure a spirit? Why, it is something of myths and legends. Something to be revered and feared.'

'But Letty—'

'That spirit has cast its mark on your daughter. It is in her.'

'Then we need to get the bloody thing out!'

Hector tilted his head and stroked the feathers on his hat in a long, considered motion.

'No,' he said with an exasperated gesture. 'We will not interfere. You said it before, and you are right. It's not our business. We will not meddle.'

'Yes, you bloody will. You will meddle. You were the ones who got her into this—'

'On the contrary, your daughter bought the Ouija board entirely—'

'You did this. You get it out.'

'Well ...'

'Now! Get it out now!'

'It's not that simple.'

Trish's fists were balled at her sides as she stepped well into the confines of Hector's personal space.

'You want to see simple?' she said. 'I will show you simple. Now, you tell me what we have to do, or I will take that feather hat of yours and stick it where the sun don't shine.'

Walter watched in awe; he was fairly certain they didn't make women like that in his day.

'Well, I guess we should get to work then,' Hector said.

They each took a book from the mountain Hector had left stacked on the table and started to skim read the contents.

The words in the book were entirely alien to Walter. Arabic perhaps, or Aramaic even. Whatever it was, it was making very little sense.

'Shouldn't there be some kind of auto-translate for these things?' Walter asked, skimming down several pages of symbols and hieroglyphs before abandoning the book altogether and picking up another monstrously heavy, leatherbound text. 'If they can turn the corridor into a fully-grown hedgerow maze, surely they can make books available in more modern languages?'

'Some of these are too old. They predate all modern language.'

'But you can read it.'

'Odd bits, here and there.'

That didn't instil much confidence.

'It would help if I had some idea what I was looking for,' Walter said.

'I second that,' Trish piped up. She was sitting in front of the hearth with the book propped up on her knees. When she read, her tongue protruded slightly from between her lips, and she seemed to be pushing the same strand of hair back behind her ear time and time again. Walter continued to watch her until her eye caught his. Hurriedly, he got back to his own papers.

'So far, I think I've learnt to disembowel a goat using only a teaspoon and make a wart elixir from urine and pigs' trotters,' Trish said after a minute.

'That's better than I'm doing. So far, the only two words I'm confident I've translated properly are conjunctivitis and mayonnaise.'

'Sounds like some interesting reading.'

'I'm not so sure.'

Walter rubbed his eyes and scanned a few more pages. When he was certain his current choice of reading was a bust, he cast it to the side and reached across for another from the stack. His fingers fell upon a smaller, softer hand.

'Sorry.' Walter felt the colour rise to his cheeks.

'No, my fault. You take this one.'

'Honestly, you take it. It's not like I've got a clue what any of it says.'

'I can't say I'm much better.'

The two stayed locked with hands on the book. Trish's cheeks had also started to darken, although with a rosy, dewing pink that only seemed to make her more attractive.

'This is it.' Hector sprung up from his seat. Walter startled backwards, slamming his elbow into the wall, which caused his cheeks to colour even more. 'I've got it. An internal exorcism.'

'A what?'

'An internal exorcism. Yes, yes. This is it. This is exactly what we're after.'

Walter and Trish exchanged a look as they crowded around Hector's faux-fur shoulders. The dusty yellow hardback had to be one of the oldest in the pile. Its pages were translucent and gleamed with a veneer of millennia old dust. It smelt of almond oil and vanilla flowers and some other fragrance as evocative and as unearthly as Walter thought a scent could be. When his senses had adjusted to the new aroma, he frowned at the dark brown squiggles.

'Are you sure that's what we want? It's a rather strange picture,' he said, commenting on the image of a naked man bareback riding a double-headed cockroach, while having his neck lassoed by a woman on a lion. Hector waved the concerns away.

'The picture is unimportant. Here it is. Everything we need to do. To rid a demon from the mind of a cursed ...' He ran his finger beneath the squiggles as he read, emitting a series of *um*s and *ah*s with the occasional *oh dear me*.

When he reached the last line, Hector shook his head and tutted.

'We have a lot of work ahead of us,' he said. 'A lot of work.'

'What do you need us to do?' Trish said.

'We need to do a cleansing,' Hector said. 'If Walter is to be able to rid your daughter of this spirit, he must be completely cleansed first.'

'How do we go about that?'

'I'll need to go get a few bits and pieces. It shouldn't take too long.' He was on his feet. 'You two wait here,' he said, slipping the book into a large briefcase that had appeared at his side. 'I don't know how long I'm going to be but stay put while I'm gone. And make sure you don't mention this to anyone. You understand? If one whiff of what we're about to do gets out, we'll be hounded from one side of the interim to the next.'

'Well, what should we do while you're gone? We can't just sit here.'

Hector shrugged his shoulder. 'Drink tea. You're both British, aren't you?'

CHAPTER 28

*W*ALTER PICKED at his nail. He crossed and then uncrossed his legs for the umpteenth time, while his fingers went from tapping his knees to fiddling with his pockets and back again.

'It's a lovely place you've got here,' Trish said, attempting to inject some conversation into the silence as she held her second mug of tea. Walter was certain she'd only drunk the first one out of politeness. He had gone over to the hearth and expected the tea to be ready made like always, but it wasn't. Once he'd found the pot, he'd shaken it, taken off the lid, tipped it upside down, and even asked it to give him tea. None of it had worked. When he'd been alive, the tea had almost always been ready-brewed for him; on the rare occasion he'd gone to make it himself, Edi would have insisted otherwise, claiming that tea was far too expensive a commodity to waste if he messed it up. And now he'd discovered what she'd actually meant. Walter Augustus made an awful cup of tea.

'It's a bit more complicated than using a bag of Tetley's,' Trish had said as Walter fussed around with the strainer, dropping flecks of sodden leaves all over the rim of the cup. What he finally handed her looked like something that had gushed out of the drains after a heavy storm.

'Look's smashing,' Trish said.

That was the last time either of them had spoken.

'So, have you always been here?' she asked, trying to force some kind of momentum into the conversation.

'All my life,' Walter said. 'Well, you know what I mean.'

'And your wife? Edi, right? She's moved on?'

Walter nodded.

'Kids moved on too?'

'They have.'

'And grandchildren?'

'And great-grandchildren. And nieces and nephews. It's just me. Always just me.'

Trish pursed her lips. Her lightness stalled, and an unpleasant hush passed between the pair. Walter blushed.

'Sorry. I suppose I'm not used to answering questions,' he said.

'I guess it's been a while. I'm not too good at knowing when to keep my gob shut either.'

Walter laughed. He caught her eyes and felt his cheeks reddening yet again.

'What about you?' he said, searching for a quick distraction. 'Who do you spend your time with up here? Letty's father?'

Trish laughed. 'God no. I mean, I'm not even sure if he's here yet. But no. Even if he was, no.'

'So, who then?'

'Oh, I've got plenty of people. Mum and Dad are still here. And my grandparents, although I don't think they'll be long off, I suspect.'

'Siblings, friends?'

'A lot of my friends are still down there. I've got an older brother here, but I never saw much of him in life so ... you know.' Her eyes drifted away and out the window. Walter's followed them as he found himself desperately wanting to know what she was thinking. A minute later and she told him.

'I guess I miss my girls, if I'm honest. I spend a lot of time down there. You know, just checking.'

Walter nodded. 'Before Edi died, I would spend all my time down there with her. Go to the shops with her. Even visit my grave.'

Trish laughed. 'I've done that too! God, aren't we strange? You'd think death would sort us out a bit. I'm more of a wreck now than when I was alive.' She laughed again, and Walter caught himself smiling back. It was impossible not to. She had one of those smiles, Walter thought, that could light up a whole room, the same way Edi's had. His lips quivered and fell.

'My eldest, Victoria, you've seen her?' Trish continued. Walter nodded. 'I worry about her. She thinks she's got everything sorted. She pretends she has, but when I see her on her own ... Oh, she's a mess.'

Walter nodded sympathetically.

'And I worry about them both, of course, I do. But Letty's always had a good head on her shoulders. Never got herself into no trouble. Not 'til now really. Now though ...' She looked down at her tea. 'You think what he says about the curse is true? That she's going to ... going to ...' Her eyes glistened with tears.

Walter's throat tightened. 'I don't know. I don't know why he'd say it if it wasn't true.'

Trish nodded silently as the tears escaped and leaked

239

down her cheeks. A dull ache spread out through Walter's chest. He leant in towards her.

'But Hector also said I can fix her. Don't forget that. He said I can fix her and I believe him. After all, he's been here long enough; he should know.' Trish nodded, clearly unconvinced. Walter leant farther forward and took her hands.

'I won't let anything happen to her. I swear. I swear on my ... on my afterlife. This is my doing. I will fix it. Your daughter will be fine. Letty will be fine.'

Trish lifted her head. Her face was streaked with glistening tear tracks.

'Thank you,' she said, her eyes meeting his.

Something stirred in Walter's gut. He lifted his hand and brushed the side of Trish's cheeks. Her eyes closed, and a tingle spread up through the tips of his fingers.

'Trish,' he said and edged closer.

'Walter?'

'Augustus?'

Walter's hand jumped from Trish's skin as he sprung backwards and slammed his heel against the hearth.

'I need a bigger house!' he yelled at the ceiling.

His outburst was met with a four-second silence, both by Trish, who appeared too shocked to respond, and by Pemberton.

'What do you want?' Walter hissed, making no pretence of niceties, even in front of Trish.

'I need a word.' Pemberton crunched a pear drop between his teeth. 'Provided, of course, that it's not too inconvenient?'

. . .

*W*alter was twitchy. Every few steps, he would cast an eye back up the narrow path towards the house and check that Trish was still there, standing by the window. He knew she'd listened when Hector had told them to stay put, but Walter couldn't help but keep checking. The last thing he wanted was to go back up there and find her gone.

Pemberton strode out in front. He had not said so much as a word to Walter since they'd stepped outside; however, he had muttered to himself continually. Fifteen feet from the shore, he stopped.

'I thought I should come and let you know, I'm off,' he said, his tone entirely devoid of emotion.

'Off?' Walter said. 'Where?'

'*Off*-off. I'm not sure when, but it won't be long.'

Walter scratched his temple. 'Sorry, I'm not sure what you mean, *off*-off.'

'I mean I'm moving. I'm leaving. I me—'

'You mean ... You mean?'

A flush of heat blasted Walter's cheeks. 'No. No, you can't be serious? How? No, you can't be? You can't.'

Pemberton's Adam's apple bounced visibly in his throat.

'I realise that this may be somewhat disappointing to you bu—'

'You're lying. You have to be.'

'I can assure you I am not.'

'How? She knows your name. She read it. I was there.'

'I can't explain it. It was in one ear and out the other. It didn't stick. I don't know what else I can say.'

'No, no, no!' Walter picked up a pebble and gripped it until his knuckles shone. 'How is this fair? How is this fair?'

Pemberton's face hardened.

'If we wish to talk about fairness, let's talk about why I was stuck here in the first place. And let's be honest, we cannot discount the possibility that I may be summoned back at any moment due to your infernal scribblings.'

'Argh!' Walter yelled as he threw the pebble into the waves and dropped to the ground, barely noticing the cold edges of the stones as they jabbed at his knees. He picked up another pebble and lobbed it out towards the horizon, followed by another and another and another.

Pemberton's hand appeared on his shoulder. He was too weak even to shake it away.

'Augustus, I don't know what you're doing with Hector, but stay safe, please.'

Walter grunted.

'He is a clever man, but he has been here a long time, and time can do funny things to the best of us.'

Walter stood up and studied the creases on Pemberton's face. He looked younger than he remembered. More at ease in his skin. Perhaps that was what happened before you moved on, Walter thought, not that he was likely to find out. He brushed off his knees and turned towards the house. A few steps down the path, he stopped and turned to his former employer.

'What's it like over there?' he said, locking his eyes with Pemberton's for the first time since his arrival. 'In case I never get there.'

'You'll get there one day. I have faith.'

'But if I don't?'

'Then it's probably better that you don't know.'

Walter walked back towards the house. Halfway from the top, he paused and turned for the second time. The beach was empty, save one small sea gull.

. . .

*'A*re you sure you're okay?' Trish said.

'I've told you, I'm fine,' said Walter with more of a snap to his voice than he'd intended.

'Well, sorry I asked.'

Walter sighed and pressed his fingers into his eyes sockets. It had been two hours since Pemberton's departure, and the four walls of his cottage were growing smaller by the second. In Trish's defence, she'd been remarkably patient with him, keeping up her cheery charade as he continued to gripe and grouse about everything from the colour of the teapot to the temperature of the tiles, none of which had bothered him before.

'I'm sorry,' he said. 'I thought Hector would be back by now. I don't know what's taking him so long.'

'It did sound like he had a lot of things to sort out.'

'I suppose.'

'We could always take a quick walk downstairs. See how Letty's doing. I don't suppose it would do any harm, just the two of us.'

Walter thought it over. He shook his head. 'If Hector said we should stay put, then we should stay put,' he said. This time, it was Trish who let out a little grumble. A second later, it turned into a low-pitched moan.

'Sorry,' Trish said when it stopped. 'Must be near bedtime I suppose. My girls always think about me at bedtime. Usually, I'd go down and see them but ... well. Never mind, eh?'

Her eyes were starting to glaze again, and Walter had an overwhelming urge to stop them. 'Maybe we could slip out. Just for a minute,' he said. Trish's face lit up.

'You mean it? Won't Hector be mad?'

'Who's going to tell him?' Walter said. Trish stepped

forward, and for a heart-splitting second, Walter thought she was about to kiss him.

His mind went into overdrive. Did he want that? Of course not, he told himself. He was a married man. Only his wife had been gone for a long time now and the likelihood of him ever seeing her again was looking slimmer and slimmer by the second. Absorbing the plumeria scent, he swallowed, closed his eyes, and waited.

'Who's going to tell me what?'

CHAPTER 29

*L*ETTY SLEPT through the night. Really slept. No stirring, no waking up, no creaking doors or shuddering shadows. No doubt it was the exhaustion from the last week, or perhaps the fact that, in a few hours, Donald would be back beside her, ready to put all this nonsense about ghosts and spirits out of her head.

In the shower, she glanced at her arm. The scratch was still there, although in the light, it looked remarkably like a cat scratch. Maybe it had happened earlier in the day, she thought. Perhaps when she'd given Mister Missy his food. It wasn't impossible. She'd had scratches before that she'd not noticed. When she was dressed, she took a lump of meat out of the freezer to defrost for Donald's homecoming dinner, before packing up the birthday cake, ready for the obtuse businessman to collect.

'What time are you taking lunch today?' Joyce asked only fifteen minutes after turning the sign on the door to open. 'Only I was hoping I could go and get my nails done. Kev hates it when they start growing out. Thinks they look well rank. I wanna give him a treat now we're back together. Just I need to ring up and book.'

Letty was using a small rag to polish up some of the girl's patent school shoes. Donald's shoes would need a good clean when he got back, she was thinking. Probably all covered in mud. Maybe once he knew about the money, he might like some new work shoes, she thought. He had always liked nice shoes.

'I've got the man collecting the cake around three,' Letty said. 'So any time before that's fine with me.'

'What about Head Office?"

'What about them?'

'Aren't they sending the kids here today? You know, from the new store?'

Letty dropped the rag she was polishing with.

'Is that today? Christ, how did I forget that?'

Letty dashed over to the calendar and flicked to the correct date. Joyce was right; the regional manager was bringing two trainee members of staff from the new store today at twelve for an induction.

'They'll only be an hour or so. They just want to have a look at how the stock taking is done and that kind of thing. Two hours at most. And I can hold the fort. It's not going to be a problem. You book your nails for whenever. We'll work it out.'

'That's why I love you, Lets,' Joyce said, and Letty went out back to check she hadn't forgotten anything else important.

～

*P*revious to that evening's affairs, Walter had come to a point where he believed it impossible to be either shocked, offended, or amused by Hector's choice of attire. His current apparel, however, eclipsed any of his former ensembles, and the less that was said about his own clothing, the better.

They had worked through the night on what Hector had called the 'cleansing.' Walter had been forced to abandon his comforting garb of a shirt and breeches and don nothing more than his underpants and fluorescent face paint. A series of strange smelling herbs and spices had been rubbed into his skin, while Hector bounced around him, chanting and hammering a long wooden stake on the ground.

'It says in all the literature that you should be naked for this part,' Hector repeated. Walter clung to his white cottons. They were out in Walter's garden, although with the high moon and series of symbols that Hector had scribbled on the trees and grass, it looked more like they'd walked into a fifteenth-century witches' coven.

'What difference does it make if I'm naked?' Walter said, fighting the urge to scratch the life out of his nether regions. A large part of him thought that Hector may have fabricated a few of these rituals for his own perverse pleasure, particularly the part of the master of ceremonies wearing a full-length cape and crow's feather tiara. 'I'll rub that stuff into my bits if I must, but I'm not getting naked, not while ... you know.'

'Know what? Good God. Don't tell me you're embarrassed. Men have been naked among men since the dawn of time. The Japanese onsen, the Swedish—'

'I don't care about being naked in front of you,' Walter said. Hector's face scrunched up, confused.

'Oh, I'm not leaving.' Trish laughed from across the garden. 'No chance. This is way too funny.'

She stood resting against one of the tree trunks. A thin veil of clouds drifted soundlessly across the sky, and while the moon's light had turned her hair silvery white, the vivid green of her eyes remained untouched.

Walter shot her a glare. She stuck out her tongue and blew a raspberry.

'Well, let's hope you keep your sense of humour when it's your turn,' Hector said.

'My turn?' Trish's mocking expression vanished. 'What have I got to do with this?'

Hector puckered his lips and put down his stake. 'Well,' he said, 'I was thinking that perhaps it would be best if Walter had a little support. I was looking through some of the books and a simple binding spell is all it would take.'

'All what would take?'

'Well, I could link you and Augustus here. Temporarily, of course. That way, where he goes, you go. And should he get into any trouble while occupying the girl—'

'What type of trouble?' Walter said.

'—then you would be on hand,' Hector continued talking to Trish. 'I'm not saying there will be any issues, of course. From what I read, these spirits are fairly easy to get rid of from the inside. A little incantation is all it should take, once you find the thing. Still, I thought it might be nice for you two to go together. Might speed things up with the removal too.'

'Removal?' Trish said.

'Of Walter's name.'

Her face fell. 'Sorry. Of course. I don't know why I forgot that.'

'Because I said I wasn't going to do it,' Walter said. He

248

stepped forward next to Trish. 'I'll find another way that doesn't include messing around in Letty's head.'

'But as you're in there anyway ...' Hector said.

'I said no.'

Walter's lips twisted. He tried to look at Trish to get some indication of her opinion on the matter, but his eyes couldn't quite make it above her knees. It didn't help matters that there was this new type of tugging behind his sternum, and it didn't feel like it had anything to do with the living.

'Hector's right,' Trish said. 'It would be silly not to. It's not like you can do any more harm than a demon in there, can you?'

'I guess not—'

'And I guess if I can help speed things along ... That's if you want me to come.'

'Of course. I mean, only if you want me to?'

'Well—'

'Only if you're sure?'

'Splendid,' Hector clapped his hands, ending the back and forth. 'Now, Patricia, if you go back into the house, you'll find a lovely looking headdress all laid out for you.'

It was Walter's turn to smirk.

And so, the three continued throughout the night. The binding spell worked well, according to Hector, although Walter had no way of knowing. He did feel like he wanted to stay close to Trish, and her smile had the uncanny ability to make him smile too, but he wasn't entirely sure that it hadn't been like that before the spell. As for the cleanse, he wasn't sure he felt particularly dirty beforehand either, but once again, Hector appeared satisfied with the results.

The final procedure consisted of Walter laying face up on the grass, while Hector flicked water over his body.

'That's it,' he said, when Walter's body had been thoroughly soaked. 'We're done. Now the minute the girl's asleep, you can go in there, do your business, and we'll all be free of this place.'

$\approx$

*T*ypically, it was the first really busy day all week.

'I don't have to go. I can cancel the appointment,' Joyce said as she struggled to fit a writhing toddler into a pair of welly boots.

'Don't be silly. This'll die down in a minute. I've already got all the books and sheets sorted for when they come. You go. I'll be fine.' Letty looked up from the floor. 'How does that feel?' Her customer, a geriatric lady with ankles swollen to the size of grapefruits, was trying their range of strappy party shoes. 'Can you wiggle your toes for me? Great. Why don't you have a walkabout and see how those feel?' While Letty watched the woman stride expertly from one end of the store to the other, Joyce led the toddler's mother over to the till to pay.

'See you in forty,' Joyce said when she was done, leaving Letty to find a size seven pair of red stilettos and thigh-high leather boots for her current customer.

As predicted, the crowd died down, and at 11:45, Letty swept through the shop, running the duster behind the shelves and straightening up the slippers and socks on their hangers. Gone were the days of being nervous about a Head Office visit. She'd been in the business longer than almost all of them, and there hadn't been a question she couldn't answer in the last decade. Still, she wanted the place to look presentable. There was a reason Head Office took new recruits to her store and not one of the others.

At 12:15, the shop was still empty. At 12:30, she headed out onto the street and scanned the road, and at 12:45, when there was still no sign of them, she picked up the phone. Before she could finish dialling, the party of three finally bundled through the doorway.

'Sorry, we got caught up. I hope you weren't about to call Head Office and find out where we were.' A woman half Letty's age emitted a throaty laugh as she plunged her hand into Letty's and pumped with the strength of an Olympic shot-putter. She was pleasant looking, with soft features and a tiny waist, although her hair was scraped back and a pair of glasses balanced on the end of her nose in a manner that was almost a caricature.

'Leticia, isn't it? Super to meet you. Geoff in the office told me I'd be fine to leave these two in your hands. We've just taken them on as part of our first "College Apprenticeship Training Scheme".' She emphasised with air quotes. '*CATS*. I came up with that acronym.'

The woman paused.

'Oh, it's very clever,' Letty said. 'Very witty.' The woman radiated smugness.

'So, I'll leave our little *kittens* in your hands.'

'Of course.'

She turned to two spotty faced trainees. 'So, I'll be back in a couple of hours, and I expect you both to be complete experts by then.'

'A couple of hours?' Letty said,

'That is okay, isn't it? I thought, while I'm in town, I have a few other errands to deal with too. Work related, obviously. And what's a little more time spent learning from the best?' The woman adjusted her glasses. 'That's not going to be a problem, is it?'

Letty glanced at her watch. The man had said he would

pick up the cake at three. Provided the woman was true to her word and back, it should be okay.

'Of course not,' Letty said.

'Super. See you later then.'

~

'*Y*ou see. That's so her. She's always been the same. Since she was a kid. Never stood up for herself. She should have told that women no. One hour. That's what she should have said if that's what they'd agreed to. Don't you think?' Walter nodded, although in truth, his attention was only partially on Letty.

As Hector had mentioned that they wouldn't be removing the spirit until Letty was asleep, the pair had decided to come down and keep an eye on her. Walter wasn't sure whose idea it was – whether he'd suggested it or merely gone along. Perhaps it was part of the binding spell, he thought; you weren't forced to be together, so much as wanted to be. So, they'd come downstairs, and now the pair were sitting on square cushions watching as the customers drifted in and out of Shoes 4 Yous.

Currently, Letty was showing a pair of spotty teenage boys how the complicated computer teller machine worked. A week ago, Walter would have had his back against the wall as far away as possible from the all-singing, all-dancing cash register. Today, it didn't seem such a big issue.

'She doesn't look sick,' Trish observed. 'You know, for someone being inhabited by an evil demon spirit thing, she seems remarkably ...' She searched for the right word.

'Normal?' Walter suggested.

Trish nodded. After a brief pause, she spoke again.

'You don't suppose he could have got it wrong, do you?

Your friend Hector? It just doesn't seem possible. Look at her? Does it seem possible to you?'

Walter studied Letty. She looked tired, certainly, but more tired than at any other time he'd seen her? Possibly not. She undoubtedly looked less stressed than she had the night before, but that was unsurprising. And as for possessive spirits, he had no idea what the tell-tale signs were, unfortunately.

'I guess we'll find out later,' he said. 'When she goes to sleep.'

'And you get rid of yourself from all her memories and disappear,' Trish said.

'I guess,' Walter said, unsure as to why the thought now made his stomach sink a little.

CHAPTER 30

BY 2:50 P.M., Letty had run out of things to do. She'd shown them the stockroom and the ordering sheets, the sales lines, and how to work the till. She'd shown them how to measure feet for width and length and gone over the key issues to point out to customers, like fallen arches and insteps. She'd looked at refunds and returns, although they didn't have a log on for the till yet, and she wasn't going to let them loose on hers. In an ideal world, she'd have got them dusting out back, but when she mentioned there was some cleaning to be done, one of them started muttering about Head Office, and the last thing she wanted was a complaint against her to top off the week.

'Well, I guess you should hang around the shop front with Joyce for a bit and get a feel of things,' she said. Five minutes and the trainees were using slippers as glove puppets, while Joyce sat taking photos of her new nails on her phone. Letty was moments away from reprimanding the lot of them when a figure bustled through the doorway.

'Thank God for that. What a morning. Tell me you've got it.' The red-haired man had a phone in one hand and a series of bags in the other. His sleeves were rolled up to show an obscenely shiny watch, and as he strode through the shop, his shoulders shimmied repeatedly to avoid making contact with any of their reasonably priced merchandise. Letty gulped. He was ten minutes earlier than anticipated. Still, she told herself, the chance of the trainees passing on any information about her cake business to Head Office seemed slim; one of them had managed to get his tongue stuck between the laces of a hiking boot.

The man clicked his fingers towards Joyce and one of the trainees. 'I'm double parked, so I need the cake now. One of you can carry it out to the car for me.'

The trainees lowered the glove puppets and looked at each other in confusion.

'Oi, you? Are you listening?'

Letty blushed and stepped in front of the man.

'Don't worry. I'll just be a second. I'll get it for you now.'

'Well, be quick. Did you hear what I said about being double parked?'

Letty ran out back and grabbed the cake.

~

'It drives me mad!' Trish was kicking furiously but to no avail. Her toes went straight through the shin of the man's neatly pressed trousers and out the other side. Next, she tried slapping his face and got an equally disappointing result. 'People like him. I can't stand them. Thinking they can talk down to her. Thinking they're better than her, just 'cos they wear some fancy expensive suit and tacky watch.'

'It's always been the same,' Walter said. 'It was worse in my day. You were lucky if you got out alive in some cases.'

'Well. It really does get my goat. Honestly. Someone needs to bring him down a peg or two.'

~

*L*etty opened the box for the man to see inside.

He gave a terse sniff. 'I thought I said no hearts.'

'Oh, I thought you said one or two would be okay,' Letty stammered. 'And they're only very small.'

He sniffed again. 'Well, I doubt it'll make any difference. She'll probably complain anyway.'

Letty smiled uncomfortably. A tightness was building up from the bottom of her intestines, intensified by the fact that the trainees had now abandoned their puppets and were focusing their undivided attention on her.

'Well, I hope she enjoys it.'

The man grunted, then reached into his pocket. He frowned then reached for the other.

'How much did you say?'

'Thirty pounds,' Letty said.

'Can you change a fifty?'

Letty glanced towards the till. Normally, she wouldn't have thought twice about it, but the two trainees were now staring at her as if this was the most exciting thing they'd seen all year.

'Well?'

A nervous churning worked its way up through her belly. You're not doing anything wrong, she told herself. You're just changing money in the till. With a deep breath, she steeled herself.

'Did you not hear me when I said I'm double parked? Have you people any idea what it's like for us with real jobs?'

Letty took a sharp intake of breath. Beside her sat a pair

of combi-leather male brogues, and for a split second, she considered picking one up and battering him with it. Yes, she wanted to say. After thirty-six years, she had a fair idea what a real job entailed, and it wasn't swanning in and out of shops on an overpriced mobile phone. This was where she wished she was more like Jean. She'd have struck him in the centre of his jaw with one of the shoes already. He'd have been lucky not to get a stiletto in the eye. After another deep breath, she smiled and lifted her feet to move to the till.

'Oh, screw this,' the man said and slapped a note in her hand before turning on his heel towards the door.

~

*H*e did not!'
'He did not what?' Walter said.

'He did! Look at that. He bloody short-changed her. Thirty pounds, that's what she said, wasn't it? He's only gone 'un given her ten.' While Letty's expression was one of slight confusion and disappointment, Trish's was of absolute rage.

Sure enough, Walter saw the part crumpled note shoved in Letty's hands, the orange writing a definite sign of a ten-pound note.

'We need to stop him!' Trish yelled.

'What?'

'Before he leaves. He's not getting away with this.'

'But—'

'We need to stop him. Stop him now!'

Walter didn't even think. There wasn't time. Trish was beside him, begging him to do something. He could, he thought. This could be his chance to show her that he wasn't a total screw up. That he really did have her daughter's interests at heart.

257

In one quick swipe of his hand, a single black combi-leather brogue flew through the air towards the man. The laces whipped around one another as it spun towards the door.

It's going to hit him, Walter thought, his insides fluttering with excitement. It's going to hit him. Beside him, Trish's jaw hung loose as she watched, half-fear, half-elation glittering in her perfect green eyes. Walter watched transfixed as the corners of her lips lifted upwards into a smile. He had done it. He had impressed the girl.

A second later, her hand flew to her mouth in a horrified gasp.

'No!' she yelled.

Walter turned back to the door. The man had sidestepped the shop's entrance to make room for oncoming traffic. The combi-leather brogue continued to hurtle towards a collision, now on a direct path, not for a mass of red hair and oversized ego as planned, but for a delicate pair of glasses perched on the end of a lady's nose as she strutted through in her pinstripe pencil skirt and high ponytail.

'So, have my kittens had a super time?' she said.

'No,' Walter yelled and lunged towards the shoe. But it was too late. There was nothing he could do.

CHAPTER 31

*L*ETTY COULDN'T breathe. She could hear the woman talking on the phone and the hushed voices of the trainees beside the cut-price wedge-heels. She could feel Joyce beside her, stroking her shoulder, saying something she assumed was supposed to be comforting, but it made no difference. Her world was crashing around her, and she wasn't even sure if she was to blame.

The shoe had been right beside her. And she'd thought about throwing it. She could distinctly remember thinking about throwing it. But it had been a thought. Surely, she would have remembered had she actually done it.

'Well, Mrs Ferguson, I have just gotten off the phone to Head Office.' The woman's glasses were now askew. Throughout the conversation, her attempt to maintain eye contact with Letty was thwarted somewhat by the need to reach up continually and stem the trickle of blood from the cut on her forehead.

'They have agreed to an immediate suspension, pending an official enquiry.' She sniffed as she spoke. 'I would recommend you pack up your things immediately. I wouldn't be expecting to return anytime soon. If ever.'

Letty stared blankly, her head too foggy to piece the words together. Joyce, for once, was on the ball.

'You're firing her? You can't do that. Do you know how long she's been here?'

'This is a case of gross misconduct.'

'He was an arse! He deserved more than a boot to the face.'

'Even if the case of assault—'

'Assault!' Joyce scoffed.

The woman coughed. 'Even if I overlook the case of assault, the very fact that you were running an illegal trade from inside company premises—'

'You make it sound like she was running a bloody crack house, not selling cupcakes.'

'—is, in my book, a case for instant dismissal. I'm sure the proper procedures will lead to the same outcome.'

'You're a bitch, you are,' Joyce spat. 'You know that. You're a right little stuck up—'

'It's alright, Joyce,' Letty said, managing to find her voice before Joyce landed herself on the same plate.

'It's—'

'It's alright, Joyce,' Letty said again. 'Don't worry. I'll get my things now. You'll be okay locking up tonight, won't you?' She found her throat constricting as she spoke. 'Key's on the hook. And don't forget you'll need to shimmy it a bit, otherwise ... otherwise ...'

'I know,' Joyce said. 'I know.'

The walk home was impossibly long, and every footstep felt like a heel kick to her chest. The smell of fish and chips wafted out from one of the cafe doors. Letty considered going in, eating her way through as many plates of haddock and batter bits as her body could withstand, but for once, she didn't.

How was she going to tell Donald? He was a supportive man, a wonderful man, but he had his pride to think of too. Goodness knows what they'd say down at the Bowls Club when they found out she'd been fired. They'd probably already found out. That was the way things worked in a small town. Maybe if she went to sleep, she thought. Maybe if she went to sleep, it would all be better in the morning.

Letty was at the corner of Hillbrook Crescent when the weather changed. The clouds adopted a mauve tint, and the wind picked up to a pace that could almost have been described as autumnal. Burying her hand in her bag, she felt around for her keys. Standing outside her front door in a torrential downpour would be the icing on the cake, she thought. It was due to the fact that Letty was so preoccupied looking for her keys and keeping her face shielded from the wind that she failed to notice the red Fiat car parked outside her drive, or the high heel standing on her doorstep until she was almost on top of them.

'Oh, ouch. Sorr ... Victoria?'

Her sister wore a red knee-length coat and ochre coloured pashmina and was playing with the ends of her nails. It was a full fifteen seconds before she looked up from her hands and acknowledged her sister's presence.

'Leticia,' Victoria said.

'Is everything alright?'

'Why don't you tell me?'

Letty closed her eyes, trying to make sense of her sister's riddles and find a way to the door before the rain started.

'Victoria, if you want something, it's been a long day.'

'Oh yes.' A strange grin was plastered across her face. 'I'm sure it has been. On your knees all day, working in that shoe shop. It can't be fun having to do that.'

'Well—'

'I was going to pop in actually, but I thought I'd try the house first. Maybe see if Donald had gotten home already.'

'Donald? Why do you want to see Donald?'

Victoria's grin spread out into full-toothed sneer.

'Why don't we go inside?' she said. 'That way we can have a proper talk.'

In the kitchen, Letty boiled the kettle. So far Victoria had offered only one-word answers since stepping inside the door. All had been served with a sideways slant to the lips that made Letty's skin crawl. Letty had avoided her by taking as long as possible to make the drinks, but given that the steam had now stemmed, and the beverages were close to tepid, she knew she couldn't avoid the inevitable much longer.

'I'm glad to see you're still using the iPad,' Victoria said as she took the cup of tea and placed it straight down on the coffee table.

'Yes. It's been rather useful,' Letty said.

'Oh, I am glad. That's part of being a sister, isn't it? Helping out where we can. Keeping each other up to speed on events in our lives. Being open.'

Normally, Victoria's cryptic comments left Letty's mind a wreck, but today she was too tired to play her sister's games. Instead, she sat back and took a large gulp of tea.

'What is it you want, Victoria? You clearly want something.'

'Do I?'

'Yes. And I've not got the energy or patience to deal with it today. So just spit it out. Whatever it is.'

Victoria stiffened and straightened her back. 'Bad day at the shoe shop, was it?'

Letty glared.

'Fine. I was hoping there was some nice way to go about this, but clearly, there's not. So, I'll get straight to it. I want to know exactly how long it's been going on.'

'What's been going on?'

'What?' Victoria's eyebrows took a trip up her forehead with amateur dramatic proficiency. 'The stealing. The money.'

Letty gulped. 'What money?' she said.

'What money? The money in your bank accounts, that's what money.'

A hot clamminess oozed over Letty's skin, and she tried her hardest not to blink. 'I'm not sure what—'

'Oh, don't you start that,' Victoria snapped. 'You know exactly what I'm talking about. And I'm telling you now, if I don't like what I hear, I'm going straight to the police.'

'The police? What? Why?'

'Embezzlement. It's a criminal offence. You'll go to jail for it, you know. You probably both will.'

'I'll what?'

Victoria steepled her fingers and sat forward in her seat.

'You know, I always thought you were a bit simple, the pair of you. Still living in this drab little house, going about your drab little lives. Never wanting to better yourselves, never wanting to make anything of yourself, but I see now.' She paused, and her eyes narrowed into thin black slithers. 'What was the plan, disappear to Mexico in hopes that they never found you? Shipping it off to an account in the Cayman Islands so that no one would ever know. My dumpy little sister, baking her cherry bakewells, on her feet all day, and all the while she's got a criminal enterprise on the go. You mark my words, I'll go to the police, and I'll go to the papers as well.'

Letty's mouth hung so wide that she could feel a draft on the back of her tongue. She studied her sister's face, hoping to find some trace of humour, or sanity, but at that moment could find neither. The clamminess on her skin was becoming hotter by the second, and when her mouth finally closed enough to speak, her voice was barely recognisable.

'How dare you,' Letty said. 'What right have you to go through my bank accounts? You want a criminal offence. Stealing the post is a criminal offence.'

Victoria scoffed. She put her hand into her bag and pulled out the ugly crocodile wallet.

'I took your purse the other night,' she said. 'By accident, before you start accusing me. And you can hardly blame me that you're still using the same pin and password that you've had for the last three decades.'

Letty's cheeks reddened. 'You had no right—'

'The money. I want my share. I wasn't joking. I'll go to the police. I'll tell them everything.'

'You'll tell them what?' Letty said.

'I'll tell them everything.'

'What are you going to say?' Then, with no breath between rage and hysteria, Letty began to laugh. It was the type of laugh that started in the belly then moved all the way up to the mouth and caused every muscle between to stitch and spasm. Soon every part of her, from her thighs to her earlobes, was wobbling and jiggling; there was nothing she could do to stop it. Tears poured down her cheeks, and her breath had transformed from ragged and irate to wheezy hysterics.

'What? What's so funny? Do you know what'll happen to someone your age in prison?'

'You're not sending me to prison,' Letty choked as the tears streamed down her face. Victoria's face shone puce.

'Don't think I won't. And Donald too. I know he was behind all this too.'

Letty continued to cough on her laughter. 'What are you going to send me to prison for? And Donald? Donald doesn't even know about the money.'

It took less than a second to realise what she'd said. Letty's mouth snapped shut, but it was too late. The corners of Victoria's lips twitched excitedly.

'Donald doesn't know?' she said.

'Victoria ...'

'No, this is priceless. Poor Donald, working all the hours in the day, looking after his poor, fat, childless wife, and all the time she's been lying to him. Stealing behind his back.'

'It's not like that. I've never stolen a thing in my life.'

'Oh no, of course not. The money just rained into your accounts I suppose?'

'Victoria, please.'

Victoria paused and glanced at her watch, after which she reached down to the sofa and picked up Letty's crocodile purse.

'Donald will be home about five you say?'

Letty didn't answer. Her legs and arms had begun to shake.

'Well, that gives me just enough time to pop into town for a manicure, doesn't it?' She pinged open Letty's purse and pulled out a crisp twenty-pound note. 'Of course, if you don't want me to come around, just let me know. My starting price is a hundred thousand pounds. It will go up though.' Letty stared dumbfounded.

'Well, I have to say I'm very much looking forward to this evening,' Victoria said as she swung her coat over her shoulder. 'Perhaps you might want to bake another cake. I know how comfort eating helps you soften a blow.'

CHAPTER 32

TRISH'S HEAD was buried in Walter's chest. While being the only companion of a crying woman was far from his ideal situation, there was something about the way her head slotted into his shoulder. The smell of peonies filled his nostrils, and the curve of her neckline exposed a sliver of porcelain skin.

'She's got so much of her father in her, Victoria has,' Trish said when she finally lifted her head. The tears had made her green eyes an even deeper hue, and Walter found himself, once again, staring at them.

'It's always been harder for her,' Trish continued. 'She was there you see; she remembers what it was like when her dad left. And I was always a bit soft, not wanting to rock the boat. Not after what she'd been through. But that's him talking. All those cruel things. How could she say those things? To her own sister?'

Walter stroked the back of her hair.

'Once,' he said. 'When my girls were young, they got into such an argument that when we were all asleep, the youngest took a pair of shears and cut off one of her big sister's pigtails.'

Trish's eyes widened.

'Oh my goodness, what did you do?'

'Well, we let her sister cut off hers.'

'You didn't?'

'We did. My goodness, the tears. They laughed about it afterwards, although not for a good few years.'

'I'm not surprised. You probably scarred them for life.'

'Nah, I don't think kids scarred so easily back then. Of course, I could be wrong.'

Trish let out a soft chuckle, but the crease in her lips quickly faded.

'But if what Hector said is right ... they don't know how long they've got left together. They can't ... they can't ... they have to ...'

And with that, she once more dissolved into the sleeve of Walter's shirt.

~

*L*etty's eyelids were lead. Her head throbbed from temple to temple and her throat felt like she'd swallowed three rich tea biscuits consecutively, without water. Perhaps Victoria finding out wasn't a bad thing, she thought; at least it would get it all out in the open now. And she could blackmail her all she wanted, but not a penny more of her money was going to find its way into her sister's pocket; of that, Letty was certain. As if understanding her sudden need for affection, Mister Missy sidled up and flopped down on her lap.

'So, dear. How was your week?' she spoke to the cat and answered her own question. 'Well dear, I got fired from my job, attacked by a Ouija board, and am now being black-mailed by my narcissistic sister. On the plus side, I have a half a million pounds that I've kept hidden from you for the last twenty years, so at least I'm not going to starve when you leave me.'

She tossed the cat onto the cushion beside her. 'What d'ya reckon?' she said. 'It'll be alright, right?'

Mister Missy looked up, his blue-grey eyes bulging, and said nothing.

'A great lot of help you are.'

Letty laid back, closed her eyes, and breathed in the scent of the old worn fabric. A sleep was what she needed. A nice long rest.

'Letty dear, is that you? What are you doing home?'

'Donald?'

Letty was on her feet as Donald hobbled into the living room.

'My goodness,' he said, sweeping down and planting a kiss on his wife's forehead. 'Am I glad to see you.'

Letty stopped and took a step back. For someone who had spent five days at an outdoor retreat, Donald looked like he'd passed the time in a broom cupboard. His cheeks were thin and sallow, and he appeared to have double the number of grey hairs. When he pulled Letty in, the smell was of cheap washing powder and greasy fry-ups.

'Long week?'

'You could say that.' He stooped down and scratched Mister Missy's extended chin. 'Did I see Victoria's car speeding off down the road?'

Letty's jaw tightened. 'She came for a visit.'

'What did she want?'

'Oh ... it's ... I'll ... I'll talk to you about it later.'

'More good news,' he muttered.

'Pardon?' Letty said, not quite sure she'd caught what he'd said.

Donald looked up and smiled before turning his attention back to the cat.

'And have you been a good boy?' he said. Mister Missy purred obligingly. After a minute or so of extreme tummy rubs and petting, Donald stood back up. His eyes locked on Letty.

Maybe it was the separation. Maybe it was simply having him there by her side after surviving such an awful week alone, but for whatever reason, for a fraction of a second, while Donald's eyes looked into hers – showing nothing but love and gratitude – Letty was certain it would be alright. Everything would be fine if she just told him then and there.

'Donal—'

'Well, I'm going to jump in the shower. You don't mind, do you? I'm sure we've got lots to catch up on, but I'm shattered. Long week. You know how it is.'

Letty nodded her head, her throat sealed shut by a large lump.

'What would I do without you?' Donald said. 'You're my rock. You know that, don't you? You're my rock.'

Letty spent the first fifteen minutes of Donald's shower pacing. She traipsed from one side of the living room to the other, then into the kitchen, then back again, after which she went to the fridge and pulled out an empty bag that had once contained Mars bars. She couldn't carry on like this, Letty told herself. She needed to do something. Something drastic.

It was a spur of the moment decision. Perhaps the thought had been implanted in her subconscious. Perhaps it was merely the stress that caused her to behave in such a manner. Perhaps the feeling that her whole life was spiralling out of control made her want to act and take charge of something. Anything.

Without so much as a flicker of hesitation, she marched into the living room, reached up on her tiptoes, and removed the small blue book from the top of the bookshelf.

'Screw you,' she said to the tattered pieces of paper. 'What's the worst that's going to happen?' Then she strode into the kitchen, clicked on the hob, and held the paper against the flame. 'Farewell, Walter Augustus,' she said, watching the book's insides curl up one sheet at a time. 'Do your worst.'

~

'I don't understand.' Walter was at a loss for words. He could feel Trish's hand in his, squeezing it tightly, but he wasn't sure he was able to respond. There was a knot in his throat, a wobble to his lungs, and a general queasiness in all the places in between.

'Am I seeing this right?' he said, his eyeballs fixed on the flickering orange flame. 'Why's she doing this? What's she doing?'

Trish was none the wiser. 'I don't know. Maybe we missed something.'

Walter watched on, trying to make sense of the scene unfolding.

'Do you think she's possessed? Do you think it's what Hector said?'

Trish's grip tightened.

'What else could it be?'

Walter's head was spinning. This was what he wanted, what he needed more than anything. The book was gone, his name almost as good as safe. So why didn't he feel better about it?

~

*L*etty wasn't sure what she expected to happen, the room to start shaking, perhaps? Cups and saucers to start flying from the cabinets? The sun to disappear from the sky in a swirl of black clouds while rain hurtled at the window and women with long noses and pointed hats dived shrieking from above? There was none of it. Nothing at all.

The flecks of ash drifted up from the cinders of the book. Letty continued to stare at the result of the cremation long after the flames had died. It was only when she heard Donald's footsteps coming down the stairs that she swept up the mess and washed her hands clean. A sad tug rose in her belly as she flipped open the dustbin and poured the ash inside. The poems were pretty, beautiful even, and she wasn't likely to forget them in a hurry, but having the book out of her life was, she assured herself, one less thing to worry about.

'I've put the kettle on,' Letty said, meeting Donald in the hall and stopping him from entering the kitchen. 'Shall we have a cuppa and go sit down?'

'A cuppa would be nice.'

'You go sit down then. I'll bring it through,' Letty said. Donald hesitated.

'I think we should have a talk,' he said.

'Yes,' Letty said. 'So do I.'

CHAPTER 33

*L*ETTY DUG her toes into the carpet pile and tried to think of a way to start. Every way of phrasing the words – I've got some secret money – in her head, made her sound at the best, incompetent, and at the worst, downright deceitful. And it didn't fare much better when she tried to explain the job. Her insides were a coiled mass of knots, and the fact that she'd not spilt her tea, the way her hands were trembling, was a small miracle.

The couple had taken their usual positions – with Donald in his armchair and Letty on the sofa – but the unnatural straightness of his back was causing her own muscles to clench. These unusual muscle responses, combined with the current episode of the shakes, were making it almost impossible to drink her drink, and as such, the sips she was taking were nothing more than noisy slurps.

'So, tell me about the trip,' she said, sucking up another half-sip of tea and trying not to burn herself with the overspill from the tremble. 'Did you learn anything good?'

Donald snorted. He caught himself and shook his head.

His eyes were rimmed red, and his cheeks in bloom with a ruddy post-shave glow.

'I'd rather not talk about work for a little bit. There's been rather a lot of it this week.'

'But it was good?'

'To be honest—'

'I mean, it was bound to be different with so many people gone.'

'It wasn't what I—'

'But you found people to talk to? You said you were sharing a dormitory. Were they all friendly?'

Donald shook his head and sighed. Letty clamped her mouth shut. The onslaught of questions was a defence mechanism; she recognised that. The minute she stopped asking questions, she had to face the reality of what they really needed to talk about. Despite the time constraints put on by Victoria, Letty reasoned the longer she could wait before her husband found out about the lies, the better.

'Who did you say it was you were sharing a room with? I'm not sure you actually told me—'

'Letty, please!'

Letty shrank back in her seat, causing the tea to slosh wildly. Donald removed his glasses and rubbed his eyes.

'Sorry,' he said, relocating his glasses to the top of his head. When he looked up, his frown lines were even deeper ingrained around his eyes. 'Letty, I need to say something. I can't go on staying silent. Not now I know for sure.'

Letty's pulse rose.

'Believe me. This is never a conversation I thought we'd be having,' Donald said. 'Not in all our years. But it needs to be discussed, Letty. I need you to give me a chance to say how things are from my side. After that, you can say your piece, of course, but I need my chance first, without interruptions. Is that going to be alright?'

Letty squashed her lips together and nodded quickly.

'Okay,' she said. She felt sick, and her insides felt as twisted as a box of self-knotting shoelaces. He had seen Victoria. It was the only explanation. He had seen her outside, and she'd already told him. Letty envisioned the conversation, Victoria's gleeful grin as she told Donald all about the years of betrayal.

'Letty,' Donald started. 'First of all, I need you to know—'

The doorbell was sharp and shrill and set Mister Missy bounding for the door.

'Fantastic timing,' Donald groused and grumbled as he pulled himself onto his feet and followed after Mister Missy. Letty buried her head in her hands. This was it. Victoria was back. It was game over.

'Oh Donald!' A familiar voice came through from the hall. 'Is she here? Is she okay? Oh, where is she?'

'Jean?'

'Letty? Letty? Oh, sweetie. Are you okay?' Jean was in the living room and crouched on the floor before Letty had had a chance to wipe her eyes. Her face was a flustered red, although her hands were surprisingly cold. 'I bumped into *whatshername*, the girl at the store?'

'It's Jean,' Donald called through from the hallway, a sarcastic twang to his tone.

'You mean, Joyce?' Letty said. 'Listen Jean,' a sudden panic rose up through Letty. 'Jean, please, you need to—'

'Of course, Joyce. That's it. Well, she told me what happened. You poor mite.'

'What happened?' Donald called through from the hall.

'Jean, I haven't had a chance yet—'

'She was a bit of a mess too, mind, but you poor thing.

275

After all you've done for them. After all these years. It's inhumane.'

'It's fine, honestly,' Letty said, the tension in her body reaching breaking point. 'Perhaps we could—'

'It is not fine,' Jean said. 'It is most definitely not fine.'

'Please, could you—'

'What's not fine?' Donald appeared in the room. The two women paused. 'I don't mean to sound rude, Jean, but we were actually in the middle of something rather important weren't we, Letty. Letty?'

It was at that point that Letty began to experience a most irregular form of heart palpitations. Her lungs could barely get a quart of air in before she wheezed it back out in a gasp. She was sweating too. And shivering. There was too much going on. Too many ropes to try to hold onto, and she was failing. Everything around her was swimming, moving in and out of focus.

'Letty? Are you okay?'

She took Jean by the hands. Her intent was to steer towards the door, but in moving discovered she could barely manage to control her own footing. She slipped and tumbled forwards.

'Letty! Come and sit down.'

'Letty?' Donald was at her side too now.

'After all you've done for them.'

'I'm fine. I'm fine,' Letty repeated, barely able to hear the words as they left her mouth. 'Everything will be fine.'

'Letty, please sit down. You're white.'

'I'm … I'm …'

'Come on, you need to sit down.'

'It's such a muddle.' Letty managed to get out as she was lowered into the chair. She gripped the cushion on her lap as she stared at the stitching. 'Everything's all muddled,' she said again. 'I didn't mean—'

'Of course, you didn't.'

'I'll put it right. I'll put it right.' Letty wasn't even sure what she was talking about. Victoria? The job? There was so much to put right, she didn't even know where to start.

'You don't need to put it right,' Jean said. 'You mark my words. Honestly, I'm in shock.'

'Would somebody mind telling me—'

'After all these years. I still can't believe it. To fire you?' Jean said. 'To actually fire you. I mean. I can't believe. I'm sure you can't believe it either, can you, Donald?'

CHAPTER 34

*T*RISH WAS ONCE again nestled in against Walter, although this time, she was facing her daughter while his arms had somehow become wrapped around her waist. It had been an emotional scene. Jean had been full of apologies as she was ushered out the door, and Donald had left for some fresh air after laying Letty down in bed. In truth, bed looked like the best place for him as well.

The woman was wiped out. She'd sobbed for a bit before heading downstairs and unearthing a long-forgotten KitKat from the back of the cupboard. After devouring the chocolate, she'd retreated upstairs and collapsed on top of the blanket. Walter's belly was racked with guilt.

The last time he'd felt this bad about something was when Pemberton died. Had it not been for Edi and the business, he doubted he would ever have pulled himself back out of that slump. Right now, he had neither.

'They'll get past this. And the money too,' Trish said. 'That's just who they are. I knew it the first time I saw them together. Me and her dad, we never had what they had. We

278

were never like these two. You mark my words; they'll be right as rain in no time.'

'If I could take it back ...'

'Pish,' Trish said. 'I was the one who told you to do something. I would've thrown the bloody shoe myself if I could. No, I'm not worried about Donald. Victoria on the other hand ...' Trish slipped out of Walter's grip and turned to face him.

'Can I ask you something, Walter?'

'Of course,' Walter said, his thoughts momentarily distracted by the infuriatingly green eyes.

'And you won't think it's silly?'

'I don't know. Probably not.'

Trish's nostrils flared as she sucked in a long breath. When she breathed out again, she looked young enough to be her own granddaughter.

'D'you believe in soulmates?' she said.

'Soulmates?'

'You know, that one person that you're destined to be with for all eternity? That one person that makes you who you're meant to be? Who'll love you unconditionally? Who'll never let you down? Who'll always be there? Soulmates, you know?'

Her big green eyes were staring straight up at him, but Walter failed to meet them. He shifted his gaze to Letty on the bed and swallowed.

'Well, you know, me and Edi we were ... yes, I guess ... I mean ...we were definitely—'

'Of course.' Trish sighed and slipped back around to face Letty.

'The thing is,' she said, 'you would've thought I'd have found mine by now, wouldn't you? I get not finding them down here, but up there. It's where all the souls are, right? If I can't find them there, where the heck are they?' Forcing her lips into a smile, she emitted a strained laugh. Walter's heart ached.

'Perhaps, when you move on?' he said.

'Perhaps,' Trish echoed.

The two stood in silence, which extended around one another and the room. Despite the heavy sentiment of the moment, there was something warming and reassuringly quiet, like being tucked up in the warm while a thunderstorm raged outside the window. A dense pressure swirled around Walter's breastbone as he realised sadly that it was the type of silence you could never experience on your own. Even in the interim. This moment of silent contemplation was the most connected he'd felt to another soul in decades. He had gotten so used to being alone in his cottage, he hadn't realised how empty it had been.

'Good God, boy.' Hector marched into the room, abruptly ending the moment. 'Do you know how long I've been looking for you? I've got blisters on my damn feet from walking up and down that damn beach of yours. Do you not know there's such a thing as sand, boy? And while we're at it, the Caribbean? Who in their right mind would have a shingled British beach in the afterlife? I swear, sometimes I worry for the sanity of the dead.'

Trish, Walter noted with disappointment, had somehow glided out from his arms and was now standing beside her daughter.

'And I thought I told you not to go anywhere,' Hector said, adjusting his black feather headdress.

'I know you did. But we've not seen or spoken to anyone,' Walter assured him.

'It was me,' Trish said. 'I needed to see her. I just wanted to check she was okay. It's been a pretty awful day. First, there was this—'

'Pff,' Hector said. 'Yes, I'm sure it was all quite terrible. Well, now that I'm here, we need to get—' Hector stopped. His eyes popped from their sockets. 'She's asleep? Why didn't you tell me she's asleep?'

'She's exhausted,' Trish said.

'Daytime.' Hector's eyes grew wider still. The headdress slipped down over his left ear as he rambled, more to himself than anyone else, Walter felt. 'Well, this will be even better, even better; at night they might suspect something, but during the day.' His tongue flickered out and ran along his lips.

'Is this good?' Trish said. 'Is it easier to get rid of the demon in the day?'

'Demon? What, oh yes. Oh definitely. Yes, yes. We must get right on it now. Get the demon now.'

Hector waltzed over to the sleeping Letty and waved his arms above her head. Her lips were parted, and a soft whistle drifted from them on every exhale.

Nerves wrangled their way back into Walter's mind.

'Are you sure we shouldn't get someone else to check?' he said.

'Check? Check what?'

'That she's actually possessed. I know about the marks on her arms and everything, but she doesn't look possessed. Surely there must be signs.'

'What do you want? A six-six-six on the back of her neck?' Hector snapped.

'No, only—'

'I'm telling you. If you want this girl to live, you need to do this now.'

'I was just asking.'

'It needs to be now. We need to do it now.'

'But maybe if we—'

'You've done the cleanse,' Hector's voice was raised. 'You're ready. I'm ready. Everything's ready. We need to do it now. Now, will you just stand there and let me finish these goddamn incantations!'

Trish pulled Walter back by the hand.

'Look,' she said, her voice a low whisper. 'If you don't want to do this, just say. I'll understand.'

'What? No, why?'

'You don't have to do it anymore. The book's gone. She's not your responsibility.'

Walter shook his head, trying to decide if his hearing was out.

'Of course, I'm going to do this. This is my fault.'

'It was an accident. You didn't mean for this to happen. You didn't hand her your book. You didn't ask her to read your name. She was the one who bought the board. I understand that. And she'll understand that too, if she ... when she ... And then you'll be free to move on.' Trish's bottom lips disappeared. Walter's chest throbbed.

'What are you saying?' he said.

'I'm saying you can back out, that's all. No questions asked. No guilt. You can back out. I won't hold it against you.'

Walter pushed his tongue onto his top lip. There was a strong burning sensation building behind his abdominals that was almost impossible to identify. Guilt? Indignation perhaps? He gritted his teeth, then clenched and unclenched his fists.

'I am doing this. We are doing this,' Walter said. 'And it's not about me getting rid of my name. I don't care. If I'm stuck here for eternity, then so be it. We are going to save your daughter, and we are going to do it now.'

A smile flickered in the irises of Trish's eyes.

'Right you two?' Hector boomed. 'Now's the time. I'm not sure how long we've got, so you need to get in there fast.' He muscled Walter towards the bed, positioning him and repositioning him by the shoulders. Once he was satisfied he went back for Trish. 'You'll need to get deep in the Athenaeum as fast as possible, you understand that?'

'I think—'

'Get up a few floors if you can.'

'And that's where we'll find the demon?' Walter said.

'Yes, yes. Keep moving inwards. If you can't find it, you may have to go deeper. Don't worry if things feel a little rocky, just keep moving. The deeper you can get the better.'

Walter's insides corkscrewed.

'Now then,' said Hector. 'If you're ready?' Walter looked to Trish who nodded instantly. It was small but certain.

'You'll need to hold hands,' Hector said. 'The bond will keep you together in there, but you'll need to be touching to pass through with him.' Trish repeated her rapid nod. Walter could feel the heat radiating from her as he took her hand. A heavy, thudding pulse passed from her skin to his.

'It'll be easy,' Walter said, catching Trish's eye.

'Of course, it will,' she said. 'Find the demon, read the incantation. Get your memories. How hard can it be?'

Walter smiled briefly then focused his attention on the rise and fall of Letty's sleeping chest.

'When you're ready,' Hector said.

It would all be fine, Walter told himself as he shut his eyes. Keep going inwards. Keep going deeper until they found the demon and ...

'Wait.' Walter snapped back out of his thoughts, pulling Trish back from her sleeping daughter. He turned to Hector. 'What about the incantation?'

'Incantation? What incantation?'

'To get rid of the spirit. You said I need to locate it and say the incantation.'

Hector's eyes widened. 'I did? Of course, of course, I did. Sorry, gosh. How silly. Good job you remembered that. Here, let me find it. Let me find it. I know I put it in here somewhere. Now, where did I put that?'

Hector rummaged around in his jacket pocket and pulled out a handful of papers. He read the first one, then tossed it aside, repeating the act with both the second and third piece of paper he found.

'Ah-ha, yes, this is it. This is the one,' he said handing Walter a scrunched-up piece of paper.

Walter squinted, struggling to read the faded scrawl.

'Poma, panem, caseus, lactis, rubus, cibus, cupam, capsicum annun ... This sounds like a shopping list in Latin.'

Hector emitted a high-pitched laugh.

'Oh, what a good one. Yes, indeed, a shopping list! In Latin! How funny! Now remember, say this when you see the spirit and it should disappear.'

'It's that straightforward?' Walter said.

'It should be. Just keep going inwards and don't worry if it gets a bit—'

'A bit rocky. Yes, I know.'

Walter took a deep breath. He held it in his lungs, let it quiver and then expelled it.

'Well,' he said to Trish. 'Are you ready to see inside your daughter's subconscious?'

'Ready as I'll ever be.'

CHAPTER 35

*W*ALTER LANDED in the stream. He picked himself up, brushed the hem of his trousers to find they were already dry, then gave his shoes a quick once over. The river was much calmer than the last time he'd been there, with barely a ripple on the surface. It carried a scent of lemon zest and was dappled with a sprinkle of a pink cherry blossom. There had always been trees here, in his previous visits, though never cherry blossom. He glanced around to get his bearings and noticed the figure sprawled out on the ground beneath a gnarled old oak tree.

'Trish!' Walter's dashed across the river, leant down, and shook her by the shoulders. 'Trish, can you hear me? Please, speak to me. Speak to me. Trish? Trish?'

A low groan rose from Trish's lips. Walter slumped in relief. A minute later, she was stirring.

'Jeez. You've done this more than once?'

She rubbed the back of her head, followed by her neck and shoulders. Walter helped her to her feet.

'It gets easier. You just need to get the hang of the landing.'

'I'll take your word for it. This is not something I'm going to repeat.'

Trish's face crinkled as she scanned her surroundings.

'I know this place,' she said, moving first to the trunk of the oak tree and then over to the stream. 'I used to take the girls on holiday here. Well, sort of. I don't remember this tree. Although I think there used to be one like it in Letty's playground at primary school.'

She drifted away from the stream and towards a shop front, squinting as she peered in through the glass. Walter stayed a length behind.

'I know this place too. It's a sweet shop. I used to take the kids here all the time.' Trish bounced on the spot. 'Look, Rhubarb and Custards. Oh, they were so sickly, but Letty could eat them by the bag load. And they've got sugar mice too. Victoria used to hate those. Letty would put them in her bed and she was melodramatic enough to think they were real.' Trish turned to Walter, her face shining with childlike glee. 'Do you think we can go inside?'

Walter bit down on his lip.

'Well ...'

Trish's face fell.

'Sorry,' Trish said. 'You're right. The demon. Obviously, we have to go.' She glanced back in through the shop window. 'It's just so funny, you know. You do all these things with them, and you spend your life with them, and you hope you're doing it right, but you never know what's going on in their head, do you? But now I do. Now I can see what she's like on the inside. That's big, isn't it? That's really big.'

Walter nodded.

'I know,' he said. 'But we need to get going if it's going to stay like this.'

'Of course, we do. Sorry,' Trish said and took his hand

again. 'And thank you.'

'For what?'

'Just thank you.'

A brief moment passed between the two.

'The Athenaeum is this way,' Walter said.

With each step, Walter's nerves quadrupled. As a child, demons – the type touted by the church and his parents – were a thing that kept him awake at night with images of horns and speared teeth. As an adult, he'd suppressed those fears and come to view them as hyperbole, amplifications of fear designed to keep young children in check. Now that he'd died, fears of the devil, the cursed, and the burning pits of hell had been all but alleviated. So, to find himself only moments away from exorcising a real demon made him more than a little agitated.

'This is it,' Walter said, stopping. 'This is the Athenaeum.'

'Are you sure?'

'Positive.'

The building had moved, although it was only a few shops down from where Walter remembered. The roof was now timber, but the panelled door remained the same, as was the feeling of immensity he felt standing in front of it.

'I guess I should go in first?' he said.

'Age before beauty,' Trish said and laughed nervously.

The door creaked on the hinges as he pushed against it. Inside had changed since Walter's last visit. Green blue marble glistened across the floor, while the staircase – still spiral and infinite – was now graced with metal balustrades. The boxes on the shelves were now decorated with iced gems and hundreds and thousands, and the birds, flying lower in the room than before, were a mixture of swallows, nightingales, and larks, their songs falling into a perfect counterpoint of melodies. Despite the confectionery, the aroma of shoe polish and clean insoles was prominent in the air, accented with hints of Earl Grey tea and lavender.

'Where do you think it is?' Trish said. 'Do you think it can hear us? Do you think it knows we're here?'

'I don't know. Hector told us we should head in deep, so I guess we should head in deep.' Still, Walter took a moment before he started to walk.

Walter let Trish take the lead as they ascended the staircase. His eyes continued to flit behind him, but there was no sign of any life, other than the birds that occasionally swept down, daring to soar more closely than he'd ever known swallows to do before.

'Shall we keep going?' Trish said as the first flight of stairs came to an end.

'I guess so,' Walter said.

Neither of them spoke and when they reached the top of one staircase, they continued silently up the next. Somewhere between the fourth and fifth floor, Walter felt Trish's hand slip into his. He squeezed it tightly but kept his eyes forward. Around the thirteenth or fourteenth floor, Walter paused. After all, they needed to start their hunt somewhere.

'Shall we try down here?' Walter said, sweeping his gaze across the endless rows of shelves.

'Looks as good as anywhere.'

It was hard to know where to look or what to look for. Walter brushed his hand along the edges of the boxes. He had to admit, he'd anticipated a demon hunt to involve more running and more demons.

'Do you think Hector got it wrong?' Trish said, apparently reading his mind. 'It doesn't seem like a demon's here.'

'Maybe we should do like he said. Get farther in,' Walter suggested.

'I guess. Or perhaps we should stop for a while, see if we

see anything.

'Hector did say to keep moving.'

'I suppose.'

Walter was about to start walking again when something darted in the shadows. His stomach jolted.

'There.' Trish pointed to where he saw the flicker. 'Did you see that?'

'I think so.'

'We should go.'

'Wait, we need to be ready. I need to find the incantation.'

'It's moving. It's getting away.'

Before Walter could respond, Trish was racing off into the bookshelves. Walter fumbled in his pockets for Hector's scrap of paper.

'Trish,' Walter yelled. 'We need to stay together. We have to stay together. Trish, Trish!'

Walter kept his head down and ran between the bookshelves. His feet stumbled as he attempted to pull the paper from inside his jacket.

'Trish?' he called as he turned one corner. 'Where are you?'

He turned another corner, then another and was partway through spinning around and doubling back on himself when he spotted it.

The figure was huddled down in a dark corner. Loud sobs rose from its shuddering back.

Walter's heart pounded. He stepped closer.

'Trish?' he said again.

Only when he was a few feet away did Walter see that it was not one figure, but two.

'Mum.' One side of the figure drew away from the other. 'Is that you?'

'It's me, my darling. It's really me,' Trish said.

CHAPTER 36

*D*ESPITE THE age difference, the resemblance between the two women was far more pronounced than Walter had realised. They had the same shaped eyes and delicate Cupid's bow. The same high brow-line and lilted smile. And the way they stood, with their weight shifted onto one side, was almost an exact mirror image of each other.

Trish lifted her hand and placed it against her daughter's cheek.

'You're here?' Letty said. 'Are you okay? Are you—'

'I'm fine, my darling. I'm fine.'

'Am I asleep?'

'You are, my love.'

'I wish I didn't have to wake up.' The child's voice struck like a knife between Walter's ribs.

Young Letty pulled herself back to arm's length, but her mother's fingers remained flush against her skin.

'I miss you,' she said.

'It's been too long. I'm sorry, my darling. I'm sorry.'

'I thought … I thought I'd never see you again.' Her lips quivered. 'It's been hard. Everything's going wrong.'

'I know my darling. I know.'

'I wish you were there to talk to.'

'I'm here now, my love. I'm here now.'

The pair fell back into one another's arms. Walter waited. His chest throbbed. There were no words, no tears, just holding. A minute passed and then another. Walter looked on at first with envy, and then with increasing concern. The embrace was at three and a half minutes and showing no signs of loosening when Walter shifted uncomfortably and cleared his throat. A minute later, he tried again.

Trish shot him a withering look to which he frowned apologetically and tapped an invisible watch on his wrist. She turned back to her daughter.

'Look sweetie. The other night, with the Ouija board—'

'You know about that? You were watching?'

'Something happened. Something not good. And we've got to try to fix that.'

'We?'

Letty stepped back and cast her gaze up and down. It was the first time she'd acknowledged Walter's presence. A rampage of butterflies danced in his belly.

'You? I told you not to come back.'

'Yes, I know. The thing is—'

'How do you know my mother?'

'Well that's—'

'You got me out of the Ouija board. You stopped it.'

'I was—'

'But the other things, you did those too. I don't like you.'

'It was rather – Sorry, what are you doing?'

Walter's need to explain the situation was derailed by

Letty's sudden peculiar behaviour. The young child had moved towards him. When she reached the limit of personal space, rather than stopping, she leant in farther. She tilted her nose towards his jacket and sniffed. The action was a cross between that of a small child and a rather hungry Labrador.

'Hmm,' she said.

'What?'

'I thought you would smell of pear drops.'

Walter grunted. 'Pear drops are not a sweet I have a great affinity with.'

'Why not?' little Letty asked.

Walter rolled his eyes. The detour in conversation was doing nothing to help him get back on track, yet he sensed it would be easier to give an answer than try to navigate whatever series of questions was to come next.

'Pemberton. He used to eat pear drops.'

'Pemberton?' Her forehead wrinkled while she spoke the name as if trying to sift through the memories and find the suitable one to fit what she was hearing.

'I know that name. He's the one you wrote the book for?' Letty said, nodding her head as she clarified the fact to her herself.

'In a manner.' Walter's foot tapped against the marble floor. The more time spent on these niceties, the more time the demon had to inflict whatever merry havoc it was planning.

'Look,' Walter began. 'The reason we're here—'

'I know it's to do with the book.'

'Yes,' said Walter. 'That was why I was here before. But that's not why we're here now.'

'I burnt it. It's gone. It's—'

'Yes, I know, and thank you. But—'

'I don't know why.' Letty's gaze wandered wistfully. 'It's

just felt like the right thing to do at the time.'

'And I'm immensely grateful, but—'

'Maybe I thought it would change things—'

'Please if you could—'

'But I guess—'

'Letty love,' Trish stepped forward, putting her hand on Walter's shoulder and moving him gently to the side. 'We're here because we need to know if you've noticed anything strange recently.'

'In here?'

'Anything out of place? Anything unusual?'

'Besides him you mean?' She shot a glare at Walter.

'Besides him,' Trish said. 'Anything odd or scary maybe?'

Letty thought for a minute. She pressed her lips together and angled her head.

'I don't think so. I don't come here that often though.'

'Anything?' Walter stepped back into the conversation. 'Something small, maybe. Noises perhaps, funny thoughts? Little men with red eyes and horns? Think back. Has anything happened since the other night?'

Letty's eyes went from one side of the room to the other, and after a minute's contemplation, she opened her mouth to speak. But nothing came out. Not until she began to scream.

～

*I*t was a dream; she knew she was in a dream. Her mother was with her for a start, which undoubtedly ruled out any real-life scenarios. It had to be a dream. Only you weren't meant to be able to feel pain in dreams, and right now, she was in pain. A lot of pain.

'Mum,' Letty opened her mouth and tried to speak, but her airway was constricting. It felt like a giant pair of hands

293

had wrapped themselves around her neck and were squeezing with all their might.

She was struggling to see, struggling to stand. Struggling to breathe. Maybe, Letty's subconscious thought, if she gave into the pain, it would all be over. Maybe that was the answer.

'Letty!' Trish was on her knees beside her daughter. 'What's wrong? Letty, what's wrong?' She turned to Walter who was, once again, cemented to the spot. 'What's going on? Is this it? Is this the demon?'

'I ... I don't know.'

'What do we do?'

'I ... I don't—' Walter stopped. 'Wake her up,' he said.

'What?'

'See if you can wake her up.'

'How?'

'I don't know. Maybe we could, maybe we could ...' Walter was trying to think, trying to remember things that had caused him to start awake in cold sweats from dreams all those nights ago, but it was no good. He couldn't think. He couldn't move. He couldn't breathe.

'Trish!' Walter gasped as he fell to the floor.

For someone who had not needed oxygen in over a century, it very much felt as though he were suffocating. His lungs convulsed, and his heart raced. Using all his strength, he heaved himself up, yet no sooner had he lifted his torso from the ground than the floor beneath him began to crumble.

The roar was deafening. Boxes tumbled one after another from the shelves above. Great cracks cleaved caverns in the walls. The birds squawked and squealed as they flew higher and higher, dodging the debris that rained down on them. Walter reached out in front of him. Trish was on the ground, her arms around her daughter, her mouth gaping as she too struggled for air. Walter reached for her, a wind howling above him, hurtling more and more boxes and books and rocks. This was the end, he realised. He wasn't sure how he knew this, but he did so with absolute certainty. This wasn't moving on; this wasn't leaving the interim. This was the end for Walter Augustus, forever. A sense of calm spread through his battered body, and a thin smile formed on his lips. At least he wasn't facing it alone. At least these last years had not been a total waste. He had figured something out, even if it had been too late. Walter gazed at Trish. If he could just feel her hand. If he could just touch her. If they could just all stay together.

CHAPTER 37

*S*O INTENSE was the light that Walter was forced to shut his eyes the moment they opened.

'Urgh,' he gasped. His lungs burnt, and the coughing that followed his first breath made him think that perhaps he was, in fact, drowning. Perhaps he'd even drowned. Even with his eyes closed, the world was spinning. Walter tried once more to move and open his eyes, but yet again, the dizziness made it impossible.

'Just stay where you are. Stay right there. I've got you. I've got you.'

Walter pushed himself up to sitting, only – he realised after his feet were lifted down and a pillow placed behind his back – he'd been helped to do so. The floor was warm beneath his feet. The light glowed pink, and a smell of sour confectionery filled the air around him.

'Pemberton?' Walter said. He blinked until he could open his eyes, and even then, it was hard to keep them open for more than a few seconds. A gentle rub of his brow sent shock waves down his spine.

'Take it easy. You've been through quite an event.'

Pemberton knelt on the ground beside him. His shirt-sleeves had been rolled up beyond his elbows, and a paper bag of yellow and pink sweets sat bulging in the top pocket.

The room they were in had walls a deep shade of burgundy, with black countertops and a cream leather suite. A spherical steel fire pit hovered in the centre of the room, beside which lay a body, cloaked entirely in black. A thin trickle of red meandered down from his ear to the floor.

'My God. Hector!' Walter made a lunge for his friend, but the dizziness caught him by surprise.

'Steady there,' Pemberton said, catching him by the shoulders and helping him back onto the seat.

'Is he ... Is he ...?'

'We should be so lucky,' Pemberton said. 'Still, I suspect, even in here, a blow like that should keep him down for a bit.' It was then that Walter noticed the poker beside him, one end glistening with a streak of congealing blood. Pemberton picked up the offending object and wiped it clean on the bottom of his shirt. Then he waltzed over to Hector's body and spat on his face.

Walter shook his head as he tried to make sense of the situation. The slight movement was enough to make his neck throb and a searing pain run all the way down to his ribs. He wrapped his hands around his throat and winced at the tenderness.

'What happened?' he said.

Pemberton moved to the coffee table. He gathered a pile of books and papers, which Walter immediately recognised.

'Those are Hector's,' he said.

'Indeed, and it appears as though our dear friend may have fed us a fair few lies.'

He handed Walter some of the pages. They were dog-eared and mustard coloured, with scribbles in the margins and annotated phrases, all in a language that well-preceded any that Walter had studied.

'I don't understand it,' he said.

'Shall I?' Pemberton asked.

'In certain rare situations where absolute occupancy is attainable, it should be sought in only the most extreme of circumstance. A delocalised spirit occupying a physical entity is subject to the frailty of the weaker physicality. As such, any afflictions caused to the host body will also be exercised within the second spirit.'

Walter took a moment.

'I don't understand,' he said.

Pemberton took the book off him and shut it with a thud.

'From what I've gathered, Hector here thought he'd found a shortcut out of this place.'

'Here? The interim? How?'

'Judging by this lot,' he tapped the stack of books, 'he figured out that if the girl dies and you're occupying her, then you go too. And a new spot appears upstairs. My guess is he'd figured out a way to be at exactly the right place when that slot opened up.'

Walter rubbed his temples.

'So, he was hoping to take my spot?'

'Indeed.'

'But that doesn't make any sense. I thought spirits couldn't hurt people?'

'Again, one of his mis-truths, I'm afraid. The incident with the Ouija board was by all accounts a test run. When he saw that you accrued the same injuries as she did, he decided it was time to put his theory into action.'

'But what about the demon? Hector had said that there was a demon in her? That's why we had to go back in?'

'All a ruse. I guess sending the other woman in with you

meant that there was no one left out here who could try to ruin his plans.'

'Trish,' Walter gasped.

'You've got to get some rest,' Pemberton said. 'You can't go through what you've been through and expect to go gallivanting about.' But Walter didn't listen. He was already stumbling out the door.

CHAPTER 38

ALTER RUSHED out of the room and through the corridor of five bar gates and grazing sheep, oblivious to the meadow of daisies, which he trampled beneath his feet. He didn't need to stop to feel the tugs or regain some sense of direction in the infinite infinity in which he stood. He knew exactly where he was going. He sprinted through the grass until he reached a wooden gate, guarded by a large and testy looking bullock. He nodded towards it politely, unclipped the lock, and slipped through.

Trish was lying on the bed, her hand moving along the line of her adult daughter's hair. Her eyes glazed with tears. When she saw Walter, she lifted her head and smiled, causing a tear to escape and trickle down her cheek. Walter tried to reciprocate the smile, but finding his own eyes beginning to glass over, he turned his attention to Letty instead.

Her skin was pallid and clammy, and the movement of the sheets almost negligible as she breathed.

'Is she ...?' Walter said, finally forcing the words up and out of his throat.

Trish shook her head, causing another cascade of tears, which she swiftly removed.

'She's just sleeping. Your friend reckons she'll be fine. Just needs some rest.'

'Trish,' Walter flopped down on the bed beside her. 'I am so sorry. I had no idea. If I'd have known ...'

'Don't be silly. He roped me in as well. Demons. God, you'd think I'd only been dead five minutes.'

Walter tried to laugh but found nothing. Instead, he sat in silence, waiting and praying for the girl to come back around.

'I don't understand how we got out of there,' Trish said. 'Your friend, he'd moved on. How did he get back?'

Walter's eyes fell once more on Letty, her quiet gentle breath.

'Pear drops,' Walter said. 'We were saved because of pear drops.'

~

*L*etty's brain was a fog. She felt simultaneously as though she'd slept for a decade yet had been awake for a millennium. Thoughts formed, but in a half-baked, fuzzy manner, as if she'd written them in icing on a warm cake, then watched as they melted away. She rubbed her eyes and winced. Her head ached – badly – and there was a throbbing behind her eyeballs that felt like she was standing next to a speaker at a heavy metal rock concert, although neither pain was as bad as the pain in her throat which felt as though she'd swallowed a string of barbed wire. She reached to the bedside table in the hope of a glass of water, and in finding none, moved slowly to the edge of the bed. She was halfway through her third glass of water when the doorbell rang.

The yellow hue of Victoria's new nails looked remarkably similar to a fungal nail infection. She brandished her arms around as she pushed her way through the door and into the living room.

'He's not here,' Letty said.

'Then I'll wait,' Victoria said as she dropped down on the sofa. 'I know you think I'm being callous about this, but you've got to understand my point of view. To have your own flesh and blood deliberately let you suffer in silence, when they could have helped. You've broken trust here Letty, and that's something I can't forgive.'

Letty inhaled. Her stomach still felt constricted, but there had been depletion in the number of butterflies that now swarmed around her bowels. In fact, if she were asked to describe her current emotional state, it would probably have been fair to say that she no longer gave a damn.

'Well,' she said. 'Since you get such pleasure in my misery, I'm sure you'd like to hear that I got fired today.'

'You what?'

'Fired. Given the boot.'

'Why?'

'Does it matter?'

'But—'

'And Donald walked out on me. I'm not sure when he'll be back. I'm not sure if he'll be back.'

'You mean that—'

'But you are more than welcome to wait if you like. You can wait here until hell freezes over for all I care. You're still not getting my money. Now, if you don't mind, I'm going to do some baking.'

It was ten minutes later – when Letty had settled on making a dark chocolate and sticky toffee tray bake – that

Victoria appeared in the doorway. She rubbed the tips of her fingers together and cleared her throat several times.

'This doesn't change anything,' she said, peering down her nose so far that the veins in her neck pinged outwards.

'I wouldn't expect it to.' Letty cracked three eggs into a bowl.

'We need that money. I needed that money. Do you know how I've struggled these last years, and you've been sneaking around in your cheap Tesco T-shirts, laughing at us? Felix nearly went bankrupt, you know that? And do you know the number of holidays we've had to cancel over the last five years?'

'Then stop booking holidays you can't afford to go on. And get a job.'

Victoria seethed. 'You've always been jealous of me. Jealous of my life. Jealous that I get to spend my days at home raising a family, while you live like a barren old spinster.'

The words stung, but it was brief, fleeting and nowhere near deep enough to cut. Not anymore.

Letty stopped stirring and faced her sister.

'Now listen to me. If you think you can come into my house and tell me how I'm supposed to behave, you've got another think coming.' Letty could feel her arms wobbling as she jabbed her spoon towards her sister. 'I'm sorry you had to look after me when we were younger. I'm sorry if you felt abandoned and let down. But you're a goddamn adult now, Victoria. Start acting like it.'

Victoria's pout bulged from her lips like a trout with an experimental lip augmentation.

'It doesn't change the fact that you lied to Donald.'

'No. No, you're right. And well done, you. You found my big dark secret. But you know what? Once again, that's none of your business. Donald is my husband, and I will tell him about the money in whatever manner I see fit.'

'Money? What money?'

Donald looked even more exhausted than before. His eyebrows tilted down, and his frown was a mass of thickly carved creases. His clean shave now looked raw and painful.

'I came back earlier,' he said. 'But you were asleep. I went to get you these, as an apology.'

He lifted a bouquet of flowers from his side. The blooms were already starting to turn, the burgundy carnations now closer to brown than red, but the sight of them made a heavy weight swirl in Letty's conscience.

'They're not the best,' he said, 'but, well, I think we'll need to rein in our spending in the next few weeks.'

Victoria squeaked. Donald's eyes slid sideways towards her.

'Sorry, Victoria. I didn't see you there.'

'Yes, well—'

'If you don't mind, this isn't the best time. Letty and I have a few things to discuss.'

'Actually,' Victoria shimmied her shoulders in preparation for her big moment. 'I've got something important to tell you.'

Donald scoffed. 'By that, I assume you mean you want something?'

Victoria's eyes widened.

'I'm sorry, Victoria. This is really not a good time. Can you come back tomorrow or something? Whatever it is can wait.'

Letty's stomach fluttered. She wanted to meet Donald's eye, but still couldn't manage to lift her gaze high enough. Next to her, Victoria gave a heavy, amateur-dramatics style sniff.

'What I want to talk about is a betrayal,' she said.

Donald's lips twitched. Victoria's smile extended.

'Yes, I discovered something rather shocking recently. A family betrayal. And a betrayal to one of us is a betrayal to all of us, wouldn't you say?'

'Letty?' Donald whispered.

Letty swallowed. Her throat had adopted the texture of sandpaper, and her eyes were refusing to look anywhere other than the submerged spoon in her chocolate and toffee batter. Donald placed the flowers on the kitchen counter and inhaled. A second later, he placed his two hands on top of hers.

'I'm sorry,' he said. Letty lifted her head and frowned. 'I've been meaning to tell you. Honestly, I have. But it never seemed like the right time.'

'What—'

'I thought it would be alright. We had a bit of money to tide us over, and I was looking. I swear I was looking. Then, when this week came up, I thought maybe I could go a bit farther, go up to London to see if there was anything there.'

'Sorry, you went where?'

'And I've tried Letty, I promise. I've tried everything. But I'm too old. I'm just too old now.'

'Donald?' Letty shook her head, trying to piece together his stream of half sentences. 'What are you saying? Why have you been to London? What are you too old for?'

'To work. To find a job.'

'What? What do you need another job for?'

'I don't need another job. I need one job. Any job.'

Donald collapsed onto a chair.

'Why? What happened?

'What do you mean, what happened? I lost my job. Redundancy. Over a month ago. Is that not what Victoria had come to tell you?'

'No,' Letty expelled a half-hysterical puff of laughter. 'No, it's not.'

'Then why?'

There was a second's pause in which Letty's eyes fell from her husband. In that moment, his hand flew up to his mouth in a gasp. Two seconds later, he cleared his throat and shook his head.

'I understand. I do. It's not been easy. I've neglected you. Not given you the attention you deserve.'

'What? No,' Letty shook her head, aghast. 'It's nothing like that. No, not ever.'

'It's not? Then what is it?'

'Donald,' Letty closed her eyes and steeled herself with a long inhalation. 'Victoria has come to tell you that I've been lying to you. That I've been hiding money from you.'

'Money?'

'Quite a lot. I'm not sure how it happened.'

'What kind of money are we talking about? Where's it come from?'

'Savings, with a few wins on the bonds here and there. I made a couple of investments too, nothing risky, just with the bank.'

Donald scratched his head. 'Well how much money are we talking here? Thousands? Tens of thousands?'

Letty's mouth twisted. Her cheeks adopted a reddish hue. 'About half a million, give or take a few.'

'You what?'

Letty nodded. 'It's probably a bit more now. You know with interest and things.'

Donald's jaw dropped. His glasses had fallen to the end of his nose, although he made no attempt to correct them. The squirming in Letty's intenseness intensified as she tried to decipher whether his expression was one of anger or simply sheer bewilderment.

'You have money?'

'I do. We do. We have money.'

'And you hid it from me?'

'I didn't. I mean I did, but I didn't mean to. It just kept growing, and I didn't know how to tell you, and I thought maybe I'd surprise you, but I was worried that you'd be cross.'

'That we have half a million pounds?'

'That I hadn't told you earlier.'

Letty finally managed to lift her gaze away from the cake mixture to meet her husband's eyes.

As her lower lids glistened with tears, his eyes were lost amid a myriad of folds and creases.

He pushed the bowl aside and wrapped his arms around her. 'Letty Ferguson, you're an old fool. But then you married a fool. What a pair, eh?'

Letty's cheeks ached as the tears streamed down them. She pressed her lips together, too afraid to open her mouth in case of what came out. Donald brushed her tears away and pulled her in.

Two minutes into the embrace and a throat cleared behind them. Letty tried to ignore it, but Donald did not.

'Victoria,' Donald said, moving back and breaking the connection. 'Thank you ever so much for bringing this to my attention. I have no doubt that you had my best interests at heart.'

'Yes, well—'

'So now, in the nicest possible way, can you please, please just bugger off?'

*T*HE AFTERLIFE smelt of cut grass and fresh laundry.

This was not an aroma that had been landed upon lightly but had been deemed by all involved to be a most wise decision. After all, there were very few who roamed the interim aspect of the afterlife that did not feel at ease in the scent of clean linen and cut grass. For Walter, it had adopted an almost nostalgic sentiment. Nowadays, his time was spent dashing from one place to another, always a job to do or a person to see. As such, he had little time to sit and absorb the aromas that had been so fastidiously picked out for his afterlife. In fact, the smells that he was most frequently surrounded by these days were ones of baked goods, peonies and plumeria.

The shop front was decked out in coloured balloons, and a scent of fresh paint rose from the windows and doors. Outside, a small crowd had gathered, among which were several familiar faces.

'Do you think she'll come?' Trish said, squeezing Walter's

hand the way she did when she was nervous. 'She'll come, won't she? She wouldn't not come, surely?'

'I'm sure she's just running late,' Walter said, fighting the urge to dash back into the interim and out through a different door just to check. 'She wouldn't let her sister down. She knows how important this is to her.'

'It looks great, doesn't it?'

'It looks incredible.'

'I do hope it'll work.'

'It'll work,' Walter said. Trish squeezed his hand once again and got back to scanning the crowd.

'They've just parked down by the church,' Pemberton said, appearing behind the pair.

'They have?'

'Unless you can think of any other woman who would find midday on Wednesday a suitable time for wearing diamanté stilettos, then yes, Victoria is on her way. And she appears to have brought the offspring.'

'Oh, I am pleased. Thank you for checking, Pemberton. What would we do without you?' Trish leant up on tiptoes and kissed Pemberton's cheek. Pemberton stiffened. Walter, on the other hand, beamed.

The *we* in Trish's sentence was still taking some getting used to.

*O*nce the incident with Hector had been dealt with, Walter had returned to his reclusive state. He spent his hours throwing pebbles out into a murky, frothy sea and plucking the endless weeds from the pathway to his house. At night, he would sit in his chair and scribble down a few lines of poetry. But his chair was harder than he remembered, and come morning, he had inevitably binned all the previous night's work. Trish had respected his decision for solitude; it was Pemberton who had brought him around to sense.

'Why are they growing?' Pemberton asked about the weeds one afternoon. Walter was on his hands and knees, soil up to his elbows, a pile of weeds bigger than Snowdon behind him.

'What do you mean, why do they grow? They're weeds. That's what weeds do.'

'Not up here,' Pemberton said. 'You know if they're growing, it's because you want them to.'

'That's ridiculous,' Walter grumbled as he plucked another dandelion out from beneath his begonias. 'Why would I want to be doing this all day?'

'How should I know?' Pemberton continued to watch, munching on a bag of sweets. Halfway through the packet, he squeezed it back into his pocket and sat down on a bench Walter had never noticed before. Walter groaned.

'Can I get you something?' he said, without looking up. 'If you're staying?'

Pemberton shook his head. 'No, no, no,' he said. He paused and gazed out at the sea. 'I was thinking actually. Did I ever tell you about my wife?'

Walter's head sprung up from the weeds. His eyes narrowed sceptically.

Pemberton's head shook again.

'No, of course, I didn't. You know I didn't. Anyway, I thought you might like to hear about her?'

Walter brushed his hands on the seat of his trousers, his eyes still slithered in scepticism.

'You had a wife?' he said.

'I did. A very beautiful wife. And a son too.'

Walter blinked, unbelieving.

'You never said. You never said anything.'

310

'No. No, I didn't. I was very young, you see, when they died. Childbirth. It's not like it is now. And we were very young to be married. Very young to be married. Very young to be separated.'

He spoke matter-of-factly, but it was clear that each word was a struggle. And while his face remained impassive, his cheeks drew in and flexed as if chewing something much softer than a boiled sweet. A prickling heat rose behind Walter's eyes.

'So, what did you do?' Walter said.

'I moved away. I took what money I had and took over the workshop, and I promised myself I would never be hurt again.'

Walter shook his head. 'I thought the shop was in the family?'

Pemberton sniffed. 'Some great uncle three times removed or such nonsense. You never saw what it was like at the beginning, a bloody barn. But I worked hard. Like I said, I was young. And I had nothing else.'

'But you never married again?'

Pemberton smiled sadly, 'No.'

'Did you ever get close?' Walter enquired.

Pemberton's eyes drifted over to the horizon, then back across the garden and finally to Walter. They stayed there, unwavering, for what felt like several minutes, until Walter could hold the silence no longer.

'I'm sorry,' he said. 'I didn't know. When you came back, I didn't realise. I didn't know.'

'Tsh,' Pemberton silenced him, then once again commenced his wistful gaze. When his eyes landed back on Walter, there was far more intention in them than before.

'I can't tell you what I saw over there, when I passed over,' he said. 'You know I can't. But I can tell you what I felt.'

Walter shuffled closer.

'Love is not limited,' Pemberton said. 'It doesn't get spread out or worn thin. I learnt that there. I learnt that, if you love someone new, it doesn't make your love for anyone else weaker. You can't love too many people, Walter. But you can miss out by not loving enough.'

An invisible force tightened around Walter's ribs.

'If someone wants to try to love you, let them,' Pemberton said. 'You have to let them try. Because if you don't, then one day, people will stop trying.'

Walter stared at the ground. He could feel the tears break free, trickling down his cheek, but made no attempt to wipe them away. He wished he could have been alone to sob out his heart in silence.

'Love is for a reason, a season, or a lifetime, Walter, and *we* have an infinite number of both. Now,' Pemberton's voice changed to a far more jovial tone. 'Isn't that funny.'

'Isn't what funny?'

Walter raised his head from the ground and cast his gaze out in front of him. He frowned.

'The weeds,' he said. 'They've gone.'

'Well then,' Pemberton smiled. 'I guess you don't have to stay around here all day anymore. Is there not somewhere else you'd rather be?'

*L*etty cut the ribbon with Donald by her side. It had cost a small fortune to kit the place out but *Let's Eat Cake* already had a queue of customers and so many orders on the books she'd already hired help. Victoria was in the crowd with the twins screaming merry mayhem as they tried to dismantle the balloon display. It didn't matter though. Letty cast her eye over the hungry crowd. There was more of a turn out than she ever could have wished for. Joyce was there. She'd even brought Kevin, who waved at Letty from the back of the queue, while Jean had shut up shop to attend. It was perfect. A lump swelled at the base of her throat, and heat rose to the back of her eyes.

'Is everything alright, dear?' Donald asked. He was kitted out in the *Let's Eat Cake* buttercup-yellow polo shirt with royal blue apron, although until Letty had him fully trained, he was to be doing deliveries only.

'I'm fine. In fact, I'm wonderful. Only ...'

'Yes?'

A thin veil of tears glossed over Letty's eyes.

'Only, I wish Mum could be here to see this.'

'I'm sure she is, my love. I'm sure she is.'

Next to Letty, but unseen, Walter leant into Trish's shoulder and whispered in her ear.

'Do you want me to throw a shoe at her?'

ACKNOWLEDGMENTS

First and foremost, to those who read my books, thank you for your support, especially those people who endured endless drafts, well before this version ever saw the light of day. To Lucy for her ridiculously keen eye. To Amy and Jacks for their advice and positivity towards my writing. To John and Chrissie, among many others, for their belief in me. To all the bloggers and my wonderful Launch Team who have helped me promote the book. And finally, Jake for his unending patience, without which I would never get my books finished.

COMING SOON BY HANNAH LYNN

EROTIC FICTION?

There's nothing sexy about her humdrum life as a mum. But is her husband's crazy scheme a bit too exciting?

Sarah's mind-numbing housewife existence is turning her brain to mush. With a third bun in the oven, this British mum is drowning under a mountain of playdates, bills, and head lice checks. But her man's novel get-rich-quick scheme of penning steamy stories and torrid tales isn't exactly her ideal way to dial up life's passion.

Drew desperately wants a break from picking up after his feral children. And if that means researching how to write sizzling lit all by himself, then he'll make the sacrifice. But as he finally warms Sarah up to his sultry side hustle, their R-rated private project gets publicly exposed...

With an office scandal brewing, it's only a matter of time before gawking workers and a perfectly nosy PTA president turn them into social pariahs.

Will they manage to inject some well-needed heat into their marriage as well as into the pages of their steamy novel, or could this be the final chapter for Sarah and Drew?

Erotic Fiction? is a charming comedy for fans of humorous fiction. If you like sweet love stories, endearing characters, and dry British humour, then you'll adore Kindle Storyteller Award Winner Hannah Lynn's delightful tale.

Pre-order *Erotic Fiction?* today on Amazon and have something sweet and funny in time for Valentine's Day!

ABOUT THE AUTHOR

Hannah Lynn is an award-winning novelist. Publishing her first book, *Amendments* – a dark, dystopian speculative fiction novel, in 2015, she has since gone on to write *The Afterlife of Walter Augustus* – a contemporary fiction novel with a supernatural twist – which won the 2018 Kindle Storyteller Award and Gold Medal for Best Adult Fiction Ebook at the IPPY Awards, as well as the delightfully funny and poignant *Peas and Carrots series.*

While she freely moves between genres, her novels are recognisable for their character driven stories and wonderfully vivid description.

She is currently working on a YA Vampire series and a reimaging of a classic Greek myth.

Born in 1984, Hannah grew up in the Cotswolds, UK. After graduating from university, she spent ten years as a teacher of physics, first in the UK, then around Asia and on to the Austrian Alps. It was during this time, inspired by the imaginations of the young people she taught, she began writing short stories for children, and later adult fiction. As a teacher, writer, wife and mother, she is currently living in the Amman, Jordan.

STAY IN TOUCH

To keep up-to-date with new publications, tours and promotions, or if you are interested in being a beta reader for future novels, or having the opportunity to enjoy pre-release copies please follow me:

Website: https://www.hannahlynnauthor.com/

Alternatively sign up to my monthly newsletter and receive two completely free books.

Sign-up to Newsletter

REVIEW

As an independent author, I do not have the mega resources
of a big publishing house, but what I do have is something
even more powerful – all of you readers. Your ability to offer
social proof to my books through your reviews is invaluable
to me and helps me to continue writing.
So if you enjoyed reading *The Afterlife of Walter Augustus*,
please take a few moments to leave a review or rating on
Amazon or Goodreads. It need only be a sentence or two, but
it means so much to me.
Thank you.

Made in the USA
Middletown, DE
08 May 2020